THE ODDS

LINDSAY PUCKETT

Scholastic Press / New York

All rights reserved. Published by Scholastic Press, an imprint of Scholastic Inc., *Publishers since 1920*. SCHOLASTIC, SCHOLASTIC PRESS, and associated logos are trademarks and/or registered trademarks of Scholastic Inc.

The publisher does not have any control over and does not assume any responsibility for author or third-party websites or their content.

Library of Congress Cataloging-in-Publication Data available

ISBN   978-1-338-80381-5

10 9 8 7 6 5 4 3 2 1   23 24 25 26 27

Printed in Italy   183

First edition, September 2023

Book design by Stephanie Yang

TO ALL FUTURE GHOSTS IN THE MAKING

PROLOGUE

If you are reading this, then you have braved the carnivorous garden, gained passage through the Weeping Tree by leaving an offering of toenails, and pried this book from the cold, dead hands of the Ghost of Swamp Root Manor's long-buried body. If you did not do these things, then you are probably an earthworm and therefore can't read anyway.

In the unlikely case that you are, in fact, a vertebrate with moderately good reading skills, I'm most disturbed to say that this book is even more foul than the journey you took to find it.

For this story contains truths that many would rather not be unearthed.

The truths of an untruthful little girl on a truly unpleasant trek, secrets of soul-sucking spirits, the mystery of a mushroom-covered man, and the clues of a cryptic chest with missing keys.

If I were concerned about your best interest, I would tell you to do something more relaxing with your time, like bird-watching, or perhaps you could practice sleeping in the grave next door. But you undoubtedly won't heed my warning.

While I may be many terrible things, a bad narrator I am not; therefore, to aid you along your reading journey, I will leave you these facts three:

Fact: Despite popular belief, platypuses and shrews aren't the only mammals that are venomous.

Fact: The great horned owl can turn its head 270 degrees. So can Ms. Majorie.

Fact: The true gift of adventure is not the friends we make along the way, but the lies we uncover about our enemies.

Fact: Kleptomania (noun) is the recurring and overwhelming urge to steal.

It was good fortune the ghost had already attacked, or the girl wouldn't have had a distraction for the heist. The staff fluttered about. Elders gossiped and clutched their rosaries. The rats in the walls squeaked and skittered. Even the manor itself was so worked up by all the excitement that it flapped its shutters as if caught in a windstorm.

Of course, this all left *his* office unattended.

The girl seemed to glide down the dimly lit hall. She knew exactly where to place each foot so as not to make a noise. For example, one would only step on the second-to-left wooden panel if they wanted to alert the whole manor of their secret wanderings with a *squeeeeeak.*

No. Not tonight.

Her calculated creeping crept to a crawl at the door of room nine, Mr. Haneef's suite. Grandpa—or Dada, as it was in his homeland—number forty-two.

Ghost attack number: Four

It was reported to the Never Odds as a coma since they couldn't understand things like magic and souls and ghosts. Most with Oddities didn't think those without them were worth the time—the girl included—but appearances must be kept up, and something had to be documented.

The child rested a hand on the brass doorknob as a buttery, flaky taste swelled on her tongue. A memory stretched its fingers across time, back to samosas and Eid and *Before*.

"Like this, meri gudiya," he had said, his soft brown hands molding over hers to shape the pastry into a perfect cocoon for the spiced goodies inside. "Fold it like it holds a secret."

The girl giggled, flour dappling her cheeks. "That's your job."

Her dada winked. "Oddity is as Oddity does."

Whatever secrets he kept were now buried within him.

She had never seen a ghost, but she liked facts, and the fact was something had left her dada Haneef stiff as a board, eyes leaking black smoke, just like Abuelo Humberto, Pawpaw Henry, and Grandfather Charles before him.

Sadness threatened to rise, but the girl pushed it down, locking it in the coffin of her mind. She had more pressing matters at hand. Her eleventh birthday, as a matter of fact, in three days' time.

Fact: On average, people have one thousand one hundred and sixty-four nightmares between birthdays.

Fact: Loud singing, cheering, and whooping noises common around birthday celebrations were once thought to scare away bad spirits.

Fact: Begonia Hollowmoor's eleventh birthday would be the worst day of her life.

4

The pipes in the walls groaned, something the manor did whenever it felt as if it wasn't getting enough attention.

"Hush," Begonia hissed, nudging the baseboard with her boot. "You'll give me away."

A hanging mirror performed a dramatic spin against its nail as the floorboards huffed.

"Don't roll your eyes at me. If you want to be part of this mission, you better *stick to the plan.*"

A tarnished suit of armor saluted as she passed, the manor's way of saying, "*Sir, yes, sir!*"

"Good," Begonia said, throwing a leg over the banister. "Now move out!"

The staircase molded into the exact shape needed for optimum sneakacy, slithering down into the belly of the manor. She pushed off, and her hair whipped behind her as she slid to the main floor.

She patted the banister. "Good boy."

The curtains hummed in delight. Or perhaps some creepy-crawly was munching the fabric.

As she snuck through the foyer, the towering grandfather clock hiccupped a loud *bong*! Begonia froze, still as a corpse, her teeth on edge. Only her heart moved, an angry rhythm tromboning against her ribs.

You see, my Advantageous Adventurer, everyone has a nemesis. If you don't, then perhaps you are too young, or too nice, or *you* are someone's nemesis and don't know that you have made such a dangerous enemy and that they are lurking behind you waiting for an opportune moment to blow a poison dart between your shoulder blades before you release a final scream for help.

Just a thought.

Begonia did have a nemesis. In fact, she had compiled a growing list of them. They were as follows, Villainous Violation rating included (scale rating 1–10, 1 being overstarched pinafores and 10 being Ms. Majorie):

1. THE NEVER-ODD CHILDREN IN THE VILLAGE

Crime: Being loud and sticky. (Always sticky? Why?) Making fun of my height, or lack thereof, and calling me "the cripple from the creep house."

Villainous Violation Rating: 6

2. MS. MAJORIE

Crime: Existing.

Villainous Violation Rating: 10

3. THE FOYER'S GRANDFATHER CLOCK

Crime: Ticking, chiming, and overall incessant timekeeping.

Villainous Violation Rating: Off the scale. DOOM IMPENDING.

The rug rolled under Begonia's feet, gently urging her on.

"Thanks," she muttered, and scurried down the main hall.

As planned, the manor clicked open the lock, and the door to the office swung inward.

Before we continue, it's important for you to understand how badly our hero—or villain, depending on who you ask—wanted the object in this office. No, *needed*. The need set a fire in her belly, tingles in her fingertips, and only the slightest tinge of guilt on her tongue.

Not enough to *not* steal it, mind you; this story is about a terrible little girl, after all. A thief.

But she would want you to know the guilt was there, Dear Reader, no matter how small.

Begonia crept inside the office. Something that smelled like gun smoke clung to the room the way mud clings to a toadstool. Every nook and cranny was filled with books, empty teacups, spare sets of dentures, and strange metal contraptions that either whistled, clacked, or sang in squeaky falsettos.

Begonia usually loved the manor's quirks—this kooky, disorganized office, the back steps that just pretended to be steps, doors that opened only on a waning moon, windows that lied about the weather. But today, each whizz of the machines sent lightning through her fingers and thunder through her heart.

She scoped out the room with a criminal eye.

Hiding places / shadowy corners: Four

Quick exits: Two

Satisfied, she slunk over to the desk.

A cracked picture frame glinted on its surface. Inside, the two of them lounged atop a picnic blanket at her favorite springtime spot—the double-heart-shaped beach by the bog.

Her stomach squirmed.

She looked the same as ever—pale white face, wispy white hair, dingy white smock. Scrawny. Insubstantial. Dandelion child, Nana Babette once called her, because if a big wind came, she looked as if she'd blow away with the wispy petals. The only thing grounding her was the tarnished silver locket around her neck. The locket she had been abandoned with as a baby. The locket she never took off.

If she looked the same as always, then the opposite must be said for David.

His neat chestnut hair fell in waves just above his neck, which grew out instead of up from all the hours spent hunched in his workshop. He had kind eyes, lanky arms, and no matter the occasion, always dressed in browns. Sprawled out over the picnic blanket, he looked warm and lazy and happy.

This was before the nursing home ran out of money. Before David's eyes stopped twinkling.

Before "the ghost."

Guilt bloomed up Begonia's throat like poisonous mushrooms. With quick fingers, she flipped the picture facedown so he could not watch, and slid open the desk drawer.

It was exactly where she knew it would be, nestled between stray paper clips, broken quills, and envelopes that screamed in bold red ink OVERDUE.

The pocket watch.

It wasn't really stealing. David had mentioned he might sell it for some extra funds, and she absolutely could not let him do that to his most prized possession. This wasn't so much a heist as a rescue mission.

She reached for the watch's chain.

"There you are."

She jumped, slamming the drawer shut.

David stood in the doorway, one of his goofy work-in-progress inventions strapped over his brow. It could have been a headlamp the way it was fixed around the skull, but with bug-eyed goggles and golden cogs that whirred around the ears like moth wings.

It looked like utter junk, but that's how David's Oddity worked. He was an inventor. Or really, an *un*-inventor. He had the specific knack of breaking things in just the right way to create something extraordinary.

"What are you doing?"

"Nothing," Begonia said, voice too high.

Normally David would have noticed something was off, but as it was, he seemed distracted. Begonia's eyes narrowed, suspicion laying eggs in her gut.

The least shabby suit in David's collection hung loosely from his frame. His hands, usually dirty from tinkering with tools all day, were scrubbed clean of grease. His hair was oiled.

"You look . . . nice," Begonia said.

Oblivious, he straightened his coat. "What? Ah, yes. Thank you. Listen, Bug—I wanted to talk to you about something. Something very important."

David sat on one of the scratched brown leather chairs, patting the seat next to him. Begonia's heart hadn't stopped its thumping. She gulped down a deep, calming breath and threw one last longing glance at the drawer before joining him, swinging her feet off the edge in an attempt to act normal.

"About what?"

"There is a particular—ah—event coming up soon that I thought we should talk about."

Grave-worms reared their vicious heads, gnawing at her middle.

"My birthday," she said.

You might think it's odd for a child to dread their birthday. You may assume it's unusual for a child to have fifty-eight grandparents. You might even consider it bizarre for that child to enjoy stealing from them all, despite her love for them.

There can be no doubt she was a peculiar girl, but the oddest thing about Begonia Hollowmoor was that she wasn't odd *enough*.

Her birthday had everything to do with that.

"It's going to be the worst day of my life," Begonia moaned.

David put a hand on her shoulder, but Begonia couldn't feel it. It might as well have gone straight through her. He blinked down at her with a gentle expression, only slightly terrifying through his bug-eyed spectacles. "Everything is going to work out. You," he said, poking her chest with each word, "are magical. You. Are. Odd."

Begonia pasted on a smile. Her eyes strayed to the pocket watch drawer.

The unspoken truth was that if she *did* have an Oddity, she could use it to help fund the nursing home, like Grandpa Clive, who sold honey from his head-hive at the farmers market, or Nana Babette, who had a fortune-telling tent at the annual renaissance faire.

Well, that, and she wouldn't get torn from her home, have her memory wiped, and be forced to live with the putrid Never Odds at a city orphanage, but we'll get to that later.

"Mr. Klein."

A woman stood in the doorway. Nay, not a woman. A Nemesis. A blight. A long shadow cast over the whole of Swamp Root Manor.

Ms. Majorie.

Begonia thought of all the residents of the manor as family, but as the nursing home's head caregiver, smile squanderer, laugh liquidator, and overall thief of joy, Begonia saw Ms. Majorie more like the feral cat that lived under your porch and hissed when you went to get the mail.

She also had an unfortunate Oddity that allowed her to twist her head nearly all the way around. Two hundred and seventy-degree vision. This used to put Begonia at a terrible disadvantage, regardless of how much of an accomplished thief she was. But lately, instead of her usual glare or snide comments or tattling, Ms. Majorie had taken to ignoring her altogether. As she stomped into the room, her eyes slid over Begonia like she wasn't even there.

Begonia did not enjoy looking at Ms. Majorie either; therefore, I will not waste my time describing her to you, my Precocious Pickpocket. Just picture the most horrible person possible.

"Sorry to disturb," Ms. Majorie said, "but Mr. Schmoob and Mrs. Pingleton are here to see you."

David sighed, looking older than usual. "Send them up."

Ms. Majorie nodded and left.

Suspicion curled Begonia's eyebrows into question marks. "Why is Mr. Schmoob here?"

"Well," David said, pulling at his collar. "That's what I wanted to talk to you about. Go wait in the hall and then we'll chat after, all right?"

Begonia did not like the smile he gave her, all weak and wobbly. It made tension cloud along her forehead, and these were the nimbus-cloud kind. The ones that brought storms.

David touched her shoulder. "Hey, you okay?"

"Yeah, just a little pressure."

His face did that strange double-emotion thing it had been doing recently, as if caught between one of his screws (sadness) and one of his hammers (discomfort). It prickled her nerves to no end. She had always been able to handle her pain on her own, thank you very much. She didn't need whatever sympathetic display this was.

"Why don't you lie down for a bit," he said. "You don't want another episode."

Begonia rubbed her temple, letting her annoyance dissolve from her body. Schmoob was the problem now. He had been coming around a lot lately, always with talks of refinancing, consolidation, and other fancy banker words Begonia didn't understand. All she knew was each time he left, a new gray hair curled along David's temple.

Her eye gave a nasty throb. From under her curtain of bangs, she snuck another glance at the drawer. Even out of sight, the ticking clock pulsed in time with her head, with the ache of her heartbeat.

Despite the pain, she tried to treasure the dull beat now, knowing it would cease to pump at all if she lost her home. Or if she was taken from it.

As always in times of stress, three pieces of trivia swam up through the murk of her mind.

1. On Mercury, a single day is two years long.

2. One hundred and eighty-four families relocate per year because they believe their house is haunted.

3. Nothing—pain, a ghost, or least of all, Mr. Schmoob—was taking her home from her.

And that, Dear Reader, was a *fact*.

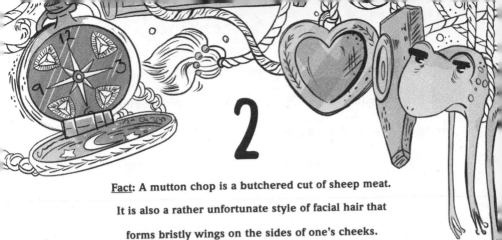

2

Fact: A mutton chop is a butchered cut of sheep meat. It is also a rather unfortunate style of facial hair that forms bristly wings on the sides of one's cheeks.

One of the worst things about being a snoop is getting told off for your snoopiness. But one of the best things about being a snoop is continuing to snoop anyway. I particularly encourage this behavior around holidays, when your parents, guardians, or captors are most likely wrapping your gifts.

Through the office keyhole, Begonia was snooping.

Mr. Schmoob, the estate's banker, was seated across from David. Though very squat and bald, he made up for both with an exuberantly bushy set of muttonchops that curled upward like warthog tusks, adding two inches to his height. Though he was a Never Odd with no magical ability, his facial hair seemed tethered to his mood. For example, his eyebrows squirmed like angry caterpillars when he was particularly excited about something. Those somethings were usually the words "overdue" and "no more extensions."

The banker was predictable—white skin, blue suit, green bottom line. But the lady next to him was a mystery.

Gold rings and bracelets glittered off her manicured hands and feet, peeping out from under an electric-pink suit and high-shined heels. Expensive-looking makeup lined her smiling lips and eyes and coated the ebony skin of her cheeks. Not a curl out of place.

A slight pain nudged behind Begonia's brow. David should have told her they were coming.

As Begonia massaged her temple, she formed a plan. Definitely *not* a revenge plan, but it did involve upgrading her heist into a more high-stakes game—a game in which she may be "rescuing" a few things from their guests as well.

"Oye," Begonia whispered. "The operation is still a go."

If she hadn't been watching the keyhole, she wouldn't have known the manor had sprung the lock, so silent was its work. With soft feet, she nudged the door open and slipped inside.

Target one: Mrs. Pingleton's ankle bracelet.

Location: Left ankle, resting atop the right.

Best point of access: Under the ottoman.

Target two: Mr. Schmoob's cuff link.

Location: Right wrist, resting on the arm of the sofa.

Best point of access: Behind sofa.

Target three: The pocket watch.

Location: David's desk drawer.

Best point of access: Directly from the front.

Escape plan: Somersault around the desk, army-crawl under the trophy stand, one-eighty spin from the potted fern to the door.

As Schmoob prattled on, Begonia leapt forward, executing a perfect roll under the ottoman. Like a swamp snake in a pinafore, she slid on her belly, whooshing forward on a gust of air until Mrs. Pingleton's ankle was in reach. The bracelet latch caught in the lamp glow. Begonia stretched out her hand and—

Mrs. Pingleton shuddered, her ankles uncrossing. Begonia yanked her hand back with a gasp.

"Ooh, it's a bit drafty in here," she said in a cheery, high-pitched giggle. "Of course, it adds to the ambience very nicely. Tell me, Mr. Klein, did you design the place with rat-eaten insulation, or is it just made to look authentic?"

David's voice started and stuttered. His shoes scuffed together.

"Wait!" Mrs. Pingleton said. "Don't answer that. It's simply marvelous either way. My guests will love it!"

"Yes, very interesting," came the uninterested drawl of Mr. Schmoob. "But if we could get back to the matter at hand."

He launched off into more big, boring words, and Begonia took her chance. Fingers feather soft, she unlatched the bracelet around Pingleton's leg. It fell into the cushion of her hand.

Begonia smiled.

Target one: Acquired.

Begonia scurried back, dropping the bracelet into one of the many pockets of her dress, sewn in for this exact purpose. Peering around the arm of the sofa, she spied Schmoob's hand keeping rhythm against the leather, punctuating each of his favorite words with a *tap tap tap*. The golden cuff link on his wrist winked in the candlelight. David sat across from him, facing Begonia, fiddling with the dials on his goggles. The thrill of the challenge sent fireworks across her skin.

"I'll need you to sign the last of these documents."

Begonia rubbed her fingers together, ready for a pinch, twist, and pull.

"You will personally be responsible for sections B, D, and F."

Breath slow. Eyes on the prize.

"It's most important you don't forget to send these to the county court."

Clink. Plop.

Begonia caught the cuff link in midair as it fell from the sprung latch. Schmoob tapped away, not missing a beat.

Target two: Acquired.

She snuck a glance up. David hadn't even raised his eyes. In fact, as he dipped his head to slip the apparatus back on, Begonia executed a perfect tuck-and-roll, landing safely behind David's desk.

She rested against the wooden leg, chest heaving, listening hard. But there wasn't so much as a hiccup in Schmoob's drone.

She had done it.

Behind the back of David's head, Mr. Schmoob's face reddened, mutton-chops twitching.

"Now, see here, Mr. Klein. I would appreciate your full attention."

David's neck straightened. Begonia could imagine him blinking up behind those green lenses, something like a swamp moth caught in a light.

"Yes, Mr. Schmoob. You are completely right. My apologies."

Mr. Schmoob chewed the corners of his mustache, his face losing some of its sharp edges. "Yes, well, this all must be hard for you. I understand you saw the last owner as a father."

His words merely floated around Begonia's ears. She already knew the story. How David had been an orphan. How Odd Dr. Yu, the then owner of the nursing home, took him in, gave him a home with the other residents of Swamp Root. Just like David did for her.

David looked away. "Yes, he left the manor to me when he died."

A scrape echoed from the desk cabinet beside Begonia, the sounds of teeth against oak. She gave it a muffled thump to keep the dust bunnies from giving her away. Angry pincers clicked, then quieted.

Begonia turned to the drawer, opened it, and snatched her prize. She squeezed its cool metal body, letting its heartbeat tick into her palm, satisfaction bubbling under her skin. Then she slipped it into her boot and braced herself for the exit plan.

"Have you made arrangements for the residents?" Mr. Schmoob asked. "Rehoming fifty-eight people could take longer than we've made allowance for."

Begonia slipped and bumped into the desk. It skidded forward with a screech, sending the picture of her and David crashing to the floor.

Mrs. Pingleton yelped and David jumped to his feet. Mr. Schmoob glared at the shards of glass on the floor as if offended they had interrupted him.

Taut as a Grave Vine, Begonia grimaced.

"Begonia," David said under his breath. He shook his head, a deep sigh billowing from his chest.

Escape plans whizzed between Begonia's ears, but she was as good as caught. The least she could do was hide the evidence.

In a flash, she shoved the cuff link between the slats of the floorboards. A rat had already dived back into the wall, Pingleton's bracelet tight in its mouth.

Undeterred by the sound, Mr. Schmoob plowed on. "We do need to talk about the—uh—more unseemly incidents that have happened here. They of course could affect the marketability of—"

"Oh, I hope so!" said Mrs. Pingleton. "What's a haunted hotel without a ghost?"

Mr. Schmoob's muttonchops flapped in alarm. He gave a dismissive chuckle. "Just whispers, my dear. Isn't that right, Mr. Klein?"

"But what about all the *attacks*?" Mrs. Pingleton asked with a wink.

David opened his mouth, but Mr. Schmoob cut him off. "Oh, pishposh. Mr. Haneef's stroke was indeed a tragedy, especially on the coattails of the a capella group—what did they call themselves, Klein?"

"The Decrepit Decrescendos," David said.

"That's it. But this is a nursing home after all. People here get sick all the time. Die, even. I see no reason why 'haunted' should be put on the listing."

"You don't believe in ghosts, Mr. Schmoob?" David asked. Begonia inched around to peep at him. He had stopped playing with his goggles and was staring intently at the banker, one eyebrow raised.

"Certainly not," Mr. Schmoob said.

"Real or not, the very *idea* of spirits makes us a killing in the haunted-attraction industry!" Mrs. Pingleton trilled. "Museums, hayrides, ghost tours—all things of the past. I plan on leading us into a new era, giving the Creep-Consumer Inc. what they want—an all-inclusive bed-and-breakfast with the undead! Swamp Root will be the *perfect* resort."

She adopted a sickeningly sweet puppy-dog face and fluttered her eyelashes at Mr. Schmoob. "Surely we can find a way to bypass the auction?"

Icicles shot through Begonia's ribs. She popped her head around the desk so only David could see her.

"Auction?" she asked, her mouth wide in outrage.

He winced at her.

Mrs. Pingleton's eyes hopped around the room. "I really feel like I understand the place, you know? The vibes. The story it wants to tell. Right. In. Here," she said, touching her heart as if deeply moved. "I'm telling you, with the lake view and this nineteenth-century crown molding, we can turn this dump into the hottest haunted bed-and-breakfast this world has ever seen!"

David spluttered. Begonia gagged. Mr. Schmoob's muttonchops fluttered.

"Now, I know this must be terribly dreadful for you, Mr. Klein," Mrs.

Pingleton said, in a tone that sounded like it wasn't dreadful at all. "But when I heard this place was shutting down, I just couldn't pass it up! Now, why don't you just sign it all over to me now and—"

"I'm truly sorry, Mrs. Pingleton," Mr. Schmoob said, "but that is impossible."

Mrs. Pingleton's smile cracked like the crown molding she desperately loved.

The icicles in Begonia's chest spread, carving through her veins and arteries until she was more glacier than girl, swelling with frost and fury and fight until, with a giant crack, the ice burst open like a dam.

"*No.*"

"Begonia—" David said. Mrs. Pingleton looked around. Mr. Schmoob started. She ignored them all and stood. "*I* want to bid."

Fact: Throughout the world and time, giraffe tails, woodpecker scalps, and porpoise teeth have all been used as currency.

Begonia's hand wiggled around in her many pockets. She didn't have porpoise teeth, but she did have a stray button, some cracker crumbs, and an enchanted frog pin she stole from Grandma Harriet that croaked when you stroked its spine. If this wasn't enough, surely the stash of stolen goodies under her bed would be.

"I will pay all I have, and if it's not enough, we can do another fundraiser or something. Right, David?" Begonia said, a plea in her voice.

She would *not* think about how much her last trip to the doctor cost him. Nor how expensive her cabinet full of pills and tonics was.

David stood and, with a deceptively firm grip on her back, led her toward the hall in silence.

"No!" Begonia said, trying to turn out of his grasp. "I'll buy it! I swear! I'll do anything!"

In a last-ditch effort to not be thrown from the room, she bucked. Hard. One foot flung wide and crashed into the door, slamming it shut with a loud bang.

"Good Lord!" Mr. Schmoob yelled, clutching his chest. Mrs. Pingleton's eyes searched the wall as if terrified Begonia might have chipped her precious molding.

David, who rarely got angry, blinked at Begonia, astonished at her behavior.

She suddenly felt very small. She just wanted to pry herself free. The door had been an accident.

Well, she would want me to tell you it was *mostly* an accident.

After a moment, David sighed and dropped his hands. He had that tortured look about him again.

Begonia's fingers ached to wring the rain clouds from his face. She wanted him to fight. To tell Schmoob to eat dirt. To not give up.

This was their *home*.

"Tell them," Begonia whispered. *"Please."*

David took another deep breath before turning back to the pair on his couch. "I believe Begonia would like to be considered for the auction."

"Oh yes, the child who lives here," Mr. Schmoob said, eyes moving through Begonia as if she were a gray sky about to ruin his cricket game. "Very sweet. But if we could get back to—"

"Surely a child doesn't have the funds?" Mrs. Pingleton said with a high-pitched laugh. Her gaze darted between them as if desperately needing someone to confirm the ridiculousness of the situation.

"I have this," Begonia said, extending her hand again with her treasures inside. "And I can get—"

"Of course she doesn't," Schmoob said with a wave of his hand. "And even if she did, there's that terrible affliction of hers." He shuddered as if being sick was the worst possible fate he could imagine. "She couldn't possibly run a nursing home in her—well—*condition.*"

The floor seemed to tilt. Begonia's vision reduced to a pinprick. It was like watching the conversation happen to someone else, floating above it all.

"It's just a descriptor," David said, pushing her on the tire swing. Her chubby fists clutched the ropes; tears dripped down a face that was still more a toddler's than a child's.

"Just like 'fat' or 'old' or 'short.' They just paint a picture of a body. A hunk of flesh. That's all. Don't let it be a dirty word for you."

"But the village children were mean! They called me the 'D' word in a bad way."

David took her face in his hands until she met his eyes. "Disabled. It's not a bad word. Say it."

"Disabled," Begonia whispered.

David smiled. "They're right, you know. You are disabled. You're disabled and smart and artistic and blond, and a little ornery, if I'm being honest—"

Begonia giggled, pawing her eyes.

"All these things make you you. Each a single cog or gear in a larger machine. And that"—he offered her his hand—"is a beautiful invention."

She took it.

David's tone turned corpse-cold. "With all due respect, Mr. Schmoob, I heartily disagree. Her illness has absolutely nothing to do with her capability to run the estate."

"It's all just nonsense!" Mrs. Pingleton said. "She's a child! If we could get back on topic—"

The office door banged open, limping from its hinges. The entire room jumped, and I do mean the entire room, as even the manor was so busy eavesdropping it didn't notice the newcomer until he was literally busting down the door.

In its place stood quite possibly one of the dirtiest, most terrifying creatures Begonia had ever seen.

The man had a patched, badly shaven head and wore clothes that could have been any color but were now so aged and filthy the only hue that came to Begonia's mind was "grave-worm brown."

She had a terrible hunch she knew what he was. And what he was doing here.

Before he could spot her behind David, Begonia slunk back into the fern.

Ms. Majorie huffed into the room, red-faced. "My apologies, Mr. Klein, I told him you were in a meeting and would see him after, but—"

"It's all right," David said, his expression strained as he turned to the newcomer. "How can I help you, Mr.—?"

"The name's not important," the man said. He extended a hand, dropping his trunk to the floor, where it issued a loud metal thunk. Begonia's insides squirmed at the thought of what could be inside.

Ever the polite host, David shook his hand, though Begonia didn't miss the white that laced his knuckles. "You're the POO, then? Can't say I'm thrilled to see you, if I'm honest."

"We prefer the title Pursuant of Oddless Occult, thanks," the POO said, sounding very offended. "From the Extraordinarily Bad Infractions Committee. Here to handle the crime that will occur in three days' time."

Fear sank its fangs into Begonia's neck. *An Oddslayer.*

For reference, Dearest Reader, Oddslayers—or POO, as those of us more villainously minded like to call them—are bounty hunters who track down and relocate Odd children who don't receive their Oddity by their eleventh birthday. At the time of this story, it was the opinion of the Committee that they were as good as Never Odds at that point anyway.

But like I always say, opinions are like corpses. We all have one in our basement; that doesn't mean I want to hear your mother's.

Oh, and there was also the tiny fact that their memories were wiped with a special instrument called an Oddbliterator, to ensure they never let slip the existence of Odds.

All in all, very charming folks.

Begonia shook so hard the fern leaves shuddered.

"*Might* occur," David said, his eyes flicking toward the potted plant. "Nothing is for sure until the stroke of midnight on her birthday."

A gold molar winked behind the Oddslayer's smirk. "I've been in this line of work for a while, and I can safely say any child who's come this close to their birthday ain't getting no Oddity. That's where I come in." He sniffed and pulled his belt buckle high as if extremely impressed with himself.

"I'm sorry—Is this about the auction?" Mrs. Pingleton said, confusion bright on her face. Mr. Schmoob glanced between the pair as if wondering whether he should call the police or county hospital.

David jumped, remembering himself. "Ah, Mr. Schmoob, Mrs. Pingleton— would you mind giving us just a moment? Ms. Majorie, I'm sure, would be delighted to show you the library."

Ms. Majorie looked like she would be more delighted to drown them in a pot of her stewed pea soup, but she gave a dutiful nod. "This way, if you please."

The banker checked his watch while stomping into the hall. Mrs. Pingleton followed but not before assessing the Oddslayer with a critical eye as if sizing up a potential last-minute competitor. Satisfied with his shabby appearance, she smiled at David and clip-clopped out after the others.

Begonia had absolutely no plans of leaving her hiding place. Maybe ever. She would simply sink into the floorboards and live with the rats and mold.

The door closed and the Oddslayer whistled a long, low note. "Business must be bad to be dealing with Never Odds, eh, boss?"

David ignored his question, eyes flicking once more to Begonia's hiding place. "Might I ask why you're here? As you said, Begonia's birthday isn't for three days."

The Oddslayer walked around the office, trailing his finger over the mantel and somehow making it even dustier than it was before. He stopped at a shelf of David's unventions.

"You make all this yourself?" he asked, picking up the barrel of a telescope David had broken into something he called an electroblaster last summer. Something Begonia wasn't allowed to touch unless heavily supervised, as it could release fifty thousand volts of electricity in one burst.

David took the blaster from him and lowered it back on its stand. "My question, if you please."

The Oddslayer continued his prowl. "The Committee likes us to be here early. You know, watch for any signs of a runner or the family trying to hide the criminal. Funny business. That sort of jazz."

An Oddchanted hourglass dinged as he flicked it in passing before turning back to David. "But I shouldn't expect any problems from you, right, boss? I'll take the girl nice and easy, and all your problems will be gone."

David leveled his stare. "Begonia is not, nor ever has been, a problem. And these archaic laws about Oddless children being ripped from their families because of magical status are utterly—"

"Oh, I'd be careful if I were you, boss." The Oddslayer stalked closer. "Seems like you've got enough problems without the Committee knowing you take issue with how they run things, don't you think?"

David's lips turned white.

The Oddslayer chuckled, then glanced around. "Where's the little beastie at, anyway?"

Begonia clung tight to the shadows.

"Around. If you are staying three days, I'm sure you'll get to meet her soon enough."

The Oddslayer's smile was a feral thing. "Looking forward to it."

Begonia gulped. Seeking the slightest bit of comfort, her fingers wove into her pocket, clutching the cold silver skin of David's watch.

Tick-tock.

Tick-tock.

Tick-tock.

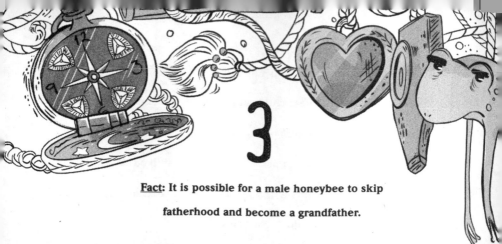

3

Fact: It is possible for a male honeybee to skip fatherhood and become a grandfather.

After the Oddslayer left the office, Begonia fled, ignoring David's calls behind her. She couldn't bear to look at him.

She hid in an alcove, pulled the watch free, and ran her thumb over its scratched face.

It was David's first unvention, a gift from Dr. Yu for his tenth birthday. He discovered after tinkering with it that it no longer told time but gave answers on a 1–12 scale (1 being the most likely, according to David).

Anticipation dry on her tongue, Begonia cupped the watch to her lips and whispered, "How likely am I to get my Oddity before my birthday?"

The watch hummed in her palms. The hands twitched, then twirled around its face, slowly picking up speed. Begonia held her breath. The hands zoomed faster and faster until they stopped on a number.

Two.

Begonia leapt forward, the balloon in her middle swelling with joy. She was going to get her Oddity. She was—

Then the dials moved again. Seven.

The balloon popped.

Four. Nine. One. Eleven.

The watch hands whirled around the clock so quickly Begonia's eyes blurred.

She shook it, gently at first, then harder.

"How likely am I to get my Oddity before my birthday?" she growled.

Twelve. One. Two. Six.

Breath hissed through Begonia's teeth. She shoved the watch back in her pocket, defeat sporing in her stomach like mold. Her eye gave another nasty throb. A promise of things to come.

You are probably wondering, my Inquisitive Interloper, how a girl could steal from those she seemed to love so dearly. Therefore, as I explain, I invite you to imagine yourself in Begonia's shoes.

You are an Oddless Oddchild living in an Odd manor full of Odd people with elders that you consider family—and they, you. You marvel at their Oddities, their gifts to the world that make them one of a kind. Special. Oddstraordinary. Over the years, you've noticed that the trinkets your grandparents are most fond of somehow take on little bits of their Oddacity. You play with the objects and are barely able to wait for your own Oddity to arrive.

But it doesn't arrive. And keeps on *not arriving*. Your family tells you it will come one day, but you aren't sure. And you begin to fear if it doesn't arrive, you may be taken from your home.

A voice worms into your head, whispering ideas to your fingers. But you ignore them. You would never hurt your grandparents. And so, you tuck your greed away. You get really good at tucking.

Until the day that tap-dancing key ring falls into your pocket. Late at night, you cradle it under your blankets, and something warm and heavy slithers into your chest. For the first time in your life, you feel the slightest bit Odd.

So you take the refilling teacup, snatch the self-shuffling playing cards, swipe the never-ending matryoshka dolls, and every time you hold one of your precious objects close, you feel as if you belong. Because petting them, holding them, collecting them . . . It's almost enough to release the strings from around your ribs and the stones from your heart and snuff out the terrible, *terrible* tick-tick-ticking of the grandfather clock that is the imminent stroke of midnight on your eleventh birthday.

Almost.

In the hall, Begonia leveled her shoulders. She would not give up like David, but she did need help. An ally. Someone to sort out this mess in front of her.

Luckily, she had fifty-eight potential allies snacking on pudding down the corridor.

As if on cue, a familiar tune swelled to life. A smile nudged Begonia's lips as she followed the notes to the parlor.

New target: Acquired.

Mawmaw Montgomery's fingers were long, dark, and covered in rings from her travels touring with Alma and the Oddettes, which she called her glory days. They danced over the keys in a pattern she knew by heart, one she had taught Begonia the duet to last summer.

Some Oddities run in families, and nearly every Montgomery Begonia knew was a famous musician. Melodies followed her mawmaw wherever she went. Quite literally, as depending on her mood, different theme songs would spring up from the ground as she walked.

"*Everyone has a song in their heart*," she would say. "*Mine just makes it to the surface.*"

Begonia plopped down on the bench beside her. She didn't expect Mawmaw to look up, as she was always in a world of her own whenever there was ivory under her fingers.

Shoulder to shoulder, Begonia plucked the first few notes of the counter-melody. It wasn't perfect—she'd never had a musical bone in her body—but it wasn't as bad as Grand Da O'Flannery's bagpipe playing either. Last time, there were no survivors.

After a few bars, Begonia felt it was safe to broach the subject.

"Mawmaw, I need some help. I was just in David's office, and—"

But eyes off the keys, Begonia fumbled, and an unruly note hiccupped from the strings. Mawmaw stared down at Begonia's hands, grimacing.

"Come on, baby. I know you're better than that."

Mawmaw patted the side of the piano as if consoling it for Begonia's lack of skill.

"I'm sorry," Begonia said, hands falling into her lap. "It sounded so good before. I just thought I could talk to you about something."

But Mawmaw was lost in her music again, swaying and humming to the rhythm. Begonia quietly stood.

"More practice, that's what you need," she said just as Begonia was about to leave.

"Of course, Mawmaw," Begonia said, warmth flooding her cheeks.

First candidate: Eliminated.

Mawmaw didn't purposely ignore her in her time of need—she was always like this around her piano. But Begonia was in a time crunch. She needed someone else to make sense of this all for her. Besides, what else were grandparents best at if not reason and comfort?

The answer, Dear Reader, is gossip.

And at Swamp Root Manor's Nursing Home for Extremely Odd Elders, there wasn't a single activity enjoyed with as much ferocity. In fact, the residents served it back and forth like a tennis ball, with many grunts, rude jeers, and sometimes street brawls, much like the actual sport itself.

The usual gossip match was in full swing as Begonia entered the lounge, a room cluttered with squishy armchairs, pipe smoke, and houseplants in different stages of decay.

"I don't like the looks of that banker. Proud as a Foxglove, that one is."

"This place can't close! I'm a fourth-generation resident—I have to die here!"

"It's absolutely subterraneous!"

"That's not what that word means, Frank!"

Begonia walked deeper into the room, eyes peeled for the perfect grandparent to fix her problems.

She sidestepped Papaw Frank, who had a charming quirk of using the wrong words for everything; missed Mamaw Betty, who loved shouting corrections at her husband; and wiggled past Grandpa Emery, busy picking his nose.

"I like the pig snout best," Begonia said as he cycled through his selection for the day.

He settled on that very one with a snort, and Begonia shot him a thumbs-up.

Then her name caught her ear.

"I had no idea. Where was she when it happened?" Grand Da O'Flannery asked, his venomous fangs slick between his lips.

Begonia spied three of her grandpas whispering over their afternoon cuppa, a rickety checker table tottering in between them. She inched closer.

"Mr. Klein's office, apparently," Grandpappy Burl answered, amidst a burst of new flurries from the half-rucksack, half-snowblower contraption David had fashioned for him. All three lumps of his body shivered, causing his carrot nose to slide down his face an inch or two.

"No. Poor lass."

"Yes, well, it was inevitable, from what the rats say," Grandpapa Sir Walter Philips said, metal arms clanking as he moved an oilcan over his armored joints.

Begonia sighed. Of course they already found out about the Oddslayer's arrival. Even the rats knew she was dead meat.

Begonia forced her chin high and continued her hunt. She couldn't allow herself to get down. She didn't have the time.

With a pop of excitement, she spotted a crossword puzzle on the end table next to either Grandpa Forty-Eight or Grandpa Forty-Nine. Even though they were two people, Grandpas Forty-Eight and Forty-Nine were twins, identical down to the ROLL MODEL and I ALWAYS WIN AT MUSICAL CHAIRS stickers on their wheelchairs. The problem was, no one could tell them apart and they never seemed to be in the same room at the same time.

She picked up the newspaper and pencil and eyed the last remaining set of boxes. The answer fluttered up like bat wings. She filled in the letters and set it back down between her grandpa's cup of tea and mystery novel.

"Here you go, Grandpa! The last word was 'peripeteia.'"

"Thank you, dear," Grandpa Forty-Eight or Grandpa Forty-Nine said, and stretched his empty teacup toward the nurse.

Bolstered, Begonia seized her chance. Speaking very quickly, she said, "Grandpa, the Never Odds are taking over the manor and my birthday is in three days and I'm running out of time because the Oddslayer is here and— what do we do?"

Grandpa Forty-Eight or Grandpa Forty-Nine yawned loudly, shaking his head at the room as he did so. "Oh dear. I'm too tired nowadays for all this excitement. I actually think I'll take a nap here soon."

"But—"

His eyes had already closed.

Disappointment sank in Begonia's chest.

Candidate two: Eliminated.

But Begonia would not give up yet. No matter how big the swamp, you trudged through until you hit the mud on the other side. Nana Babette had taught her that.

Begonia slapped her forehead. Of course.

Turning on her heel, she darted around stray walkers and embroidery baskets until she reached the tent at the back of the room.

Why didn't she immediately think of Nana Babette?

You see, Begonia was blessed with many types of grandparents. Formal ones who preferred to be addressed as Grandfather or Grandmama. High-maintenance ones liked Glam-maw Charlenne. Ones who preferred no gendered titles at all, like Elder Kai. There were wai pos and wai gongs who she celebrated New Year with, and babushkas and dyeduskas who taught her to ice fish, and too many more from places all over the globe to name.

But of them all, Nana Babette was her favorite.

Maybe it was because they were so similar. They were both grumpy and short, neither of them liked other children, and both had parts of their bodies that didn't seem to work as well as they should. Or maybe because it was Babette who had named her after David found her baby bassinet under the begonia bush that fateful day.

Whatever the reason, Babette always felt a touch more like blood than the others, though she would never admit it.

Begonia parted the tent fabric and stepped inside.

Nana Babette had constructed a sanctuary of scarves, shawls, and NO SOLICITING signs so as not to be disturbed when she left her suite. The space was quite cluttered with worn tarot cards, chipped teacups, pillows, poufs, and cedarwood incense smoke.

To Begonia—the only guest allowed inside—it was nest-like. Warm. A cozy chrysalis and she was a sleepy caterpillar.

Another layer of tension peeled back from her bones like a graying onion skin. The problem was she felt like a really, really big onion.

A crotchety voice echoed from outside the tent flap. "When's that darn radiator getting fixed? It's colder than a witch's glass in here. No, I said 'glass,' Howard."

The fabric *whooshed* aside and Nana Babette entered the tent.

She looked—bless her heart—much like a very old, very agitated beetle. Round, stubby-legged, and hunched under a mound of shawls, sweaters, and beads. Milky gray eyes blinked out from behind bottle-cap glasses as she broke into a wide, toothy grin.

"Ah, pet. Hope I didn't keep you waiting. Those cabbage-brained workers left those paint cans blocking the bathroom, so I had to go *all* the way down the hall to David's office. For his sake, he better let it air out—we had lima beans for lunch." She barked a laugh. "It's his fault anyway. Hideous paint color he picked. Chartreuse. Really, the color of an old bruise."

Begonia didn't feel the need to remind Nana Babette once again that the residents had voted on the paint color, not David. She had a hunch her nana remembered this, but she just liked to complain.

Babette tottered to her favorite wicker chair, muttering curses more loudly than she probably thought she was. Begonia pretended not to hear, watching her plop down with a grunt and take a gulp of cold tea. She rubbed her knee—a pain that had been with her since a childhood illness—and smacked her lips before glancing at her granddaughter.

Her brow crinkled, all signs of anger gone.

"What's wrong, pet?"

Begonia opened her mouth and words came tumbling out. And then didn't stop. David keeping secrets; the auction; the Oddslayer; the weird, magical strokes befalling her grandparents; even her piano skills being worse than normal. And that was saying something.

"And my head is hurting again," Begonia said, toying with the locket around her neck.

"Oh dear. Another migraine." Babette opened her arms, the white skin mapped with hills and valleys of blue veins and liver spots. "Come here, baby."

"I'm too young to be this overwhelmed," Begonia said, words muffled as she buried her head in Babette's shoulder.

"You and me both, pet."

That got a small smile out of Begonia.

"There's that grin. Now, what do I always tell you?"

"Always go to your friends' funerals, or they won't come to yours."

"Not that one."

"Never trust Papaw Rusty in poker?"

"The one about handling our problems."

"Oh yeah. Tackle one problem at a time."

"And if they attack you at once?"

"Knock the smallest one out cold to build your confidence and intimidate the others."

"Good girl. And what is your smallest problem?"

Begonia didn't have an answer. All her problems were towering sea serpents and she, a limp piece of kelp. But she hoped at the very least Nana Babette's Oddity could help her with one.

Seeing the unseen—futures, auras, spirits. That's what Nana could do. Her entire family had Oddities that toed the line between this world and the next, and if there was an invisible creature attacking her grandparents, Babette would know.

Begonia told her as much, but Nana Babette shook her head.

"I've told you about a million times, my dear—if there was a ghost, I would have seen it."

"But a stroke? Black smoke from the eyes? Never-waking sleep? It's at the very least something Odd."

"This house is old and very Odd, so who knows. It could be another infestation of hobgoblins."

Begonia sighed. "No. The gardener sprayed for them last week."

Nana Babette kneaded the lumps from Begonia's shoulders. "Oh, pet. I was in the room with Haneef when he had his stroke, and I can promise you—if there had been a ghost in the room, I would have spotted it. Right away."

Begonia wasn't quite ready to let her sour mood go.

"And everyone's being weird around me. Like I'm made of glass or something, and others ignore me like—"

"Like you've already been taken away."

Taken. Evicted. Kidnapped. Forced to live with terrible Never-Odd children in their terrible orphanage. To never remember David or Babette or her hate for Ms. Majorie, even if she saw them across the street.

Begonia's throat threatened to close. "Yes."

Her nana sighed. "Everyone copes with loss differently. Maybe they are trying to separate themselves from you before—"

She stopped at the look on Begonia's face.

"Oh, come now. There, there. Dry those tears." Babette wiped Begonia's face with her least scratchy shawl. It smelled of old mothballs and floral perfume. Of home.

"You've got to forgive your nana Babette. She's gotten rotten with words in her old age."

Begonia swatted her tears. She hated letting others see her cry.

Her nana booped her nose with the tip of her thumb, her eyes twinkling. "Much better. Now—down to business. Tell me about your plans to ignite your Oddity."

"Nana, it's not coming. I've only got three days and—"

"Well, it won't with that attitude. No, now listen, Begonia—" she said as Begonia opened her mouth to argue. "There isn't a soul who's lived in this manor who hasn't gotten their Oddity by their eleventh birthday. Yours *will* come. You just have to make it show."

"But *how*?"

"That's the question, isn't it? Mine came after I took up chain saw juggling at summer camp."

Begonia's mouth opened in horror. "I have to juggle chain saws?"

"Oh, nothing so dramatic. Flaming torches would probably suffice." Babette cackled. "No, no. Any good scare would do the trick. What are you afraid of? Werewolves? Goblins? The dark?"

"I don't know. What are you scared of?"

"Me? I'm your nana. I'm not scared of anything! Well, maybe the Decrepit Dunderheads, or whatever they call themselves, waking up. You know I despise show tunes."

"Nana!"

"All right, all right. That was out of tune, I'll admit."

Begonia could have sworn she heard her nana add, *"But so is their tenor,"* under her breath, but she decided not to press.

Instead, Begonia pondered her fears, conjuring fanged beasts and clawed monsters from the shadows of her mind. But only the thought of losing her family sent shivers down her back.

She reached once more into the pocket housing David's watch. Babette's eyes followed the motion, but she didn't say anything. Begonia had always had the feeling Babette knew about her sticky fingers—she saw the unseen, after all—yet she had never scolded Begonia for it.

"Now, now, pet," Babette said, rubbing Begonia's hand over the watch. "Don't worry your pretty little head. We'll work on it together, yes?"

Begonia nodded.

"Good. And it will come. Babette can't lose her favorite granddaughter, now, can she?" she said with a wink.

Even though her eyes were still watery, Begonia rolled them anyway. She was Babette's *only* granddaughter.

But Begonia couldn't lose her either. Couldn't lose any more of them.

Even if that meant she would need to find a hardware store and some blade-proof gloves.

4

Fact: The moss that covers most swamps is not moss at all.
It's a flowering plant related to the pineapple.

All the residents of Swamp Root knew that the fastest way to the graveyard was through the Whispering Woods. Since you had to travel there yourself to obtain this story, you know the name of the path is far more sinister than the wood itself. Yes, the trees are alive, and yes, sometimes they stick up a root to trip you, but it's all in good fun.

Honestly, the worst part, according to Begonia, was their terrible puns.

"Pssst."

A deep rumbling moved through the earth, a sound only one who spent time in the company of trees would recognize as laughter.

Begonia heaved out an annoyed breath and rolled her eyes up to an old sycamore.

"Pssssssst. Begoniaaaaaa."

"Hi, Gary."

"I've got a good one for you today," Gary said, his voice full of creaks, crunches, and snaps.

Begonia checked her—David's—pocket watch. "I'm actually in quite a hurry to—"

"Knock knock."

Begonia glared. "Who's there?"

"I could tell you, but you *wooden* believe me."

The woods erupted in creaking laughter. Leaves all around rustled in applause.

"Very good indeed," said a pine.

"Yes," agreed a spruce. "I'd say you definitely *stumped* her with that one."

"Aww, I missed it," whined a crabapple. "Can someone repeat the joke?"

A shrub shivered his leaves to get everyone's attention. "Yeah, Maryanne was left out of the *oak*."

The woods fell silent.

"Get it, guys?" The shrub's branches swayed nervously. "Oak. Joke. Ha ha."

"Get out, Herman," Gary said.

"Ah, man," Herman said, and pulling up his roots, he scurried like a spider to the edge of the forest, leaves downturned.

"Um," Begonia said. "Am I allowed to leave now?"

But the trees, so caught up in their own chatter, paid her no mind. With one last glance over her shoulder, Begonia followed the path out into the open air of the graveyard.

The sun had set behind the storm clouds. Begonia sloshed in the mud all the way up the hill, weaving through the tombstones that rose like crooked gray fingers from the ground. The hill ended in a cliff that overlooked her and David's double-heart beach and the swamp below, looking much the same as it did the day they took the picture in his office.

Holding a stitch in her side, she peered down at the thick green water.

Her heart *tha-dum-bummed* extra hard. It was a long way down.

She wasn't about to juggle chain saws, but tricking her Oddity into thinking she was about to fall might scare it out just the same.

Begonia swallowed the stone in her throat.

Anything for her family. Anything for her Oddity.

She closed her eyes and inched her boot tips over the rocks.

It might just have been the autumn breeze, the rain, or those tricksy bog fairies fluttering about her ears again, but it was as if something changed around Begonia. The air charged. Her skin tingled. Her heart expanded in her chest.

This was it. This was *it*.

Elated, Begonia smiled and stuck one foot out to hover over the ledge.

"Nooo!"

Something barreled toward her, moonlight glinting off glass. The breath *oomphed* from her lungs as she was knocked into a slimy pile of leaves, cold muck dampening her backside.

"*What was that for?!*" Begonia said. She pulled a twist of muddy hair from her eyes and glared at her assailant.

The boy—for it was a boy and not a motorcar, regardless of how Begonia's sore behind told her otherwise—got to his feet gingerly, massaging his shoulder.

Mud clung to his light brown skin, his sweater, his cargo pants. Even his glasses had flecks of earth clouding the lenses. He took them off and rubbed them—well, not clean, but less muddy—on his chest before grimacing down at his loafers.

"Ah, man. Mom is going to kill me."

"Barnabas Montgomery," Begonia spat through gritted teeth. "I should have known."

Barnabas Montgomery was the short, chubby, ten-year-old grandson of Mawmaw Montgomery. Begonia had so far avoided formally meeting him— thanks to all the manor's hidey-holes—but she should have known he would eventually run into her at some point during his two-week stay. She just didn't think the run-in would be literal.

David said it was a regular visit, that he was happy to have another person under the age of one hundred and seven staying at the manor, but Begonia had a hunch Barnabas's moms dumped him here during his autumn vacation in the hopes Mawmaw's musical prowess would coax his Oddity out of him early. They just couldn't wait for another prodigy in the family.

Barnabas, now picking twigs out of his short Afro, smiled up at her with gapped teeth. "I'd prefer Bass, if that's okay. That's what my friends call me."

"We are *not* friends." Begonia huffed. She crossed her arms over her chest.

Barnabas—Bass—was not to be deterred. "Not yet, but we can be!" He held out a pudgy hand.

Begonia could already tell it would be sticky, like most children's. Nasty things, they were. She backed away as if he were contagious. Which he probably was.

"I'm Bass. I like taxidermy and meat loaf with hot sauce—not ketchup—and hate when people call me Barney. Oh, and I have this kazoo!"

His cheeks puffed as he blew on the mouthpiece. It made a pitiful whine. He frowned down at it.

Begonia blinked at him for several seconds. She had never been cursed with a little brother, but if she had, she assumed he would have been something like Barnabas Montgomery.

Which is exactly why she loved being an orphan.

"This might be rude, *Barnabas*, but I just thought you should know: I really, really don't care."

Bass's grin slackened. "But I just saved your life! I feel like that's what friends do, you know? And I could *not* let a friend fall to their death in that swamp. Don't you know the first body part to naturally fall off when you decay in water is your *feet*? And that's only if the turtles don't get to your fingers first."

Begonia did not, in fact, know this odd bit of trivia, but instead of telling him, she filed the information away to use—or hopefully never use—at another time.

The migraine behind Begonia's eye gave a nasty throb. She quivered from head to toe.

"You absolute cabbage, Barnabas Montgomery! I was just about to coax out my Oddity when you knocked me over. I felt it and everything!"

"Wait—you can do that?"

"Yes. Why else would I be on the edge of a smelly old swamp about to fall to my death?"

Begonia unpeeled herself from the mud with a wet plunging sound and stomped to her feet. "My nana Babette says you can make your Oddity show by scaring it into thinking you are about to get seriously hurt. Like, it will show up to save you or something. I was just about to get mine when *you*—"

"Cool! Let's do mine next! Where were you, here? Ooh, I can't wait to see what I get!"

"Absolutely not."

His lip pooched. "But I don't have my Oddity either."

"Listen, small child," Begonia said, placing a consoling hand on his shoulder. "I have my own problems. Way bigger than anything your pea-brain could ever, and will ever, comprehend. Now, Barabbas—"

"Barnabas, but call me—"

"Whatever. Just do one little thing for me."

Bass's eyes lit up. "Anything!"

"*Never* seek out my company again." She patted him thrice and turned on her heel. "Fare thee well, Barney!"

I did try to warn you Begonia wasn't a nice girl.

She was halfway down the hill before she heard clumsy feet squelching in the mud behind her. Something jingled in rhythm to his footsteps, setting Begonia's teeth on edge.

"Are you always this mean?" he asked, catching up to her.

"*Go away, Barry.*"

"Mawmaw always says people that act like they hate others really just hate themselves but aren't smart enough to know it."

"And my nana Babette says the only thing worse than forced conversation is a violent bout of the winds."

"That's a good one!" He giggled. *Giggled.* Followed by a snort.

Tension from her head crept down Begonia's neck. She tried another tactic.

"You better go inside, where it's safe. You don't want the big bad ghost to get you!" Begonia lunged for him, wiggling her fingers menacingly.

Bass swatted her away with a grin. "There isn't a ghost. Mawmaw says that's just superstitious talk."

"But are you *sure*?"

"Of course."

"*Sure-sure?*"

"Yes."

"Like, 'cross your heart, wish on a magpie, pour some poison in your chai,' *sure?*"

His eyebrows fell. "Um, I think so?"

"Well, you know what I think, Barry? I think you should run to your room and lock the door. In fact, just to be safe, I don't think you should come out until your moms come to get you. And don't worry—we can have meals brought up. You can even borrow Papa Newget's bedside commode."

They walked in silence for a few steps, Bass's eyes roaming the dark corners of the grounds and Begonia smirking.

"There isn't a ghost," Bass said under his breath, but he was looking over his shoulder so often he didn't notice how close he was to Begonia's heel.

"Ouch!"

"Sorry! Sorry!"

Begonia stopped; mousetraps *clack-clack-clacked* under her skin. She took a deep, steadying breath to let the steam out of her ears.

"What are you doing skulking around the graveyard at night, anyway? That's what murderers do."

"I'm not a murderer! The opposite, actually."

"What's the opposite of a murderer?"

Bass puffed out his chest. "I am a mortician. Or—well—I want to be one. A mortician-in-training. That's why I was in the graveyard."

Begonia's eyebrows lifted. "Sorry, what?"

"Yeah, I thought I would get a sample of the dirt back here! Some soil is more acidic and affects decomposition differently. I was just scooping this up when I saw you." From deep within one of his pants pockets, he tugged out three different glass jars, all with different shades of brown muck inside. He rattled the contents in Begonia's face as if this was a real treat for her.

The jingling sound suddenly all made sense.

"A mortician?" Begonia asked, hand on her cocked hip.

"You don't believe me? Ask me anything!"

"I'd rather not."

Begonia turned to go, but Bass jumped in front of her, sliding in the mud a little.

"Did you know that if you lined up all your blood vessels, arteries, and blood capillaries, they would roll on for sixty-two thousand miles?"

Begonia crossed her arms, uncomfortable. "Well, of course—"

"And rigor mortis rolls down head to toe, then recedes toe to head?"

"I—"

"But my favorite death fact," Bass said, stars reflecting in his glasses, "is the story of Oren Maffick. Ever heard of him?"

Begonia rolled her tongue over her teeth. "Who hasn't?"

Bass continued as if he hadn't heard her.

"Maffick was a world-renowned coffineer, works envied around the world. No one else could quite get their coffins to be as lightweight, as stylish, or as comfortable."

"How would they know if it was—"

"Maffick was selfish though and kept his coffin-making secrets to himself. Worst of all, he sold his coffins for three times the normal price, ensuring all the poor people in the village had to buy cheap coffins, so their corpses rotted faster and much less comfortably.

"But one night, as he was working under the light of the full moon, lightning struck his workshop, causing the building to shake and a stack of coffins to rain down on him like an avalanche. He died and was buried in one of the coffins that killed him—that *he* made!"

His chest heaved, eyes wide as dung beetles. If he expected Begonia to share his enthusiasm, he was sorely mistaken.

"Mortician, huh?"

"Yeah," Bass said, his excitement waning. He rubbed the back of his neck. "I know it's kinda weird, but—"

"Not musician?"

His face fell. "Oh, yeah. Or I guess I will be anyway. That's why Mawmaw got me this kazoo." He tugged out the orange whistle from the string where it hung around his neck. "I think she's hoping it'll spark some talent in me."

Begonia had a feeling she knew how he felt. Someone else, *something* else deciding your fate. Your worth.

Movement caught her eye. A figure drenched in fog and shadows wove through headstones, and suddenly, music tinkled deep in Begonia's ears. A slow, suspenseful melody. Something that reminded her of scurrying mice and trench coats in back alleys. It made her toes feel like sneaking and her fingers like thieving.

"Mawmaw?" Bass said, squinting into the shadows.

It was Mawmaw Montgomery. Her heart-song crescendoed and her gaze flared as she spotted them.

"Barnabas Lee Isaac Montgomery the Third, what in the name of all things dead and unholy are you doing out here?"

"I'm hanging out with my new friend! Um—playing a game!" Bass said, winking at Begonia.

She acted like she didn't see.

"You better not have snuck out to dig up more animal carcasses. I will not come back to my suite to find another autopsy being performed on my coffee table."

"No, ma'am," Bass said, pushing his jars deeper into his pockets.

Mawmaw Montgomery's eyebrow quirked in a way Begonia hoped it never would at her. "You better not be. Regardless, you know you aren't supposed to be outside alone at night. In a graveyard of all places. The rougarou could have got you. You know he liked that swamp back there."

Bass's forehead creased. "You told me he was taking some time off to travel and find his inner child."

"Did I?" Mawmaw said, her eyes rolling down their muddy bodies. "Lord, look at your shoes. Your momma will skin me alive. Now, inside."

"But—"

"Uh-uh. I don't wanna hear it. *Inside.*" She pointed back to the manor. A letter crinkled in her fist below as she ushered the children up the walk.

"What's that?" Begonia asked.

Mawmaw Montgomery ignored her. Instead, she peeked over her shoulder, a high burst of heart-song wavering through the air. Between the suspenseful melody and Mawmaw's nighttime wanderings, fingers of suspicion were beginning to play notes on Begonia's spine.

"Have you seen David?" Mawmaw asked.

"No," they answered.

Bass pointed to his grandmother's hand. "Mawmaw, who's that letter for?"

"What? Oh. David. I've been looking all over for him, but he's not at any of his local haunts." She laughed, but it rang false.

Begonia studied the letter with her thief's eye. The paper was floppy, moist, and creased as if she'd been worrying it in her hands for hours. Begonia fell a step behind to see if she could make out what it said, but the moonlight was too dim.

She huffed. "David's probably still with Mr. Schmoob, Mawmaw. They sometimes have drinks in the billiard room after meetings when—"

Her lips smooshed against Mawmaw's backside as her grandmother stopped in front of her. Bass *oophed* and Begonia looked over to see the same thing had happened to him.

Something high and shrill exploded in her ears. A violin's cut strings. Wind screeching through dead branches. Broken fingernails on glass.

Begonia had never heard Mawmaw's heart-song play a tune like that. For the first time since entering the graveyard, she was afraid.

Mawmaw's eyes were full moons, searching for a terror she could feel but not see. Begonia did the same.

A pearl-gray figure slid free from the mausoleum. She was old, wrinkled from boots to face. Pale starlight oozed through her transparent skin, her hair, the spindles of ribs exposed through the torn fragments of her dress. A clawed hand stretched toward them as she glided forward, mouth open with a gurgling wail.

Begonia froze, eyes wide, lungs full of stones. But it *couldn't* be a—

"Ghost!" Bass screamed.

Mawmaw turned, disoriented. Arms thrown wide, her hand knocked

Begonia in the chest. Begonia tripped back and grasped at air to keep from falling.

Her fingers found Mawmaw Montgomery's but slipped, ripping the letter from her clutch instead. Begonia landed in the dirt beside a cowering Bass.

The ghost flew at Mawmaw, nails outstretched, mouth open too wide, teeth too long. The ghost screamed, and the sound was unlike anything Begonia had ever heard. Worse than the shrill song of Mawmaw's fear or the Oddslayer's smirk or Mr. Schmoob's favorite words.

The ghost's claws found Mawmaw Montgomery and sank inside, fingers parting her chest like smoke before a knife. There was a brilliant flash of green, a sigh sung from Mawmaw's lips, then, with barely a sound at all, her body crumpled to the ground.

"Mawmaw!" Bass squealed.

Begonia could not think. She could not feel. Her feet had grown roots in the ground. All she saw was her grandmother's face stretched in a silent terror, tendrils of black smoke leaking from black eyes.

The ghost's head swiveled in her direction, her gaze pinning Begonia to the grass.

The scream unclogged from Begonia's throat and flew full force from her body. Mud splattered as Begonia and Bass scrambled over each other, tripping in their haste to flee. They scurried up the path and through the Whispering Woods.

Begonia's lungs burned. Her mind spun. She did not look over her shoulder to see if the ghost was following. She didn't want to know. She did not want to think.

But as the blessed, beautiful, crystal-bright light of Swamp Root Manor came into view, one thought pestered Begonia's mind like vultures circling a dead opossum.

No, not one thought. A truth. A verifiable certainty.

Fact: The ghost of Swamp Root Manor was *real*.

5

Fact: Dentures were once all the rage as wedding presents.

Begonia tugged Bass inside. In the door, up the stairs, down the hall, and then down another hall because the manor had swapped them midway. All the way to Nana Babette's room before busting in the door.

"What on earth—?!"

Nana Babette creaked to her pink-slippered feet, pulling a matching robe tight around her waist. Her dentures swam in a glass of water next to a massive crystal ball and tin of butterscotch candies. She fished them out and plopped them back in.

"What is the meaning of this?"

"It's Mawmaw Montgomery," Begonia said.

"She's dead!" Bass wailed.

"She's not dead. She's just—"

Begonia kneaded the stitch in her side. She didn't know what the ghost had done to their grandmother. Frozen her heart? Spelled her into a forever sleep? Just like her other grandparents. Alive, but wrong.

She couldn't get the image of greasy black smoke oozing from Mawmaw's eyes out of her head. Her chest ached. She wanted to scream, to throw something.

She wanted to steal.

Her head throbbed. She reached to rub it, and something crinkled in her hand.

The letter Mawmaw had for David.

"Alma?" Nana Babette asked, alert. "What happened?"

Begonia slipped the letter into her pocket as the story tumbled free—almost getting her Oddity, the weird way Mawmaw was acting, the ghost attack. Bass interrupted from time to time, adding in details like "leaking black smoke!" and "terrible scream!" and "leaking black *smoke*!"

Nana Babette listened to every word, hand clutched over her heart, scowl growing on her face. By the time they were done, Bass's bottom lip quivered.

"Oh, come here, baby," Nana Babette said to Bass, who let her lead him to her comfiest chair, covered in wool blankets and oatmeal cookie crumbs. She tucked the throw over his shoulders and handed him the dish of butterscotch candies.

A worm of jealousy inched under Begonia's skin. She decided not to warn Bass that those candies were stale enough to break his teeth. He'd figure it out.

She followed behind them and plunked down on the sofa.

Nana Babette's suite was much like her tent downstairs—mismatched fabric-patterned, pills and tonic bottles, and lots of crystals, cards, and clutter—except this room could fit a cozy sleeping nook and wash closet.

It usually felt like home, but there was currently a very squeezy boa constrictor living around Begonia's neck that was making it very hard for her to feel comfortable anywhere.

The netted curtains parted as Nana Babette squinted out the window. "The night shift must have been looking for her. They're bringing her up to the manor now."

Begonia leapt to her side. Through the haze of twilight and window grime, she could just make out a group of nurses hauling a limp form across the grounds on a stretcher.

Dots danced in Begonia's vision to the matching rhythm behind her brow. She had to bite back a growl. It wouldn't have surprised her if one day her fingers permanently fused themselves to her eyes from rubbing the pressure so often.

Pain. Always pain.

It did, however, chase away some of her fear and anxiety, leaving the one emotion she could deal with.

Anger.

"You said there's no ghost," Begonia said, glaring at Babette.

Babette had bumbled off to the portable kettle, measuring tea into strainers and clacking saucers. "I don't know if now is the time to talk of such things. Given your friend's state."

"Well, I disagree. And so does Barry. Don't you?" Begonia threw him an encouraging look.

"Bass," Bass corrected.

"See?" Begonia said.

The kettle screamed. Babette took her time filling the chipped china and loading the tea tray with cookies before setting it down on the coffee table between them. She eased herself into an armchair, massaging her knee.

Begonia didn't touch her cup. "You do believe us, don't you?"

"I believe that you believe you saw something in the graveyard."

A sourness slipped down Begonia's throat. Slimy and wriggling. Her face must have said aloud what she could not, because Babette jumped to continue.

"If there was a ghost, I promise I would have told you about it. You know that."

But Begonia had *seen* it. Bass had seen it. Mawmaw Montgomery certainly saw it too.

Her mind spun webs in all directions. Maybe since the ghost had been seen by many now, it didn't count as "unseen," and Nana Babette's Oddity would pick up on it.

Although vexing, the thought made Begonia feel slightly better. She explained her theory to Babette, who listened carefully, but Begonia felt that she was just appeasing her.

After a long sip of Earl Grey, Babette set her mug down. "I still think I would have seen a ghost if it were in our own house, but"—she added as Begonia opened her mouth to argue—"things *could* slip through the cracks, I suppose. I am getting older."

Begonia groaned and collapsed into the armchair. If the ghost was real, which she knew it was, it would be the lock on the coffin lid, sealing her family's fate inside, six feet under. Because a real ghost in a haunted resort? Mrs. Pingleton would be unbearable.

Well, more unbearable.

"There has to be something we can do," Bass said, popping a candy in his mouth. He broke into choking coughs. Babette patted his back.

Bass was right. There had to be a way to fix all of this, and like any good thief, Begonia knew a successful heist was planned from the ground up. So Begonia started at the foundation.

"What do you know about the ghost's story?" Begonia asked Nana Babette.

Nana helped herself to an oatmeal cookie. She offered one to Begonia, but she waved it away.

"The same superstitions as everyone else. It's all phooey, if you ask me. These old people have nothing to do but talk."

"But you've been here forever. You must have heard something else. Something we've missed that could be important!"

"I haven't heard the story," Bass said, still massaging his throat.

Nana Babette snapped crumbs from her fingers, looking ill-tempered. "Oh, all right, all right, but don't get your tarantulas in a twiddle, there's not much of a story here!"

"Tell it anyway," Begonia said.

"All I know is people say a witch used to live here. Edith Hollowmoor. The Hollowmoors built Swamp Root Manor, which is why I thought it made sense to give you that as a last name."

Begonia frowned. She didn't like sharing the ghost's last name, even if it was only because she didn't have one of her own.

"What did she do?" Bass asked.

"Dark things, I guess. Whatever it is witches do. Then a spell went wrong, and she got sucked into the walls or some other nonsense."

"Sucked into the manor?" Bass said, eyes roaming the ceiling.

"Your guess is as good as mine," Nana Babette said with a dismissive wave. She took another swig of her tea.

Bass shivered. "That's horrifying."

But instead of fear, fire scorched through Begonia's veins. "If I had my Oddity, I bet I could defeat her."

"You don't even know what your Oddity will be," Bass said. "It could be something like growing extra-long, luscious nose hair—"

"Then I would use my luscious nose hair to set a trap, tripping the ghost, then tying her up with it until I find a way to banish her."

Fact: **The longest nose hair recorded by Never Odds was 0.7 inches.**

Fact: **The longest nose hair recorded by Odds was from Grandpa "Nosy" Norman, whose length reached 8.2 yards. Norman, in fact, set this very same trap for his mortal foe, Grandad Theodore, after a nasty incident involving garden shears, a wet suit, and a rather ill-tempered porcupine.**

Bass shot her a droll expression. "I don't think that's how ghosts work."

"What do you know about it? You're the only Montgomery in four generations without a musical Oddity."

Bass's chin fell to his chest as he sank into the folds of the armchair.

"Begonia Hollowmoor!" Nana Babette said, eyes flashing behind her spectacles. "I didn't raise you to speak so rudely to your friends."

But Begonia wasn't paying attention. A cauldron's flame sparked to life inside her, potion bubbling silver white. For in the flash of Babette's glasses reflected the crystal ball.

"That's it!" Begonia said. She slid to the floor and huddled around the edge of the table, eye level with the glass orb. "You can use your crystal ball to tell us how to defeat the ghost!"

"Oh, I don't think—"

66

"Pleeeeease!"

"Is it even real?" Bass said. He quickly sank deeper into the armchair cushions under Nana Babette's glare.

"Prove it to him!" Begonia said, crawling before her nana, hands clasped as if in prayer.

"You know I don't have to prove myself."

"Come on, Nana!"

"Will it help my mawmaw?" Bass asked.

He peered up at Babette, face still red with admonishment, but there was hope there too. Eyes big and wide like furry forest ferrets. It was a nice touch.

It seemed to soften Babette. Or at least, dissolve the angry V on her forehead.

"Oh, all right. Let's see what the spirit world has to say."

"Yes!" Begonia said. She shot a look of glee to Bass, who cracked the smallest of smiles.

They gathered around the table as Babette adjusted the light knob, dimming the gas lamps with a soft *shhh*. She then took her time lighting candles and some incense that tickled Begonia's nose before placing the crystal ball in between them. She settled herself back in her armchair and leaned over the table.

"I'll need quiet to reach the Beyond," Babette said with a stern glance at the two.

"Where's that?" Bass asked, gaze roaming over the room as if expecting to find a signpost. Then, noticing Babette's raised eyebrow, he fell quiet.

Babette closed her eyes with a *hmpf*, hands hovering above the crystal ball. Bats fluttered in Begonia's chest as the seconds ticked by. Within a few minutes, Begonia was squirming, unable to keep still.

The air hummed. The watch in Begonia's pocket ticked. Bass huffed, recrossing his legs for the fifth time.

Bass opened his mouth, about to break the silence, when a breeze tore through the room. The candles flickered out, the gas lamps sputtered. Bass gasped and Begonia gripped the edge of the tablecloth. Babette remained motionless.

The crystal ball flared to life, bright blue mist swirling within. The light cast long, haunting shadows on the walls and drenched Babette's face in an eerie glow.

She opened her mouth and words erupted, but the words didn't seem to come from her body—they echoed from the floors and walls, from Begonia's skull itself. It boomed so loud Begonia covered her ears and Bass dove under the table with a squeal.

"An Oddject of power resides on this hallowed ground
Where twin hearts are affixed and grief goes to drown.
Kindred souls on an odyssey to reveal their powers,
Their fates intertwined until the final hours.

The Oddject is precious; breathe a word to no one.

Follow this clue and the prize will be won:

Up and up, go clippings to weep.

Yearn for the dust of that true deep sleep.

Now hurry, keep quiet, for enemies abound.

But the reward is great if it is to be found."

The sound died. The wind stilled. The crystal ball dimmed and the candles fluttered happily as if they had never been blown out.

Begonia's heart slowly moved back down her throat. She had seen Babette do a lot of Odd stuff, but this was a lightning storm when everything else was a spring shower.

Babette blinked as if awaking from an afternoon nap. She fumbled for her teacup, downing the remains in one gulp.

Begonia swallowed, reaching out a tentative hand. "Nana? Are you all right?"

Bass's head peered out around the leg of the table, hands still clasped over his ears.

Babette slumped back in her chair and gave Begonia a weak smile. "That took a lot out of me, I'm afraid."

"Here," Begonia said, placing a pillow behind her head and pulling a tartan blanket off the couch. She tucked it around her until her nana looked like a large, misshapen burrito.

"Thank you, pet. But don't worry, I'm tougher than I look."

Sure her nana was safe, Begonia turned her thoughts to the riddle still echoing in her bones. Her mind whirled, higher and faster, a kite caught in a tornado.

"Um, what did that mean?" Bass said. With shaking arms, he pulled himself up on the armchair.

But Begonia's mind was already worlds ahead.

"An Oddject of power resides on this hallowed ground . . ."

She turned to him, a wild glint in her eyes.

"It means there is a magical object hidden at Swamp Root that will ignite my Oddity."

6

Fact: Solid black cats are more likely to be male than female.

"Most of it's straightforward," Begonia said, refilling everyone's teacups. They had been poring over the pages where Bass had copied down the prophecy for the last few minutes.

"Number one," Begonia said. "We can't blab to everyone we know about what I'm up to. Number two: I follow the clue at the end to find the hidden Oddject and reveal my Oddity."

She was still stumped over the second line, however. She had no idea where twin hearts were affixed—whatever that meant—or how grief could drown in the first place.

But she *would* figure it out. This was her one chance to find her Oddity and, with any luck, to use her power to rid the nursing home of both the ghost and Mrs. Pingleton. Failure wasn't an option.

"*Our* Oddities," Bass reminded her. He squinted at the ink-smudged paper before him. "It says, 'kindred souls on an odyssey to reveal their powers, their fates intertwined until the final hours.' That has to mean you and me are going on an adventure! To get our Oddities and save Mawmaw!"

Begonia scowled. "Absolutely not."

"It's what the prophecy said!"

"Nana!"

Nana Babette dunked her tea bag in the steaming water, still more pale and weak than Begonia would have liked. "I think Bass is right, pet. It does seem to refer to two people needing their powers revealed. You and Bass are the only ones in the manor without Oddities."

Bass smirked at her, an imp in glasses.

"I can handle this heist on my own, thanks."

Bass's eyes lit like Granny Jean's eyebrows whenever the milkman stopped by. "Oh, a 'heist' is a great word for it! It will be like a game!"

"This is not a game!"

But Bass was practically bouncing out of his seat. "Ooh, you know what we need? A name! All good crime organizations have one."

Begonia's mouth fell open in outrage.

Nana Babette shrugged and said, "I think it's a lovely idea."

Begonia made a choking sound. Over the top of her teacup, Nana Babette mouthed, *Be nice,* and Begonia's insides liquefied like a month-old corpse. Overruled, she slumped back in the sofa.

Bass punched the air and whooped. Then his quill feverishly started to scribble its way across paper.

"Okay, okay, okay—what about the Order of Odd?"

Begonia rolled her eyes. "Too on the nose."

His pencil scratched.

"The Global League of Oddity Experts?"

"Too much."

Scratch.

"The Odd Company?"

"Speak for yourself."

Scratch.

"How about the Oddacious Operative Alliance. OOA for short."

Begonia sighed, pinching the bridge of her nose. "Fine. But I'm the ringleader and you are my lowly henchman, understand?"

Bass pumped his fist. "Yes!"

Begonia's eyes rolled open, heat scorching the side of Bass's face.

His smile dropped, and he saluted her. "I mean, sir, yes, sir!"

"Well," Nana Babette said, clapping her hands. "If you are an official organization now, you need badges."

She got to her feet and walked toward her dresser, rumbling around in the drawers.

Begonia winced. "Badges?"

"Great idea!" Bass said. "Like a secret way for members of the gang to recognize other members."

"It's just you and me though."

But no one seemed to be listening. Poison simmered in Begonia's gut. No one but her understood how important this was. How serious. How not like a game this was.

This was life or death, and technically the ghost was already dead, so life or death or undead. Even more serious.

"Here we are," Babette said, pulling something shiny free from a stray pair of pantyhose. She walked back to her sitting area. "Now close your eyes."

Bass shut his right away, hopping to his feet. Begonia managed to shoot one last round of eyeball-daggers at him before doing as she was told. Nana's fingers pinched the fabric right above her heart. She peeled open an eye and found a brooch shaped like a daisy pinned to her chest.

"Now look!" Nana Babette said.

"Whoa, neat!" Bass said, holding his shirt out so he could see the black cat brooch on his chest.

They were both very old-fashioned and old lady-ish, which was normally Begonia's style, but she wasn't going to be happy no matter what until she had snatched that Oddject.

"They don't even match," Begonia said.

"You don't want them to match," Nana said with a wink. "Too much uniformity will make it easier to spot the other if one of you is apprehended."

Bass gulped. "Is that likely?"

"Of course, Barnabas. You are going on a quest. And what did the prophecy say? 'Enemies abound'?"

Something seemed to click inside Bass's brain. And that something was probably his own mortality.

"Um, Nana Babette? How many people die on the quests your prophecies send them on?"

Nana Babette patted his shoulder and gave him her best toothy smile. "Don't worry yourself over such silly matters, my dear. Sure, there's been a few deaths, but none of them serious. Now"—she clapped her hands once more and turned to Begonia, failing to notice the delicate shade of green Bass had turned—"what do you make of the clue?"

Up and up, go clippings to weep.

Yearn for the dust of that true deep sleep.

Begonia smiled. "I think I know exactly where to look."

A knock rattled the door, and all three of them jumped. Babette's brow wrinkled. She grabbed her walking stick and inched toward the door.

Begonia held her breath as Nana Babette turned the handle, swung open the door, and—

Saw Ms. Majorie towering right outside. She sneered at Babette and Begonia hiding behind her, before her eyes trained on Bass.

"I'm so pleased to find you, Mr. Montgomery," Ms. Majorie said, looking anything but. "Mr. Klein wishes to see you in his office."

"Me?" Bass asked, voice high.

"Yes, terrible news. It seems your grandmother has suffered a stroke." Her wide mouth slithered into an oily leer. "Shame."

Begonia caught Bass's eye. She shook her head a fraction of an inch. Trying to convince Ms. Majorie of the truth about Mawmaw Montgomery would be a waste of time.

"A-all right," Bass said.

Ms. Majorie turned, not waiting to see if he would follow. Begonia linked her arm through his.

"I'll go with you."

His eyes danced in their sockets. "Because us OOA squad stick together!"

"No, because I don't want you to bungle the story up in front of David."

"Children! Be careful," Nana Babette called from her door as they made their way down the hall. "And if you see the ghost, give her a good kick up the—"

The manor pipes issued a loud whistle.

"—for me!"

Begonia tightened her hold on Bass's arm. It was high time she brought everything she'd learned to the one person who maybe knew Swamp Root Manor better than anyone else.

David.

7

Fact: Goggles are worn by many people in different occupations—chemists, hot air balloon drivers, and botanists that work in close contact with the Spitting Sanservieria Vinus, though their venom has been known to melt plastic.

"Pushing Daisy, this is Nine Lives. Do you read me? Over."

"Keep it down," Begonia hissed.

Bass's hands cupped the cat pin on his chest as he talked into it like Begonia wasn't just a foot in front of him.

She ground her teeth, wishing they were fangs.

Bass was a terrible henchman. He never stopped talking. His nose whistled. His shoes clattered against the hardwood like bones. Worst of all, every time she looked at him, Bass gazed up with wide puppy dog eyes, full of admiration and wonder, as if she were the final stitch in a beloved taxidermy project.

The sooner she talked to David, the sooner she could find the Oddject and be rid of Barnabas. She quickened her pace down the dark corridor.

A part of Begonia wished Ms. Majorie had escorted them to David's office, if only to be the sacrifice Begonia would offer if the ghost showed up again, but alas, she had rushed off to listen to her nightly romance broadcast, leaving Begonia and the Worst Sidekick Imaginable to make the journey alone.

"So I was thinking. We really should have a panic word. Just in case one of us needs backup or to shout for a fast escape, you know? Personally, I like 'undertaker.' It's an old term for—"

"Those who took care of the dead, I know."

Begonia stopped by the cracked bust of Duke Penwalfus Redicklington mounted against the peeling wallpaper. He was carved entirely of stone, from his full cheeks to the false mustache hanging from his lip like a broken spider leg. She gently straightened it and the stone clicked into place.

"Thank you," he said, swinging forward to reveal a secret door handle in the wall. Begonia turned it and pushed until the wall opened into a low-lit passage-way, her trusty shortcut to the foyer. Most of the time anyway.

"No funny business," she said to the manor, stepping inside. "I won't have you dumping me out in the toilet again."

The walls hummed in laughter. Bass followed behind, taking in the wood rafters and cobwebs with wide eyes.

"Wow, I've never been this way before. Are we in the walls? Creepy."

"It's only creepy because you don't live here."

"*Psh.* No one lives in the walls."

"The rats do. And Grandpa Fitz from time to time."

Bass prattled on through the maze of wood beams, babbled while they slid down a dusty fireman's pole, and waxed poetic about the Seventeen Laws of

Moral Conduct in the Art of Corpse Positioning during Wakes as they climbed to freedom through the hidden exit in the grandfather clock.

She might have slammed its door a little harder than necessary. It did seem to tick extra loud at her.

The foyer was still, moonlight gleaming against the chipped marble floors and oil paintings. Begonia could just make out yellow candlelight spilling from David's office at the opposite end. She trudged for it, Bass on her heels.

"—and that was the fourth time I learned the hard way, but as Dr. Mort Acini always says, '*Gloves finger to elbow every time, lest your nail beds host corpse slime!*'"

Begonia whirled around. She closed her eyes and took a deep breath. "Peevish Child."

"Bass!" he corrected, beaming up at her.

"Just—please, *please* stop talking."

"Wow! You're as red as a tomato!"

Begonia massaged the tension in her forehead, feeling herself give way. "I hate tomatoes. They aren't even really vegetables."

"I know! They are a fruit in the nightshade family! My favorite is belladonna—one of the trickiest poisons to detect in autopsies. Did I ever tell you about the time—"

Heels clicked across the floor. Begonia's heart hopscotched through her rib cage. She grabbed Bass by the scruff of his collar and yanked him into a coat closet.

"Hey!" Bass said, voice muffled. He spat as Begonia smooshed him into a fur-trimmed collar.

"Shh!"

The clomping stopped outside the door. Barely daring to breathe, Begonia peered through the crack.

Fact: In some ancient societies, high heels were banned because the style was associated with witchcraft.

Fact: The ancient pyramid builders forced their butchers to wear high heels in order to keep their feet out of the animal blood.

Fact: High heels push the body's center of gravity forward, placing the spine and the brain—especially in the case of the villain before Begonia—out of alignment.

Mrs. Pingleton stood facing the opposite wall, smoothing flat a split in the wallpaper. "Positively derelict!" She pulled a notepad and pen from her massive handbag and flipped open to the first page. Her hand swirled across its surface.

"Add—more—stylized—rips. The more—clawlike—the better."

She punctuated her note with a sharp jab of her pen and, with a giggle, slipped her notepad away.

"Who's that?" Bass asked, wrestling forward to see, stepping on Begonia's foot. She retaliated with a swift jab of her elbow.

"Ouch!"

Begonia clapped her hand over Bass's mouth as Mrs. Pingleton's head shot up. Bass gasped between her fingers. Mrs. Pingleton glanced around, eyes finding the closet door ajar.

With a smirk and a hair flip, she strode forward, heels piercing the marble like knives. She bent down so her lips pressed between the door and the wall, right in the shadow hiding Begonia's face.

"Is that you, little Begonia? That's your name, right?"

Begonia didn't breathe. Neither did Bass, but that was probably because her grip was blocking his airway.

Her words were sticky and sweet, honey mixed with tar. "I'm glad I found you. I've been wanting to have a little chat. You see, I admire your determination to save your home, I really do. And business is never personal. You'll understand that when you're older. But just so we're clear—this manor is *mine*. It will be the crowning glory in my haunted resort empire." Her tone, if possible, rose to an even more sugary pitch. "And there is nothing you, or Mr. Klein, or anyone else can do to take that away from me. Am I understood?"

Begonia's vision flashed red. Bass made a choking sound between her fingers. She eased up on his face and he heaved in a grateful breath.

Mrs. Pingleton straightened, smiling like a fox who ate the egg, the hen, and the farmer to boot. "Splendid! And don't worry, dear—when you turn sixteen, there will always be a job for you here. I'm sure a place like this never runs out of toilets to clean!"

She sauntered away, heels clacking, curls bouncing. Once she had disappeared down the hall, Begonia burst from the closet.

"What is that horrible woman still doing here?"

Bass peeked out around her, eyes following Mrs. Pingleton's fading shadow. He bit his lip. "I don't know. Maybe scoping out the location?"

"Sneaking around is more like it. I bet David doesn't even know she's still here." Begonia's smile was a mean thing. "Be nice if the ghost got her next."

"Don't say things like that!" Bass said. Sweat had broken out on his forehead. He tugged her sleeve, eyes roving the darkest corners of the room. "Come on. David, remember? We have my mawmaw to save."

Begonia let him pull her forward, but not before she vowed to add another name to her nemesis list.

"Keep an eye on her," Begonia whispered to the walls. The picture frames quivered with excitement.

Raised voices echoed from the office.

"Don't you have something more useful to be doing besides torturing the bloody bejeezus out of me?"

Interest piqued, Begonia peered around the doorframe.

David stood behind the seated Oddslayer, wrestling a pair of goggles matching his own around the grungy man's head. The Oddslayer winced as the band snapped onto his brow.

"This junk is interesting and all, but I'm here to discuss the girl. Wouldn't it be best to take her now, get one more flea out of your wig?"

He tried to rise, but David clamped a hand on his shoulder, throwing him back down with an "Oy!"

"Begonia is not a flea," David said, adjusting the nozzle on what looked to be a small tank of goo duct-taped to the side. "And if you're going to be here for three days, then you can at least make yourself useful. I can't afford to house people for free."

"Doesn't look like you can afford much of anything. Ouch!"

"Is that a POO?" Bass whispered, frozen.

"Unfortunately," Begonia said. Her stomach felt heavy as a tombstone. She grabbed the locket around her neck, rubbing its smooth surface for comfort.

The POO spoke again. "What about the sick old bag who was all stiff and smoky? Shouldn't you be with her?"

David took a while to answer, and when he did, his voice came soft. "Mrs. Montgomery has been moved to her suite. An Odd Doc will be here in an hour to look her over, but until the rest of her family arrives, *you* hold still. I want to see if these work on—"

Bass leaned into the door. Begonia gritted her teeth, but it was too late. It squeaked open, revealing the two of them standing in the hall, ears forward and eyes wide.

The Oddslayer's face broke into a vicious grin. "There she is. The belle of the ball."

He shook David off, standing to his full, lanky height. His beady pupils, amplified to the size of tea saucers behind the green lenses, cut through Begonia's very bones.

Shock registered on David's face for a moment as his eyes swung from the POO to Begonia. Then his gaze fell to Bass.

"Come here, son," he said, and Bass stumbled forward.

David put a hand on his shoulder, crouching to eye level. "Barnabas. I'm so sorry I have to tell you this, but—"

"I already know about Mawmaw," Bass said, glancing at Begonia, "but it wasn't a stroke! It was the ghost. We saw her. I promise we did. She—"

"I believe you, Barnabas."

Begonia's mouth dropped open. She knew he would believe them, but she didn't *know* know.

"You do?" Bass asked.

"Yes, actually. You live in this manor long enough, you start to believe anything's possible."

Begonia mirrored Bass's grin.

David leaned back on his desk. His hand bumped a book off the stack in the corner and it landed on the hardwood with a *thwack*.

Seances and Science: Gadging Ghouls with Gadgets and Gallantry, by Flanus Thopman.

David noted Begonia's interest and slid the text away.

"But this isn't something you children need to be concerned with. I'm going to sort this out. Promise," he said. "Both of you are to keep to your rooms. At least until the rest of your family arrives, Barnabas. I don't want you two meddling in such dangerous affairs."

"But we can help!" Bass said. He glanced to Begonia for aid.

Begonia addressed David. "Could we speak to you in private?"

"Don't think so, love," the POO said, inspecting his filthy fingernails and crossing his muddy boots over David's desk. "Surely whatever you have to say can be said in front of me."

Begonia's foot toyed with a loose floorboard. "Well, it's a really serious matter—"

"Then as the Committee's representative, I'd love to hear it."

Begonia glanced back and forth between David and the Oddslayer. Concern and condescension.

The Oddject is precious; breathe a word to no one . . .

But David might know something she didn't. He could help her with the twin heart–grieving clue, and maybe what the dust of true sleep was, as those two lines continued to stump her. As things were going, she'd never figure it out on her own.

"Begonia?" David said, concern etched on his face.

She flinched. He still didn't say her name right. Not like he used to. Before, it had been as if the very word was an exclamation point, or a sunset, or a shiny new toolbox filled with all his favorite knickknacks.

Now the letters dripped like tears.

Begonia shook her head clear, remembering why she was there. She launched into an explanation of everything Babette told her about the ghost, the prophecy, and the Oddject hidden on the grounds.

David's frown deepened the longer she talked. She swore she even saw a chestnut wave near his temple boing into a tight silver curl. The Oddslayer, who was a terrible audience, tutted every few sentences and spat his dirty nails on the floor.

"*'Reveal your powers'?*" David said. "If this is about your Oddity again, Bug, I told you—*it will come.* You're just a bit of a late bloomer."

The POO cleared his throat. "If I may be so bold as to give my professional advice—not likely, chap. Once a lame duck, always a lame duck. Quite unfortunate, that."

Begonia's throat filled with grave dust.

"Give me three facts," David said, holding her braids as she leaned over the bedpan. Her head hurt. Her gut rolled. The floor was no longer under her knees.

"I can't," Begonia panted. She pressed her fist into her eyes, biting down another heave. "It hurts too much."

David rubbed her back. "Deep breath in and out. There you go. Good. I want you to breathe deep, and each time you let it out, think of a fact from the book I gave you."

"Why?"

"Because you have been given a weight others haven't. And I want you to learn to deal with it the best you can. This is called relaxation and diversion. Do you know what that means?"

Begonia didn't want to rattle her head, so she just closed her eyes. David understood. They didn't have to speak to talk sometimes. That was one of the things she loved about him.

"It means we are going to think about something else to take your mind off the pain. Because focusing on it makes it worse."

"But it won't help!"

"It won't make it go away, but it will help you carry it."

Tears leaked over Begonia's chin. "David. I—I don't want this."

David hid his face, voice jagged as cliff rocks. "I know, Bug. If I could take it from you, I would. But you are strong. You will survive this one, just like you did the last one, just like you will the next."

He smoothed back the hair from her damp brow, and she leaned into his touch. He pinned on the bravest smile he could. "Now, the fact. Which one will you tell me?"

Begonia nodded and slowly pushed herself upright, even though thunder and lightning *warred behind her eyes. She set her jaw, deciding then and there she was stronger than any storm.*

That she was the storm.

And with a wobble in her chin, she spun through the list of trivia in her mind.

Back in the office, David's voice came sharp and dark. "I will not tolerate talk like that in my manor."

The POO smirked but said nothing, ripping into his next cuticle.

"Besides, I found that in the time I waited for my Oddity to arrive, I learned some truly valuable life lessons." David got up and spun to his glass display cabinet, where he kept his more delicate unventions. His finger traced the glass over a whirling Doohickey and buzzing Thingamabob. Brown eyes, which always seemed sad and misty of late, shone with the starlight of memories. "Being resourceful is an important skill, with or without powers. I made these before I knew what my Oddity would be, and now look what I can do." He gestured around to all his unventions filling the room with their disjointed metallic song.

Begonia shook her head once more. "David, there's only three days until my birthday. Really two, because today is almost over. I can't wait. And neither can the nursing home."

"She's got a point, you know," the Oddslayer said.

"Oh, do shut up," David snapped. The POO chuckled.

Begonia bit the inside of her cheek to keep from screaming. Her fists balled in her pockets and something crinkled against her skin.

Mawmaw Montgomery's letter.

"Wait!" Begonia said, struggling to rip the note free from her smock. With everything going on, she'd forgotten about it. "Mawmaw Montgomery had this on her when she was attacked. She said she was looking for you!"

"That's right! It might help!" Bass said.

"She was looking for me?"

David unfolded the mud-splattered letter, and Begonia and Bass peered over his side to read. The POO leaned over as well.

"Do you *mind*?"

The POO threw up his hands in penance and backed away.

Dearest David,

The most grievous news has come to my attention. The information is so shocking, so unbearably sinister that I cannot find the proper words. Therefore, I will find the notes.

Down the rest of the page sprawled a hand-drawn music staff titled "Confessions," by Alma Montgomery. There were no words, but it was clear from the jaunty cape-like flourishes on the backs of the eighth notes that this sang of Mawmaw Montgomery's signature flair.

Begonia deflated.

"What did she need to tell you?" Bass asked, shoulders slumped, no doubt just as disappointed by the lack of information.

David took his time pressing the letter into a neat, tiny square before tucking it into his back pocket. "I have no idea."

"I bet she memorized whatever she was going to sing to you. That's her style," Bass said. He then gasped, startling everyone in the room. "Ooh, Begonia! Maybe she found out something about the hidden Oddject. Or even the ghost!"

Begonia nodded, hope trickling into her limbs once more. "It's definitely a possibility. David, could you help me with the prophecy clues? I don't know what certain lines—"

David held up a hand. "Now, hold on just a minute. I cannot allow the two of you to traipse around the manor at night—alone—with an angry ghost on the loose."

"Then come with us!" Begonia said.

"I can't, Bug. Someone has to be here when the Odd Doc arrives. In fact, he should be here soon."

David felt around the many pockets of his jacket and trousers. Frowning, he pulled open his desk drawer, shuffling the contents around.

Begonia paled.

"Bug, have you seen my pocket watch?"

Fact: People on average lie four times a day.

Fact: Statistically, people lie more in January than any other month.

Fact: It is easier to keep up a lie with one-word answers than by concocting elaborate stories.

Therefore, Begonia lied with a simple—

"No."

David's hand ran through his hair, goggled eyes roaming the cluttered office. "I'm sure it's around here somewhere. But all the same—I want the two of you to stay in your rooms, understand?"

"But—!"

"No *buts*, Begonia. I'm serious. And I'll be having a word with Babette about encouraging you to get involved. Now come on. I'll take the two of you up to your suites."

David steered them from the office with a hand on their shoulders. Begonia glanced back at the Oddslayer, who was struggling with the goggle strap around his skull.

"Oy! Can I take this thing off now?"

David didn't answer until they disappeared from the POO's sight, heading toward the stairs. "Just place it back on the desk. *And be careful.*"

Begonia paid them no mind.

Because Mawmaw Montgomery knew something. Something that may have been the reason she was attacked.

And Begonia was going to find out what it was.

91

8

Fact: Each day, 4.5 pounds of sunlight hits Earth.

None of that light reached Swamp Root Manor. This was because storm clouds were lazy, according to Pepaw Leroy, who, besides growing nails where his hair should be and hair where his nails should be, had a deep love of meteorology. The cloud that took up permanent residence over Swamp Root—Reba, as Pepaw Leroy had named her—snored over the ground nearly 365 days a year.

None of us are perfect, however, and as we all sometimes do, Reba would stretch herself a little too thin. At the first offensive sprinkle of sunlight, the manor would shift a hair to the left, dousing itself in cozy gloom once more.

While no one ever caught the manor doing this, it wasn't uncommon to wake up to all your belongings having shifted two inches to the left overnight or, say, experience walking down the hall with a brimming bowl of tomato soup when there is a great lurch and suddenly you are covered head to toe in a steaming fruit that is not a vegetable.

The manor did love chaos, after all, and all chaotic things stick to the shadows.

Sticking to the shadows, Begonia and Bass snuck down the main hall. Sure, they were supposed to be captives in their rooms, but Begonia had a mission.

The night before, she had stayed up formulating, plotting, and rolling the prophecy riddle around in her mind until she could recite it in her grave.

"An Oddject of power resides on this hallowed ground

Where twin hearts are affixed and grief goes to drown.

Kindred souls on an odyssey to reveal their powers,

Their fates intertwined until the final hours.

The Oddject is precious; breathe a word to no one.

Follow this clue and the prize will be won:

Up and up, go clippings to weep.

Yearn for the dust of that true deep sleep.

Now hurry, keep quiet, for enemies abound.

But the reward is great if it is to be found."

At the first crack of Reba—thunderstorm forecast, again—Begonia crept from her bed and slid open her bedroom door, only to find Bass glaring up at her.

"We have to find the Oddject together, Begonia! The Oddacious Operative Alliance unite! OOA! OOA!" he said, pumping his fist and tooting his kazoo until Begonia threatened to shove it up his nose.

So, unfortunately, Begonia whispered her plan to her annoying sidekick as they crept downstairs. Quickly his excitement turned into apprehension.

"I don't know," Bass said. "It sounds really risky."

"Stop being such a baby, Montgomery," Begonia said, checking both sides of the corridor before crossing into the open. "I'm a professional."

Bass looked unconvinced. "I'm down for a heist to find the lost Oddject, but stealing?"

Begonia rolled her eyes. "Relax. It's just Ms. Majorie."

In fact, Begonia thought she might even enjoy this bout of thieving more than usual.

Bass followed silently for a few steps, chewing over his thoughts before eventually shrugging. "Well, it's your funeral if she catches you, and I'm really good at working the crematorium now, so I'm in."

"Good. So what's your assignment?"

"Keep a lookout for David."

"And?"

"No code names!"

"And?"

"Stay hidden so well it's as if I never darkened the doorway of existence in the first place!"

"Perfect," Begonia said, and peered around the corner into the heist zone.

The morning room ("The *mourning* room, you mean," Babette would correct anytime the brunch parlor was mentioned, "*because that's where all the old farts sit around waiting to die!*") was crowded with rickety tables and irritable elders gumming their porridge and arguing about whose rheumatism was the worst.

In short, it was a hotbed for disaster.

A line of elders had formed around the far wall, awaiting their pills, tonics, and tinctures. The only grandparent away from the others was Nini Zehra, Begonia's smallest, oldest grandma, who leaned against the window breathing in the weak sunlight as little whiffs of her dandelion curls floated serenely around her face. She photosynthesized her breakfast.

Ms. Majorie stomped into the room. She looked sour as ever, bearing her basket of morning doses. Her frog-like voice croaked over the din. "All right, you lot. Line up alphabetically by height, in no particular order. Hurry up, hurry up! Form a circle, I don't have all day!"

As Begonia's grandparents moseyed about in their general confusion for the medicines, Begonia spotted exactly what she had been searching for dangling from a shiny belt loop off Ms. Majorie's uniform.

Her face split into a wicked grin.

Up and up, go clippings to weep . . .

Fact: **Fingernails grow 4x faster than toenails.**

Fact: **Toenails grow faster in the summer than in the winter.**

Fact: **Toenails are made of the same protein as hair.**

That last piece of trivia would be very interesting to Pepaw Leroy, but at that current moment, Begonia was more concerned with the first two.

Now, I must stop you here, my Tiptoeing Toenail, to explain a few things necessary for your understanding. As you will have learned, Swamp Root

Manor was an unusual place, full of impossible impossibilities. At establishments such as these, it is best not to question the reality of such things and just accept them as they are.

For example, if I were to tell you a villainous woman carried a satchel of summer-grown toenail clippings on her belt, you should reply with a firm *"Well, logically!"* Or if I mentioned said toenails were offerings needed to enter a door to the attic, you would not argue. And if I stated that door was actually a magical creature known as only the Weeping Tree—yes, a real tree—that one day sprang up through the ground in the middle of the manor and formed a door at the top, and still lives there only because David thought it would be rude to ask it to leave, you would reply, *"But of course!"*

If Begonia was right about the riddle, the Oddject would be "up and up" to the highest point of the manor—the attic—and the key to gaining entrance was tied to her nemesis's dress loop.

With a sneak in her step and a fizz in her fingers, Begonia scurried into the morning room and ducked under a tablecloth, Bass on her heels.

"You stay here," Begonia whispered. Bass gave her a silent salute and inched the tablecloth up just enough to spy from under.

Scurrying on her hands and knees, Begonia moved from table to table, dodging wayward canes, slippered feet, and—in Mimi Arnetta's case—hooves until she had reached her target. She peered around the table leg to the grandparent above her.

Grandma Minnie, a towering beast of a woman, sat with her eyes closed, slurping a steaming bowl of pea soup. Though she never smiled, Begonia knew she was happy due to the delicate shade of lilac on her thick, twisted horns.

Time slowed. Jitters traveled up and down Begonia's arms. Mouth dry, she watched and waited. Calculating the rhythm of each dip of the spoon, timing every swallow. Holding out for the opportune moment.

And then, as the spoon hovered between bowl and babushka, Begonia made her move. She swiped the stew from right under Grandma Minnie's nose, sliding it below her feet without spilling a single drop. Begonia grinned.

Plunk.

The spoon thwacked against the table. Grandma Minnie peeled open her eyes.

There was only one other soul at Grandma Minnie's table, and that was Grandpa Bonic, who told everyone his first name was Beau for ironic reasons, but Begonia had it on good authority his real name was Fitzgerald.

He had a special Oddfinity for rats, and this morning they were jumping shoulder to shoulder, stopping only to lap at his bowl of stew. Which, unfortunately, happened to be the exact same kind as Grandma Minnie's.

He smiled at her, waving his spoon in hello.

Now, under no circumstance would Begonia consider herself an expert in rat language, but she had been around this mischief of rats—yes, that is the real name for a group of rats—so long, she was getting quite good at translating.

For example, she knew that *squeak-squeak-sniff* meant "What absolutely remarkable storm clouds we're having today." And *scratch-sniff-squeak* meant "My! Grandma Minnie looks quite affronted indeed!"

Grandma Minnie's horns had turned bright red. With a grunt, she lunged across the table, snatching Grandpa Bonic's bowl. Rats skittered. Grandpa Bonic's mouth dropped. Begonia grinned.

Grandpa Bonic slid the bowl back, huffing. Grandma Minnie took it again. Then Grandpa once more. Soon they were locked in a vicious battle of tug-of-war, rats squeaking and circling the table in excitement.

The entire room stopped to watch as the bowl of stewed peas ricocheted into the air, arced over the tables, and landed with a wet plunk on Grandpa Clive's head.

Fact: Some bees have hair on their eyes.

Fact: Grandpa Clive had bees on his hair.

An entire hive, in fact. Their buzzing went deadly silent as Grandpa Clive slowly lifted the bowl from his head, shriveled vegetables oozing down his face. His gaze fell directly on Grandpa Bonic, who wiggled his fingers nervously at him with a pale smile.

Grandpa Clive roared, his bees awakening, flying from their hive, and forming attack patterns in the air. They swarmed into the crowd of elders, buzzing, stinging, swirling. Shaking their angry little fists to instill fear in the hearts of their enemies.

And just as Begonia hoped it would, the room erupted in chaos.

Grandpa Bonic and his rats fled into the walls, mushrooms popped from Grandad Merl's arms, and Nanny "Cloning" Claudette transformed into her neighbors.

Some did try to take hold of the situation. Mamaw Myrtle lunged for bees as they zoomed past, using her dust touch to dissolve them. More often she missed, hitting a lamp or wig and turning the grandparents' retreat into a hairless, slippery stampede.

The manor relished in the pandemonium, in fact adding to it by banging the doors and windows open and shut with rattling force.

Begonia emerged from under the table just in time to see Ms. Majorie trampled under an assortment of feet, walkers, and rats. She rolled into an Oddchanted tapestry, which proceeded to wrap itself around Ms. Majorie like a boa constrictor. It did not much appreciate being awoken from its nap.

"Begonia!" Bass shouted from his post. "Get the pouch!"

The plan clunked back into Begonia's brain. She sidestepped shattered plates, loose bingo chips, and knitting that tangled around her boot toward a flailing Ms. Majorie. She was facedown, coated in thick green soup, swimming in dust, and peppered with something that looked suspiciously like rat droppings.

The pouch peeked out from her side.

Before anyone noticed, Begonia tugged the pouch free, bindings ripping at the seams. Ms. Majorie, busy suffocating in stew and stitchwork, didn't notice.

99

Elation swirled like dust motes in Begonia's belly.

One step closer.

On light feet, Begonia darted for the hall. She whipped around a table where a content Grandma Minnie sat, tucking into a new bowl of stew, and passed Nini Zehra by the window, who either couldn't hear or didn't care about the commotion. Begonia grabbed Bass's arm and tugged him with her.

"Yes!" Bass said. "You got it!"

"Of course I did."

Slam!

The morning room door banged closed. But this time, it stayed shut.

Begonia grabbed the handle and yanked, heart crashing into her ribs. She wedged her foot against the wall and tugged with all her might. But the manor was in a right fit now—walls humming, windows banging, smoke belching from the chimneys.

"Come on!" Begonia yelled.

With a roar and much flying of soup, Ms. Majorie flung herself free of the tapestry. An enchanted pair of dentures chomped idly at a tendril of hair loosed from her bun.

Begonia crouched low, dragging Bass down with her, but not before she thought Ms. Majorie caught a glimpse of them. Her head swiveled, eyes roaming the room.

Begonia tried to remember how to breathe. She crouched lower, waiting.

"Who's there?" Ms. Majorie snarled. She clomped closer, her foot landing by Grandad Vernon's armchair. He hissed and slid lower into the shadows.

"Begonia," Bass whispered, his hand a claw on her arm.

"Shush," she said. Her mind whirled. In all her excitement, she had forgotten the first and most crucial rule in thievery—always form an escape plan.

The wet squelch of Ms. Majorie's shoes drew nearer. Nearer.

Nearer.

Then stopped right on the other side of the tablecloth.

Bass whimpered. Begonia pushed the pouch deep inside her pocket and closed her eyes.

A crash split the silence, followed by the strangest hum Begonia had ever heard. She peered around Ms. Majorie's ankle.

Nanny "Cloning" Claudette stood in the middle of the room, somehow having put her foot through a wayward accordion. It breathed a mournful sigh as she freed herself. And then, in the space of a breath, she shot Begonia and Bass a sly wink.

Ms. Majorie turned a moment later, but when she did, it was not Nanny Claudette standing in the middle of the room she saw, but Bass.

Or at least, a clone of him.

The real Bass's hand was starting to sweat against Begonia's arm.

"Whoa," he breathed. "That is so, so weird."

Ms. Majorie exploded. "What are you doing down here?! You're supposed to be in your room until your family arrives!"

Claudette-Clone-Bass put her thumbs in her ears, wiggled her fingers, and stuck out her tongue in a way that clearly said, *"Well, I do say, my dear Ms. Majorie—I think you're scum!"*

Ms. Majorie screamed and lunged forward. With the dexterity of a much younger woman, Claudette ran for the window and leapt through just before it slapped down behind her.

Ms. Majorie charged like a bull.

Fact: **Over a million birds die per year from smashing into windows.**

But no one ever talks about the windows that die from the birds smashing into them. Of course, no one would think to care about that unless you were a manor with quite a few cracked windows as it was.

Sensing danger, the manor flung open all its windows and doors, and with a wail, Ms. Majorie toppled outside.

"Begonia, come on!" Bass said.

She turned. The morning room door was open.

Begonia raced for the hall. She wished she had more time to engrave this moment in her brain. The stew. The window. The way Ms. Majorie squealed.

That alone was worth it all.

"Yes!" Bass said, clacking his heels midjump. "We did it! OOA! OOA!"

Begonia allowed him a ghost of a smile. Then she turned to glower at the wall.

"When you calm down, we are going to have a serious talk," she said to the manor.

They passed bee-stung residents smelling strongly of produce, limping, swearing, and throwing accusatory fingers in one another's direction.

Begonia was just about to suggest going through the laundry chute secret passage when she stopped dead. She stared into an open room.

"Hey, what's up?" Bass said, looping back. He peered into the room. "Whoa. What is this?"

"The Odditorium," Begonia whispered.

Inside the normally dark and cobwebbed ballroom, dozens of workers milled about. Some dusting, some setting up chairs, others attaching festive streamers to the banisters. Against the far windowed wall, a woman in overalls unfurled a long banner.

ESTATE AUCTION

Under those words was a date.

Begonia swallowed the bile in her throat. She went cold head to toe, filled with static, and somehow felt equally too big and too small for her skin. Maybe this was what Oddbliteration was like. Or death.

She didn't know which she preferred.

"Oh no," Bass said. "That's only—"

"Two days away," Begonia said. "I know. That's—that's my birthday."

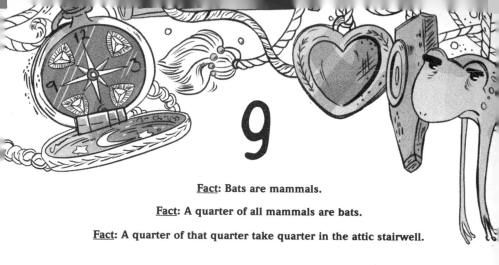

9

Fact: Bats are mammals.

Fact: A quarter of all mammals are bats.

Fact: A quarter of that quarter take quarter in the attic stairwell.

This particular colony seemed to know something was going on because instead of their usual screeches, chirps, and wing-whooshes, they clung to the ceiling beams like stalactites, gaze red and watchful on the children's feet.

Bass eyed them warily, nearly tripping over more chartreuse paint cans. He caught himself on the slick wall.

"Oops," he said, and rubbed his green hands clean on his pants. Begonia rolled her eyes.

What luck to be stuck with a henchman that has eggplants for brains.

They continued up the rickety stairs and under a row of arched windows streaming with rain and moonlight.

It had been hard to wait for the cover of darkness to head to the attic, but Begonia knew Ms. Majorie would be on the lookout for them after the brunch fiasco. Her nemesis had been ever so confused when, dripping stew and mud, she stomped up to both Bass's and Begonia's rooms to find them each curled up with a book in their bed as if they had never left.

But now Begonia was on the hunt. A ruthless wolf in the night. She had two days until her home and her memories would be taken from her, and she refused to let that happen.

Movement caught her eye. Begonia stopped, holding out one arm for Bass. Her heart was a drumbeat in her ears.

Someone was walking below the foggy pane of glass.

Begonia pressed her nose to the window, trying to peer down on the grounds.

"What is it?" Bass squeaked. "The ghost? Ms. Majorie?"

Begonia flung the latch and eased the window open. Rain pattered on her hands as she squinted into the dark.

Beyond the murky line of shrubs, a figure stooped just under the conservatory awning, two wings of facial hair drooping from either side of their face.

Begonia rubbed her eyes clear, blinking rapidly.

Mr. Schmoob?

He wore his usual blue suit, dyed black by the rain, and was leaning over in the shadows, speaking to someone in the dark.

Begonia strained her ears, but she could only catch snippets over the gale.

"Of course I'm still keeping my part of the deal . . . five resident attacks . . ."

"Why is the banker here so late?" Bass asked, peering out beside her.

She had no answer.

As her shock abated, Begonia's eyes narrowed. Mr. Schmoob shouldn't have known about the attacks. He was a Never Odd. Her grandparents' assaults were reported as strokes, their bodies seen as comatose to Oddless eyes.

And what *deal*?

Begonia squinted, searching for the person Schmoob was talking to in the shadows, but she couldn't make them out.

After a long moment, Schmoob ran off around the building, holding his jacket over his head.

"What do you reckon that was about?" Bass asked.

Begonia shook her head. "I have no idea."

She stared after the place where Schmoob's form had vanished before tugging Bass's sleeve.

"Come on. The Oddject, remember?"

He nodded.

Mounting the final set of steps, the two paused, gazing up.

If one wasn't accustomed to the manor's Oddities, they might at first believe the attic stairs ended in a straight wall of rock. But what looked like stone, Begonia noted, was actually textured and knobby the closer she came. Treelike.

In the center, an ancient, gnarled hand had formed in the bark, jutting out like the claw of a monster frozen in time.

The Weeping Tree might not speak like those in the Whispering Woods, but anyone who had come close could feel its presence. Powerful and intelligent.

Begonia suppressed a shudder. A rhyme Begonia had known since childhood swam up through time.

> *A curl, a tooth, or the heart of your beau,*
>
> *But none so delicious as the nail of a toe.*
>
> *A world revealed as long as the price is paid.*
>
> *Only fear if my request be disobeyed.*

Bass gulped. "You sure about this?"

"Of course," Begonia said. She charged forward, head high, but if she was being honest with herself, most of it was bravado. Begonia had never been in the attic, had no need to pass through the Weeping Tree.

And the ghost seemed much closer now that the sun was down.

At the top, she handed the pouch of toenails to Bass. "Here, you do it."

Bass's face was caught somewhere between fear and repulsion. "Why me?"

"Because the prophecy said our fates are intertwined or whatever, and so far you've helped on this mission squat."

She crossed her arms and raised her eyebrow at him, channeling her best crime-boss energy.

The wood groaned ominously in the wind.

Bass looked like he wanted to argue but took the bag from her anyway. He plucked a half-moon from the pouch and held it up in the moonlight.

"One on each finger?"

"One on each finger."

It may not make sense to you, fitting toenails on a hand, but I've learned in my many years it's best not to question the request of ancient beings, especially one so Odd as the Weeping Tree.

"And it won't lock us in there?" Bass asked, concerned.

"The toenails won't fully dissolve into the wood until we leave. That's what I've been told, anyway."

Bass stared at Begonia.

"We *will* be able to get out. Now hurry up."

Bass took a deep breath, then one by one, fed the nails in place on the hand. They locked like puzzle pieces, the bark growing over each, vining around the cuticles and nail beds.

The moment they left the attic, the nails would be dissolved into the bark, feeding the tree and locking the passageway shut.

When the pinkie nail slid into the wood, a crack split the air. Begonia jumped. Bass leapt back with a cry as the fingers awoke, flexing their joints and sending little puffs of dust into the night.

Wood groaned. Splinters loosened. They twisted and wound around themselves until a dark, oval path gaped in the doorway.

Begonia's stomach hollowed.

For Mawmaw. For Dada Haneef. For Swamp Root Manor. She trudged forward, Bass whimpering behind.

The tunnel was tight but shallow. Within a few steps, the two were free on the other side.

Begonia gaped.

Half a tree house, half an antique shop, the attic took shape in the moonlight. The room—the Weeping Tree itself—breathed around them. Vines stretched and contracted over old trunks, broken furniture, crates, and windows as if they were valves of a giant heart.

On the far wall towered a precarious stack of coffins. You truly could never have enough in a nursing home.

"Wow!" Bass said, fear forgotten as he ran to them. "Fillaman's caskets! These are really, really rare."

Begonia stalked over, eyebrow cocked.

"Fillaman is super famous. Like, he had his own spread in *Mildly Mortuary*'s winter catalog and everything. He makes the hardest caskets in the business— completely grave-robbing proof—but never shared his secrets before he died. I'm thinking it has to do with the steel lining."

Bass gave the side of the casket an enthusiastic slap. A deep *wong-wong-wong* echoed around the attic. Starlight and wonder shone from his glasses. He bent closer for further inspection. "These might have been some of the last he ever made."

A loud creak made Begonia's hair stand on end. She turned back to the tunnel, but it was empty. She frowned.

The tree groaned and the walls flexed. Above Bass, the topmost coffin swayed.

Begonia pulled Bass back, squared his shoulders, and looked him dead in the eye.

"Focus, Montgomery. A crucial rule of the school of thievery, my young cadet—"

"You're literally nine months older than me."

"—is to get in and get out. No lollygagging. Understand?"

Bass nodded, all business now. "Sir, yes, sir!"

"And keep an eye out while I search for the Oddject."

"I wanna help!"

Begonia's temple throbbed, a different caliber than before.

Her migraines were thunder and lightning. And this was a storm cloud on the horizon.

She probably had just hours until she couldn't continue.

David's watch thrummed in her pocket.

Tick-tock. Tick-tock.

"What did the prophecy say again?" Bass asked.

Begonia swallowed her nausea. *"Up and up, go clippings to weep. Yearn for the dust of that true deep sleep."*

"Okay," Bass said, glasses flashing in the dark as he scoped out the room. "We got the first part. But what's the dust of true deep sleep?"

Begonia had been working that clue over in her head all night. Deep sleep sounded like a metaphor for death, but dust? Surely the Oddject wasn't a disintegrated skeleton hidden in one of these boxes.

As soon as the thought left her mind, her eyes snagged on something. For resting atop an old china hutch sat an ornate vase.

"That's it!" Begonia said, darting to the cabinet. "It's urn, not yearn! And the dust of deep sleep—cremated remains—it all fits!"

Bass's lip wrinkled. "That's dark, man. I mean, I love it, but that's reeeal dark."

The urn was up too high to see inside, so with trembling hands, Begonia lifted it, finding its weight surprisingly light, and set it on the floor between them.

She peered into its inky depths. "I'm guessing the Oddject must be inside."

She looked at Bass expectantly.

He threw his neck back. "What—you want *me* to stick my hand in there?"

"You're the one who wants to be a mortician!"

"Yeah, but that's sticking my hands in corpses, which is a controlled environment with protective gear, not my raw skin in creepy vases with mysterious contents! What if there's a gnome in there?!"

"They have a vaccine for the venom now."

"Still!"

Begonia shot him her most Babetteish glare. "If you would rather stick your hand in a corpse than a slightly dusty but overall *clean* vase, then there is something seriously wrong with you."

Bass stared at Begonia. Begonia stared back. She refused to break the gaze.

The walls creaked around them. The pocket watch ticked. Slowly, the fight drained from his body. She worked to keep her smile under her skin.

"For Mawmaw," she said, this time using her gentlest grandma voice, all oatmeal cookies and hand-stitched mittens. She patted his shoulder in soothing circles.

Bass gulped. "For Mawmaw."

He blew out two quick breaths, then plunged his hand inside.

As you may know, my Brave Tree Traverser, sometimes when you're least expecting a scream, it can startle you, causing a chain reaction where one person yells and then another and another until everyone is screaming and no one knows why. Which is exactly what happened when Bass's hand went inside the urn.

"Ahhhhh!" Bass screamed.

"Ahhhhh!" Begonia screamed.

"Ahhhhh!" you may also scream, and if you are either lucky or unusually vindictive, you may be able to cause the scream-spree to continue in the classroom, library, or freshly dug grave you are sitting in.

"Sorry," Bass said, flapping his hand. "The ceramic was super cold."

Begonia clutched her chest. Her molars would definitely be worn to nubs by the end of this heist. She snatched the urn from him.

"Really great job, Barney. I'm sure the whole nursing home heard that."

Bass picked lint off his sweater, face pink. "I don't think it's in there, anyway. I didn't feel anything."

Begonia peered inside. Blackness peered back. Not to be deterred, Begonia flipped the urn upside down and shook it.

A crumpled piece of paper floated to the ground.

Begonia dove, but Bass got there first. They wrestled for a moment before Begonia ripped it from his hand and ran to the window. Weak starlight sprawled across the parchment, illuminating words.

You have followed the clue without a doubt.

But next find this where poison things sprout:

You need me when your way is barred,

when there's no code that can be crunched.

I'm old enough to be a skeleton

With teeth, yet cannot munch.

"Um, is this the object?" Bass asked, reading over her elbow. "Kinda puny."

"It's a clue, Barry."

"BAR-NA-BAS."

"Bless you," Begonia said. "Now shush. I'm trying to think."

The words swam behind her eyes, head now positively pounding. The constant sounds of splinters breaking was really getting to be too much.

"What has teeth but can't munch?"

"Keys," Bass said.

"What?"

Bass, who had been staring down at the pouch of toenails in his hands, lifted it for Begonia to see. "Keys! The answer is a key!"

Begonia's head shot up. "When your way is barred!"

"Skeleton!"

"Teeth that cannot munch!"

"It all fits! I was looking at the toenails and thought, our way was barred to get in the attic until we stuck them in the door like keys." Then his face fell. "But where is it?"

"But next find this where poison things sprout . . ."

Begonia grinned. She had already worked that one out.

"The carnivorous garden."

"Um, is that a place?"

"Yes, on the far side of Swamp Root grounds. We grow all the healing herbs for my grandparents there. And the ones that keep Grandma Cathy at bay during high tide."

Bass fidgeted with the kazoo around his neck. "Carnivorous though?"

"You'll be fine. I've been in there hundreds of times and haven't died yet."

"But I thought the prophecy said the Oddject would be here."

Begonia shrugged, trying not to act as disappointed as she felt, and shoved the paper into her pocket. If it could only have been that easy. "Maybe the original owners of the house found it and moved it or something."

The room shifted. Trembled. Groaned.

Begonia eyed the ceiling. Surely it wasn't always this loud, or the residents below would complain. She couldn't help but shudder. The tree seemed . . . angry.

"Let's head out," she said to Bass, then marched for the tunnel.

She skidded to a stop.

There was no tunnel. The pathway had sealed itself flat.

"Montgomery?"

"Yeah?" came a trembling reply.

"Where's the door?"

Bass stumbled forward and patted the wood with quaking hands. "I—I don't know."

A chill inchwormed up Begonia's spine. The air in the room suddenly had a charge. All at once, the groaning in the floor and walls peaked to a dull roar. The window burst open with a cold breeze, ragged curtains blowing like a ghost. Bass all but jumped into her arms.

"L-let's get out of here!" Bass said, clawing up her shoulder.

Begonia frowned, shoving Bass off. She skated a finger down the gnarled bark. She didn't understand. The toenails didn't dissolve in the wood until those who put them there left the tunnel. They obviously were still here, so the passageway should have remained open.

> *A curl, a tooth, the heart of your beau,*
>
> *But none so delicious as the nail of a toe.*
>
> *A world revealed as long as the price is paid . . .*

As long.

Something plinked in the back of her mind. Literally a *plink*, just like the scratching, groaning, wood-bending sounds she had heard since entering the attic.

Her blood chilled.

Someone had stolen the toenails while they were still inside. Pried them away.

Someone had locked them in.

10

Fact: By the standards of instrument classification, the kazoo is more closely related to the bongos than a flute.

Begonia's heart was a moth in her throat.

The wind picked up and sent her hair up in spirals. The wood creaked and moaned like an old ship in the middle of a maelstrom.

She slapped her palm against the door that was no longer a door. "Hey! Hey, let us out!"

Bass pounded his fists in rhythm with hers.

No one answered. The manor couldn't help them; this was out of its domain.

Suddenly, all sound died. The wind, the tree, the rain. Silent as the grave.

Begonia turned to Bass, his face a full moon of terror. Spiders danced on the back of her neck, and she knew. She just *knew*.

Someone—*something*—was behind them. Slowly, she turned.

The ghost of Edith Hollowmoor gazed back.

Breath slithered from Begonia's lips. She could only grasp what she saw in flashes—mouth slack, jagged teeth, broken fingernails, hand outstretched.

Coming toward them.

Bass screamed and flung himself at the passageway. Begonia whirled back, and together they prodded, pounded, kicked at the wood, battering every inch they could. Searching for a knob, a hinge—anything to free them.

"What do we do?!" Bass said.

"I don't know, I don't know!" Begonia shouted, fingers raw against bark.

If only she had her powers—something defensive like bees, horns, or even dust touch. Her head screamed in protest as the blood rushed through her veins. Her vision blurred. She howled in frustration.

Useless. Useless. Useless.

And still the ghost moved closer.

"Up!" Begonia yelled, pulling Bass toward the nearest tower of junk. She flung both of them on the pile, and hand over hand, they climbed. Higher and higher. Begonia's knee banged a rusted trunk and sent a broken mannequin flailing to the ground. She spared a glance downward and her stomach dropped.

The ghost had followed them up. Not floating like one would think a ghost would, but dragging herself as if out of quicksand, clawed hand over clawed hand, mouth hinged wide, sharp teeth glowing.

A scream died in Begonia's throat. "Hurry!"

She had no idea what they would do when they reached the top. She just wanted to be as far away from that creature as possible.

Bass needed no encouragement. He scaled the mountain like a pack of dust bunnies were hot on his heels. Reaching the top a moment before Begonia did, he hauled her to her feet. Her ankles wobbled and she windmilled her arms to keep from tumbling to the floor. The table they stood on swayed precariously, and with a sinking feeling in her gut, Begonia saw it only had three legs.

The ghost was only a cabinet, a chipped dollhouse, and a broken viola away. Her eyes were hollows of dead smoke.

"Help," Bass whispered, bouncing on his heels. Searching for something, anything, that could save them. "Help!"

Trivia facts popped in and out of Begonia's brain, her tried and true, the skill that had never let her down before. But each she swatted aside. All useless.

"Once a lame duck, always a lame duck."

Begonia had nothing. She was as empty as the coffins beside her. They were belly-up, daisy-pushing, worm-counting casket carcasses.

Caskets.

"OREN MAFFICK!" Begonia shouted. She clutched Bass by the shoulders. "Oren Maffick's death avalanche!"

To Begonia's surprise, Bass understood straightaway. His eyes lit, his mouth set in a determined line.

As you well know, my Careless Casket Crusader, most coffins are built for only one occupant, and under normal circumstances, it is recommended that the occupant be dead. But in this case, I think even Maffick would make an exception.

"Get in!" Bass said, heaving one of the caskets loose. It slammed between them as he shoved off the lid, dust flying.

Begonia flung herself inside. An umbrella with a torn canopy fell into her lap as Bass grabbed a chipped cane for himself. He propped a leg up against the coffin stack.

"On my whistle—row!" Bass said, tugging his kazoo free.

Begonia nodded, her mouth a hard line. Unlike Maffick, she planned to stay above this tide.

The ghost slapped a hand on the side of their coffin. Then another. She hauled herself up the rim, nails scraping, teeth gnashing.

Begonia jerked away with a scream, stabbing the ghost with her umbrella bayonet-style. It whispered through the ghost as if she were made of smoke. Which she probably was.

Unbothered, the ghost clawed for Begonia. Lunging for her chest, for the heart hidden beneath. A piercing wail tore from her grave-stained throat.

"Hold on!" Bass yelled. He kicked at the casket pile and, with a decidedly undignified, high-pitched scream, cannonballed into the coffin.

With an explosive crash, the stacks of odds and ends collapsed around them. Something hard hit the back of their coffin, and like a ship at sea, Begonia and Bass were swept into the cascade of caskets.

The ghost screamed, and her grip was lost, buried under a mountain of junk and dust. Wind whipped at Begonia's hair. She pulled it out of her eyes in time to see they were sailing straight for a very sturdy, very thick armoire.

"Row!" Bass said, stabbing his cane into the coffin current and blowing his kazoo with all his might. Begonia plunged her umbrella down and heaved. The casket veered left, narrowly avoiding the armoire's swinging doors.

Begonia rowed to the rhythm of Bass's kazoo, stirring past an antique sewing machine, around a rusted birdcage, and over a cracked telescope. She rowed until her shoulders ached and her body was coated in dust.

The Weeping Tree non-passageway came closer, still very, very solid. Begonia braced herself, sinking into the plush lining of their makeshift boat. She shut her eyes, ground her teeth, and—

BOOM.

Wood splintered. The tree howled. The children screamed.

They crashed through the tree, flew down the stairs, and skidded to a stop halfway down the hall.

For a moment, Begonia lay there making sure she could still breathe. That no bones were broken. Concluding that she was still, in fact, alive, she slowly raised her head, brushing Bass's leg off her shoulder as she did so.

Bass lifted up on his elbows, glasses askew and white from dust, but seemingly unharmed.

As one, the children looked up the staircase.

The ghost wasn't there.

Begonia's muscles relaxed, although she did spare a wince at the hole in the Weeping Tree door. A moment later the bark swayed to life and slowly began to knit itself back together.

Begonia slumped back in the coffin, corpse-style. Bass let out a long whistle.

"I told you these coffins were the best," he said, wiping two clean circles in the dust on his glasses.

"We didn't die," Begonia said. "I can't believe we didn't die."

"Not yet. David might kill us though." Bass nodded toward the newly painted wall they had just scraped down.

"At least Nana Babette will be happy."

"She had a point. I mean, chartreuse?"

Begonia couldn't help herself. Laughter bubbled from her throat. She couldn't remember the last time she had laughed, or even wanted to.

Excitement lit Bass's face.

"Did you see that though? We were like whoaaa"—he mimed something that looked like a surfer on a wave—"and then the ghost was like 'grrrr,' but we were like 'bam-bam-bam!'"

Begonia grinned. "You did good, Barnabas."

He glanced at her, happiness a bloom on his face.

Remembering herself, Begonia let her smile fade. She swiped the dust from her dress and made to haul herself free.

"We better get out of—"

A wave of nausea washed over her, stars popping behind her eyes. She swayed.

Bass was at her side in an instant. "Hey, you okay?"

Begonia mashed a palm into her eyes, hissing in pain. Lightning and thunder.

"Let's get you downstairs. Maybe you could rest for a—"

Begonia shrugged out of Bass's hold. "I'm fine. Let's go. We have to get the Oddject before it gets—"

But she couldn't bring herself to say *gets worse.*

Because it would get worse before it got better. And then it would be worse again. And even in the periods of no rain when she got to run and play and just *be*, thunder and lightning always lurked in the shadows. Souring her cloudless days.

She was always prepping for the next thunderstorm.

"Begonia, I think you should at least—"

"I said I'm *fine*. Half the manor could have heard this crash. We need to get out of here."

Bass toyed with the debris at his feet. "I'm worried you're not okay."

"Maybe you should worry about yourself, Montgomery. If you had kept a lookout like I told you to, we wouldn't have gotten locked in. I need a competent henchman for this treasure hunt. Got it?"

Bass's eyes sparkled with hurt and anger, but he kept whatever he was thinking tucked behind pooched lips.

Swallowing bile, Begonia steadied herself before stomping from the wreckage and toward whatever awaited them in the carnivorous garden.

She didn't look back, but if she did, she would have seen the redness circling Bass's eyes as he turned and followed.

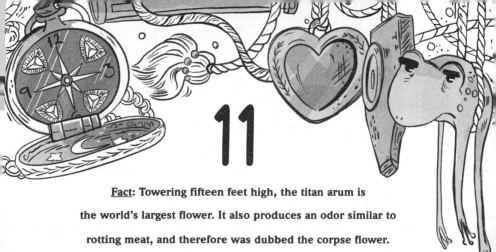

11

Fact: Towering fifteen feet high, the titan arum is the world's largest flower. It also produces an odor similar to rotting meat, and therefore was dubbed the corpse flower.

An iron gate so tall its pointed tips melted into the starless sky towered before them. The spiked tops were necessary, of course, since some highly temperamental plants called the carnivorous garden their home, and they kept trespassers out.

"*Or the inhabitants in!*" as Nana Babette would say, which is also true. Luckily only one species of fern had evolved fingers capable of climbing, and the elders kept the gardener stocked in tight, hand-sewn mittens to prevent their escape.

Begonia stared at the rusted sign that hung from the front gate. It groaned in the wind.

DO NOT TICKLE THE MARSH WORT DURING BREEDING SEASON

And just under that, in smaller print:

SHEAR AT YOUR OWN RISK

"Nope," Bass said, spinning on his heel.

Begonia caught him by his kazoo loop and dragged him back. "Quit being such a baby."

"I'm not being a baby."

"Then help me find those keys."

"It looks locked."

"Of course it's locked. But I'm a professional. I spotted these rusted bars the moment we came over the hill."

Mud squelched as Begonia trampled over to the bars, indeed quite rusted. She reached for them. "A crowbar is more traditional, but—"

"No!" Bass said, slapping her hand away. "Tetanus! Trust me—you do not want to die of lockjaw."

"All right, all right," Begonia said, rolling her eyes.

Bass went back to his moody silence. It was a nice change from him prattling on all the time, but she didn't like how he had been acting funny since the attic.

She *had* snapped at him, but it wasn't her fault her tolerance cauldron was filled to the brim, what with her pain, the nursing home's lack of funds, her Oddlessness. Adding a ghost and a deplorable henchman to the list of ingredients was just enough to send her poison boiling over the edge.

He really should have kept a lookout.

But Begonia was less concerned with Bass's feelings and more worried about the fact that someone might have purposely locked them in the attic.

With the ghost.

She would need more time to investigate that after she found the Oddject.

She motioned for Bass to step back, reared her boot, and kicked the bars as hard as she could. One bar snapped, and with two more kicks, the second bar followed, leaving an opening just big enough for two children to fit inside.

Pain pooled at the base of her skull, but it was the flutter of crows' wings in her heart that Begonia clung to. The thrill of knowing she was at least useful for something, even if these acts were a little more on the wicked side.

Begonia slid between the bars and, a heartbeat later, heard Bass follow.

The muddy path cut like a wound through the garden, and if the path was a wound, then the tangle of weeds were the jagged stitches holding it together. Most of the plants had died in the first frost, but those that survived swayed as the children passed, some spitting venom, some singing very off-tune.

"Keep your eyes peeled for anything that looks like a key," Begonia said. "And for goodness' sake, stay away from that Witchroot. It's drooling."

Bass bypassed the purple shrub oozing goo and hurried up to Begonia's side.

Through the garden they searched, decay and earth heavy in their noses. They stomped around prickly Drearyweed and Waisy Nettle, tromped through a patch of Groggy Gardenias that snored against neighboring stalks, and leapt over the clusters of teeth sprouting up like cabbages, ripe to be plucked and molded into dentures. And still no sign of a key. Begonia was beginning to worry when a yelp came from behind. She whirled.

Bass, arms windmilling at his sides, had been thrown off-balance by his leg, which seemed glued to the ground. Earth grew at his ankle, churning and snapping, until with a gasp, Begonia saw what it was.

A yellowing tentacle had coiled around Bass's boot, roping itself farther up his leg.

Bass yelled. He grabbed the root and tugged, but the plant only flexed, squeezing until Bass collapsed in pain. Begonia ran to his side.

"Getitoffgetitoff!" Bass said, clawing the rising tendril.

"Move your hands!" Begonia said.

Bass did as she asked. Begonia zoned in on the sturdiest root, wound up, and gave it a good slap.

The vine released a high-pitched whimper, withering brown. Bass scrambled back as it let go of his leg and mournfully swayed back into the earth.

For a moment, the two sat in the mud staring at the place where the vine had receded. Then Begonia rose, wiping her muddy hands off on her backside. All in a day's work.

"What was that?" Bass said, absently massaging his calf.

"Grave Vine. So named because—"

"Because it will drag you to your grave? Yeah, worked that bit out for myself, actually."

Begonia glared at him. "Yes, well, just in case you stomp on another one, know they hate to be slapped."

"Why?"

Begonia shrugged. "It's degrading. Now come on, we don't have all night."

"Right," Bass said, wincing to his feet. "And thanks for that."

"Don't thank me. Just be less helpless all the time."

Begonia knuckled her forehead. Nausea crept up her body like—well—Grave Vine. It boiled in her middle, snapping and frothing. If she could just hold out a little longer—

Her skull throbbed as a shard of something bright hit her eyes. She squinted, following the source of light through the greenery. Her pulse sped.

"Montgomery—look!"

Bass turned, then his mouth went slack in horror. "What is *that*?"

A poisonous green stalk loomed before them, thick as a tree trunk. A large bud protruded from the top with thorns for teeth and petals that tufted its wolfish face like fur. Six meaty tentacles writhed through the air, each ending in white flowers that were suspiciously shaped like gloved hands.

And on a chain around its neck lay an antique key.

Fact: In the past three hundred years, more than five thousand plant species have gone extinct. Unfortunately this plant was not one of them.

Begonia winced. "Foxglove."

Trivia whirled through Begonia's mind as she recalled everything she knew about the species.

She knew Foxgloves were never grown, but sprang from the ground fully formed. She knew that no one knew why or how they appeared, but some

129

carniviotologists believed the placement of Pluto and migration pattern of mosquitoes were involved. She knew they were incredibly proud creatures, highly reactive to both compliments and insults.

What she didn't know was who placed the key around its neck and why.

The plant sniffed the air as a vine-like tail whipped in irritation. Its head swiveled to the children. A deep growl rumbled from its stalk, gloved hands cracking their knuckles menacingly.

Bass shivered, licking his dry lips. "Um, I think you should take the lead on this one."

"Relax," Begonia said, waving a hand. "I know all about these guys. Foxgloves are super sensitive. All we have to do is flatter it enough and it will bow its head in a blush. And when it does, the key will slip off its neck and we grab it."

"That means we have to get closer?" Bass said, voice high.

Begonia stomped forward, rolling her eyes. "Really, these things are all bark and no bite."

The Foxglove hissed, and Begonia flung up her hands in apology.

"Sorry, sorry. You are *very* terrifying."

"And what if it does bite anyway?"

"It's super easy to make them pass out. Now, will you come on?"

Begonia glanced back at Bass, half-hidden in the shrubs.

She stalked back and pulled him forward until they were right in front of the beast, but the action loosened some dizziness inside her. She hunched to her knees, steadying herself in the mud.

"Begonia! Are you—"

"I'm *fine*," she spat, clenching her throat to keep the bile inside. Her breath appeared in gasps. But she had a job to do.

She straightened her spine, rigor mortis tight, and gazed at her subordinate.

"Time to focus, Montgomery. And past time for you to prove your worth in this organization, young initiate."

Bass's eyes were crinkled with concern, but that melted away as the Foxglove gave a growl of impatience.

"Um, Begonia? See, the thing is, I usually pride myself on being a pretty self-aware person and—uh—I don't think I can do this."

"No cowards in the OOA! What is our mission, Initiate?"

Bass gulped. "To save Mawmaw and the others from the ghost."

"Correct. And to do so we must?"

"Find the Oddject and get our Oddities."

"Correct," Begonia said, motioning him forward. "Then proceed."

For a long moment, Bass wasn't capable of movement. Then he took a deep breath and whispered, "For Mawmaw."

He threw out his chest, fists trembling, and stepped before the creature.

The Foxglove cocked its head. Bass had to look straight up to see the thing's face. He stood there so long Begonia thought he might have chickened out, when Bass's voice quivered, "M-my, what big teeth you have."

The Foxglove's eyes narrowed, a low growl moving through its chest. Bass's gaze darted back to Begonia, who gave him a droll look.

"That was embarrassing."

Bass swallowed and turned back to the creature. Then something bright broke across his face. Fumbling in excitement, he tugged the kazoo string from under his sweater and popped the whistle in his mouth.

He blew a long, shrill note, then broke into song.

"Fur so soft, like the winter snow.

Foxglove, you have my heart wrapped around your big toe."

Bass drew out the last note with a very high, very off-key exuberance, followed by another screech of the kazoo.

Begonia covered her ears, eyes watering, while the plant tossed its head as if trying to shake off a horde of flies.

Bass took a step back in alarm. "I-I don't think it likes music!"

"Well, to be fair, that definitely wasn't music."

Begonia wanted to add that if Bass did receive a musical Oddity, it would be a miracle, but didn't think that particular fact would help them achieve their goal at the moment.

Besides, Begonia was practically bouncing on her toes now to keep her dinner in place.

Bass tucked his kazoo away, forehead damp. "Okay, okay. Something more direct."

He nodded shakily to himself and stepped forward once more. He studied the Foxglove, taking in every thorn and root of the quivering plant. Once more, an idea crossed his face. He wet his lips and tried again.

"What a beautiful color you are."

The Foxglove stopped its head slinging, ear-petals perked. Bass's smile grew.

"Yes, so beautiful. That shade of green. Chartreuse, they call it. Back up at the manor, the elders loved your color so much they wanted it painted on the walls."

The Foxglove's tail wagged. A tentacled hand swatted the air in a shy "*No, please*" gesture, the way Begonia had seen adults do at the nursing home.

Bass beamed at her. Begonia shot him a weary thumbs-up.

"Yes," he continued, with a bit more bravado. "It's a stunning color. My favorite, in fact. The exact shade of a corpse, thirty-six hours after death, my favorite stage of putrefaction—"

The plant snapped its fangs, and Bass fell back with a yelp.

Begonia glared down at him in the mud. "Seriously?"

"I thought it was a good compliment!"

Begonia covered her eyes. She felt so weak, so powerless, having to let this foolish henchman do her work. If she just had her Oddity. Even if she only didn't have this *pain.*

Anger and frustration flared white-hot. Her voice came out in a vicious whisper. *"Do you even want this to work?"*

Bass climbed to his feet. "Of course."

"Well then, *try harder.*"

"I'm doing my best!"

"Well, that doesn't mean much, apparently."

Hurt flashed pink on Bass's cheeks. "Why don't you try, then?"

The throbbing. The pain. Begonia gnashed her teeth. "Because I'm the ring-leader of OOA and ringleaders give tasks below their station to their inferiors. I don't have time to milk fake compliments to this dirty, yellow-leafed, aphid-bitten weed of a plant—"

But she had said the wrong thing. For never, Dear Reader, insult a Foxglove.

With an earsplitting snarl, the Foxglove lunged. All six tentacles jutted forward, snatching, grasping, clawing.

The children screamed. Begonia tripped back, barely missing one of the creature's razor-sharp talons. Unfortunately Bass was not quick enough. A tentacle hooked around his ankle and hoisted him up in the air.

Bass squealed once, then all sound left his body. For a moment, Begonia feared the worst, but from way up in the clouds, she could make out his mouth moving, saying something to her that was lost in the plant's roars.

"Hold on, Montgomery!"

She searched the ground for a stick, a rock, even a Grave Vine to fling at the

Foxglove, but sensing danger, the entire garden had sunk below the mud like crabs cowering in their shells.

Vines whipping, roots thrashing, the creature dangled Bass upside down over its head. Its mouth opened wide, long, poisonous thorns oozing slime.

To Begonia's surprise, Bass didn't scream. In fact, he seemed to have made peace with his death, his arms already crossed over his chest like a mummy in the tomb. As the Foxglove lowered him closer to its mouth, Begonia was finally able to make out Bass's words.

"Tell my moms I don't want to be embalmed! It's bad for the environmennnnnnt!"

Her head spun into overdrive, searching the library of facts in her mind, everything she knew about the Foxglove.

And then it came to her. The one way to make a Foxglove faint.

For the tiniest moment, guilt coiled in her gut, but she quashed it and raised her voice to Bass.

"Shame you're about to get eaten and can't even sing your own funeral dirge!"

From above, Bass twisted. "What?"

"Yeah! You're going to die being the only Montgomery in four generations without their musical Oddity. That's your legacy."

The Foxglove stopped Bass's descent and cocked its head once more. Listening.

Despite herself, Begonia felt a thrill in her chest.

"Your whole family must be ashamed! The one worthless Montgomery!"

"That's—that's not true," Bass said, brow furrowing.

The Foxglove's tail wagged. Maybe Begonia was imagining it, but she could have sworn she saw the plant lower Bass away from its mouth by a hair.

"Oh yes it is. I know you, Montgomery. I've spent more time with you these past few days than anyone else, and I see you for what you are. Worthless."

"I'm not—"

"It's time to face the music! You're a waste of space. An embarrassment to your family. A sad boy who spends so much time hiding from his own pointlessness by distracting himself with a stupid death obsession. Everyone sees right through you."

Bass's mouth trembled. A single tear dropped from the corner of his eye, down his brow, and off the top of his upside-down head.

Like a Venus flytrap snatching an insect, the Foxglove opened its mouth and snapped up the tear. It smacked its lips, mouth pulled back in a toothy grin. It began to quiver and shimmy, raising its face like a wolf and howling with delight, before crashing to the ground, unconscious.

Bass yelped as he fell, and delighted, Begonia ran forward.

If she were a nice person, Begonia would have noticed Bass, glasses askew and mud-caked, glancing up hopefully as she drew near, hand raised to be hauled to his feet. But as I have said many times before, Dear Reader, Begonia Hollowmoor was not a nice girl.

Bass's face fell as she darted past him and slipped the key from the Foxglove's neck.

"Don't worry about me," he said, wincing as he stood. "I'm fine."

"I know. I saw you land in the leaves."

Her mind was already a million miles away.

A tag clung to the key, the large kind looped around holiday presents. She brushed it clean of dirt and held it up in the moonlight.

The Oddject's resting place has already appeared on this list;

Start from the beginning and revisit what you missed.

Begonia's chest collapsed, a waterlogged grave. She turned to Bass, her eyes never leaving the words.

"Montgomery, what do you make of this?"

When he didn't answer, she glanced up.

Bass stared determinedly at his bootstraps, toying with a stray string from his sweater.

Begonia crossed her arms. "All right, out with it, then. What is it?"

"You know what it is."

"I'm not a mind reader, Montgomery. Spit it out."

Bass lifted his eyes to somewhere near her chin. "Why'd you say that stuff?"

"What stuff?"

"That stuff about me. My music Oddity."

Begonia looped the chain safely around her neck, the key and tag resting against her locket. "The only way to calm an angry Foxglove is for someone else to be humbled in front of it. Their body overexcites and shuts down." Begonia nodded to the snoring Foxglove. "You're welcome, by the way."

Bass's next words were so quiet, Begonia had to lean forward to hear.

"You could have told me first."

"I said what had to be said for it to drop you. Don't be so sensitive."

Begonia turned and began to trudge back through the garden. Bass splashed up behind her.

"You could have said anything. My clothes were ugly. I talked too much. My lineup was crooked. Anything, and the Foxglove wouldn't have known the difference. But you picked the one thing you knew would bother me the most."

"I'm sorry, but you were *upside down* above the mouth of a vicious plant-beast. I don't have time to stroll through a catalog of Barnabas Montgomery–related flaws. I just picked the first thing that came to mind, and look! Now you are on the ground. Keep in mind what is most important here."

"I just think that—"

"What is our objective, Initiate?"

Bass glared at her. Begonia glared back. Finally, he sighed.

"To get our Oddity and save the nursing home and our grandparents."

"Right." Begonia's finger stabbed at his chest with each word. "Whatever. It. Takes."

Begonia turned, catching herself on a tree. The last few minutes had drained what little strength she had left.

She did notice, this time to her annoyance, that Bass did not check to see if she was okay.

But she had to keep going. She had to. She just needed a quiet, and less poisonous, place to sit and go over the clues again.

She pushed off from the tree and trudged back into the mud.

After a few uneasy steps, Bass's voice rang out behind her.

"What's that?"

Begonia stopped and looked back. Bass was pointing to something hidden behind the willow she had just come from. She held her head, eyes closed.

"I don't know. Let's just get out of here, all right?"

The sound of branches rattling caught her ears, and she opened her eyes to Bass pushing through the trees.

"Montgomery. Come on!"

Bass's voice was different this time. High and quivering. "Begonia."

Her spine snapped to attention, weakness forgotten. She crashed through the underbrush, picturing a Spitting Sanservieria Vinus or man-eating earthworms. But she only found Bass, staring at something in a clearing of mournful willow trees. She drew close and looked down.

It was a headstone, old and weathered. Weeds curled up the grave like sickly opossum tails over a thick layer of green limestone.

"Why's this back here?" Bass asked.

"I have no idea."

Begonia squatted, a bit unsteady, and peered into the face of the grave. Vines and roots ripped under her fingernails as she cleaned the surface, some of them grumbling before sinking back into the earth.

For a heartbeat, Begonia took in a small divot in the stone's front, as if someone had carved out the shape of a heart. Then she gasped.

She ripped her hands free and scurried away until she hit Bass's leg. It trembled against her.

"Is that—? Begonia, is that who I think it is?"

"It has to be." Begonia got warily to her feet. She read the words once more, a chill seeping into her bones.

EDITH HOLLOWMOOR

MATRIARCH. MOTHER.

And in red paint, graffitied across the whole of the stone, was one final word.

Witch.

"The ghost of Swamp Root Manor."

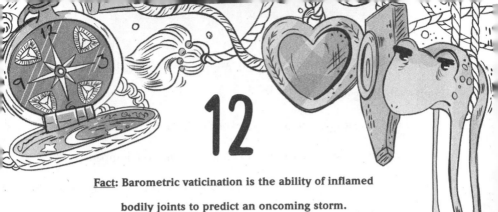

12

Fact: Barometric vaticination is the ability of inflamed bodily joints to predict an oncoming storm.

Wind whipped through the clearing, sending Begonia's hair skyborne. For the first time in a long time, she felt cold.

"Why isn't she in the graveyard with the others?" Bass asked. Begonia bent down, inspecting the grave with a thief's eye. Her fingers brushed the heart-shaped design at the top, feeling for answers in the smooth carving. Absent-mindedly, her hand found the locket at her throat.

"Montgomery?"

"Yeah?"

"Why does my locket look like it will fit perfectly in that space?"

Bass glanced back and forth between her neck and the gravestone, eyes rounding out like moons. He fingered the cat brooch on his chest nervously.

Begonia's breath came very fast. Heart fluttering in her fingertips, she closed her fist around the locket and pulled. The chain broke free with a *snap*. With measured slowness, Begonia inched the locket toward the stone.

"Begonia, don't—!"

But too late. Begonia pushed the heart into the carving, the pieces locking with a satisfying *click*.

Begonia's breath caught. She waited one heartbeat. Two.

A crow screeched somewhere above and both children jumped.

Brows pinched, Begonia climbed to her feet, refitting the locket around her neck. Disappointment sat heavy against her lungs.

Bass's shoulders had slumped, no doubt relieved nothing bad had happened.

Begonia circled the grave, eyes roaming every curve and chip. "Do graves normally have cutouts like these on them?"

Bass leaned in for a closer look, all business now. "It's not uncommon. Some have decorative carvings or figurines on them."

The answer wasn't what Begonia was looking for. Her necklace didn't fit perfectly into the grave of a ghost for no reason. She wasn't sent on a quest to find the Oddject for no reason.

She pawed her eyes, trying to focus.

The Oddject's resting place has already appeared on this list;

Start from the beginning and revisit what you missed.

She was missing something. Something big. It felt like a hair on her tongue or a pebble in her shoe—right there, but she just couldn't grab it.

Begonia needed to start back at the beginning, just like the clue said. She shut her eyes and recited the first line of Babette's prophecy, the one she had never understood.

"An Oddject of power resides on this hallowed ground

Where twin hearts are affixed and grief goes to drown . . ."

Her eyes flew open, hand clawing the chain at her neck. She ripped it free again, staring at the rusted metal locket.

A locket shaped like a heart.

She gasped. "This is what we're looking for! *This is the Oddject!*"

Bass's face shifted from alarm to confusion. "Your locket?"

"No, but one just like it! A twin heart!"

Begonia whirled back to Bass, who still looked skeptical, and pulled out the second chain, holding the key.

"This will open—I don't know—a door, a cabinet, something! And the twin locket will be inside! The second locket is the Oddject we need to get our powers and defeat the ghost and save the nursing home!"

Her chest heaved. Bass stared. He took a long time to answer, but when he did, it was with a measured tone.

"I think that's a great theory, but you can't know that for sure, Begonia."

But Begonia *did* know. She felt it in her bones the way Nana Babette's bad knee felt an oncoming storm. This was the missing piece.

The look on Begonia's face must have frightened Bass. He cautiously walked to her, like she was an escaped lion at the circus.

"I think we should slow down. Think about this more."

"There is nothing else to think about—it all fits!"

"But *why* does your locket fit in there in the first place? If there is a twin, why was it moved from the headstone? And by who?"

Begonia caressed its cold surface—a crystal ball holding all the answers. It was her longest companion, the friend she had had since her bassinet under the begonia bush nearly eleven years ago.

She let the locket thump back against her chest, determined. "I don't know. But I'm going to find out."

Then, in the space between one breath and another, the night changed. The wind howled, plants writhed on their stalks, and finger bones slid down Begonia's spine as darkness smothered each star one by one.

Her gaze found the grave, and she remembered where they were. What they were standing in front of.

Behind the gravestone, the ghost of Edith Hollowmoor appeared once more.

13

A scream lodged itself in Begonia's throat. She tripped back, tumbling over Bass, as they both hurtled to the ground. With a wet slither, vines sprang from the mud and curled themselves around Bass's legs, arms, and chest.

"Begonia!" he yelled, wrestling the Grave Vines.

But Begonia couldn't move. The world had exploded behind her eyes; everything she had kept bound, coffined, and buried rattled loose. Her vision sparked, her stomach roiled, her head split in two. It was all she could do to keep breathing.

The world softened. Slowed.

The ghost trudged toward her, moving as if her feet were clasped in heavy chains. Every inch an odyssey, every second a lifetime. Bass's screams pounded in Begonia's ears as Edith Hollowmoor knelt at her side.

She couldn't move. She couldn't think. She would die, there in the mud, completely helpless under this crushing tide.

Spiderweb hair tickled Begonia's neck as Edith bent down, their cheeks a whisper apart. Black teeth and tongue emerged as Edith's mouth gashed open, papery lips moving a breath away from Begonia's ear, but she couldn't hear over the wind and Bass's screams and the blood pounding through her skull.

Edith's gaze burned with rage. Her hand rose; long, jagged nails hovered just above Begonia's chest. Sinking lower.

Begonia couldn't even shut her eyes.

As the tip of the ghost's nail touched Begonia's pinafore, Edith froze.

As if electrified, her spine snapped straight as she stood. And those black eyes, where just before had brimmed so much hate, had glazed over, dull and placid.

Then, as silent as she came, Edith Hollowmoor turned and floated out of the garden.

Begonia's head sank back into the mud; her chest was heaving. The wind died and crickets once more began to chirp.

A rustle and whimper sounded beside her. Begonia turned.

Bass was covered in Grave Vine. It had not only wrapped itself around his entire body but had dragged his leg down into the earth like a spoil of war.

Using the last of her strength, Begonia flung out her arm, hitting the vine with a resounding *fwap!*

It squealed, releasing Bass and withering back into the ground.

Bass gulped in air, massaging his throat. He was so coated in mud and leaves he looked like a creature of the garden himself. He shook the rest of the vines free and crawled to Begonia's side, panting.

"Are—you—all right?"

Begonia had just enough time to turn before she vomited in the bushes amidst many cries of "I say!" and "Really, now!" from the disgruntled shrubs.

She moaned as serpents wriggled in her gut.

Bass trembled to his feet and hauled Begonia up by her armpits. "We need to get inside."

"No—the prophecy. We have to open whatever the key—"

Begonia retched again, flopping back in the sick-splattered mud.

The next thing Begonia knew, her arms had been flung over Bass's shoulder.

"Lean on me. It's going to be all right," he whispered.

The night wore a gray coat, as if the world was covered in fog. Begonia worked to put one foot in front of the other, which was difficult to do because for some reason her boots were filled with cement.

Her head lolled on Bass's chest, and for a brief moment, she worried her puke would get on him. But then she remembered he wanted to be a mortician and it was best he got acquainted with body fluids sooner rather than later. She almost laughed, delirious.

Another burst of lightning shot over her eyes and a flash of memories sparked.

The ghost's fingers playing in the air above her chest. Her mumbling lips. Those inky eyes. How her entire demeanor shifted in a blink.

Up the manor steps and over the threshold they went, panting and sweating despite the frigid air.

"We should find David," Bass said, hauling Begonia through the foyer. "He'll be able to—"

He stopped. Begonia cracked open an eye, ears ringing from the pandemonium before them.

Elders hobbled to and fro, some screeching, some cursing, and others sprouting feathers.

Bass grabbed hold of Grandma Whitman's sleeve as she passed.

"What's going on?"

"Oh, it's awful!" she said, wrapping her robe more tightly around her. "Didn't you see?"

"No, we've been outside!"

"It was awful!"

"Dreadful!"

"Simply subcutaneous!"

"That's still not the right word, Frank!"

Begonia's vision swam. She tried to look around, but even the dimmest light was a needle point in her eye. All she knew was the warmth of Bass's arm and the roar of the hall's hullabaloo.

And then different arms were around her. The smell of cedarwood and butterscotch. Dry, warm hands and a scratchy shawl.

"Come on, pet. Let's get you upstairs," Nana Babette said.

"What happened?" Begonia heard herself ask. Her head lolled, trying to see what her grandparents were huddled around.

"Never you mind, Begonia," Nana Babette said, gently tucking her chin against her chest as she led her to the stairs.

But Begonia had seen, and even through the haze of pain, her skin crawled.

For on the floor, eyes leaking black smoke, was Ms. Majorie.

"It was as if an invisible hand punched through her chest!"

"Oh, but the rumors are true! There is a ghost at Swamp Root!"

"Shh, shh," Nana Babette said, brushing Begonia's face. She hadn't even noticed the tears rolling down her cheeks.

As they mounted the landing to Begonia's bedroom floor, a single image burned through her mind. Not of the Grave Vine or the Foxglove, or even Ms. Majorie's body downstairs.

No, Begonia knew that the memory her mind would keep her up with all night was that of the ghost's lips against her ears.

And how—with no other evidence than simply a gut feeling—she knew Edith Hollowmoor had desperately wanted to tell her something.

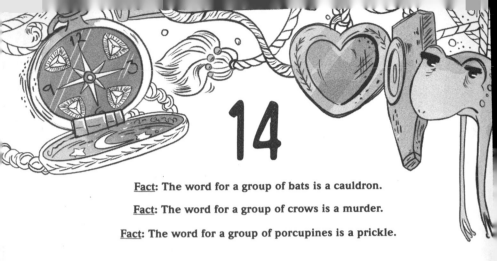

14

Fact: The word for a group of bats is a cauldron.

Fact: The word for a group of crows is a murder.

Fact: The word for a group of porcupines is a prickle.

Begonia thought the word for a group of elders would be a gaggle. All her grandparents quarantined in one room led to much ruffling, squawking, and territorial displays over the best sunbathing spots, quite like a flock of agitated geese.

· David had decided everyone would gather in the parlor, both for protection from the ghost and to keep the last dregs of the Never-Odd auction setup crew from noticing anything—well—odd.

That didn't stop the elders from trying to reveal themselves, however. David and the remaining nurses had been bustling around all morning plucking mushrooms, shoving rats into walls, concealing lizard scales with makeup, and making sure they hid their Oddities.

"This is far too tight!" Grandpa Clive complained to anyone who would listen, scratching the turban David had wrapped around his head to cover his bees, the fabric buzzing in agitation.

Then there had been a loud confrontation in which David gave Babette a serious telling off for "putting nonsensical and dangerous ideas in the children's heads," and by serious, I mean he didn't say "My apologies, but—" or "I must politely disagree, however—" once.

In short, everyone was on edge.

Begonia shifted uncomfortably on the window seat, propped up with many plump cushions and worn quilts. She had lain there all night and most of the day, an ice pack over her head and a puke bucket at her feet.

She called the phase she was in now pain echoes. An aftermath of her migraines that left her with chills, aches, and a bone-deep tiredness, much like how one feels with the measles.

All day, Begonia had tried very hard not to think about the Oddject somewhere just out of reach, the ghost with her mumbling lips, or the grandfather clock in the foyer chiming out its countdown.

She even tried to distract herself. Begonia had spied Mamaw Myrtle hunched over an old chessboard, one in which only half the pieces were playable since the rest were piles of grit at the bottom of the chess box, compliments of her dust touch.

Mamaw Myrtle hadn't made a move in thirty-three days. She studied the board every afternoon, her expression growing more and more defeated. She knew Begonia had her.

Needing a win more than ever, Begonia had dragged herself up from the couch and wandered over to Mamaw Myrtle. Just to see if she had cracked.

"Ready to admit defeat?" Begonia said.

"Oh, Begonia." Mamaw Myrtle sighed and prodded her king with her finger. It burst into dust.

"Ha!" Begonia shouted. "About time. We should—hey! Where're you going?"

Mamaw had shoved back her chair and walked from the board, muttering under her breath.

Begonia harrumphed and collapsed back on the couch. "Spoilsport."

She then drifted back into an uneasy sleep.

It was dark when she awoke. Her grandparents were snoring, mouths open, by the fire.

Part of her wanted to lie back down, but the clock chimed on the wall. Seven o'clock. Five hours until her birthday. Until the day of the auction. And she was further away from finding the Oddject than ever.

Her fingers inched to her locket as she tried to think, but her skull seemed full of Ms. Majorie's pea stew.

"An Oddject of power resides on this hallowed ground

Where twin hearts are affixed and grief goes to drown."

Fact: The original meaning of the word "clue" was a ball of yarn or thread. This is where the modern idea of unraveling a mystery came from.

Fact: Banging your head against the wall burns around 150 calories an hour, which was what Begonia was about to try next.

A sound startled Begonia from her thoughts. The familiar click of knives on marble. Biting back a gasp of outrage, Begonia flung herself up and glared down the hall.

Mrs. Pingleton made her way along the corridor, throwing cautious looks over her shoulder every few steps. Before Begonia had time to blink, the tail end of her power suit whipped around the corner and was swallowed by shadows.

"Begonia?"

Begonia jumped. Bass stood beside her, following her gaze. His eyes rounded out like warning bells.

"What was it?"

"Nothing. I mean, not the ghost, just Mrs. Pingleton. Again."

Sourness sat on Begonia's tongue, and it wasn't all from her pukiness. "I don't get why she's still here. The auction isn't until the morning." Surely David wasn't letting her stay here. Surely.

Bass pulled his kazoo from under his top and ran it up and down the string. He threw another glance down the hall and ushered her back. "Let's just get inside. I brought you some crackers! Good for settling sick tummies."

The thought of eating anything made Begonia's stomach squirm. She nudged Bass's hand off her back, glancing down the dark hall once more.

Begonia stared for a moment, then her shoulders slumped. "All right, fine."

Bass sighed in relief as they made their way back to the bay window.

The snores of her grandparents and low hiss of the fireplace filled the room with a sleepy haze. Bass inched down on the cushions beside Begonia. She rested her head against the cool windowpane, mind and body at war. She both wanted—*needed*—to continue her search for the Oddject and needed to sleep for a thousand years.

For the hundredth time that day, she cursed her body.

"I brought you this," Bass said, breaking her thoughts.

He held out the daisy brooch Nana Babette had given her, a token of her OOA membership. It must have fallen off her dirty clothes as Babette had helped her into her nightgown.

Not having the strength to roll her eyes, Begonia took the brooch and pinned it back on her chest.

"Do you really think that stuff about me?" Bass asked abruptly.

"What stuff?"

He shot her a droll look. "You know."

She did know. She just didn't have the energy to get into it. "Really? Now?"

His eyes roamed to the sleeve of crackers in his hand as he toyed with the crinkly wrapper. "I bet that's what my whole family thinks. I'm the dud. Can't even play a kazoo. Who can't play a kazoo?! You just blow!"

Begonia's tone was sharp, the way Nana Babette's was when Begonia would get weepy about the mean kids in the village. "Why does it matter what your family thinks? Or me? How do *you* feel?"

"I don't know. I have to get my musical Oddity. I have to be a musician. I'm a Montgomery."

"Is that what you want to do?"

"It doesn't matter."

Begonia shrugged. "Well, maybe it should."

Begonia would take any Oddity at this point and, to be completely honest, had a hard time feeling bad for Bass. He had plenty of time for an Oddity to show up, musical or not.

Still, she thought of all Bass's death facts, his fascination with the caskets upstairs. His excitement reminded her of the way her Pepaw Leroy danced a silly jig as he tracked a warm weather front, or how David's gentle hands would caress a new wrench.

Bass's solution seemed simple to her, but he'd have to get there on his own.

Heavy boots sounded in the hall. Only one person wore such heavy, squeaky boots, and the realization sent lightning down Begonia's spine. Her eyes flew to Bass, and his to her.

"Hide!" Bass yelled.

Begonia plopped down from the window seat as Bass lifted the top, pillows and quilts flying like popcorn kernels. Begonia eased herself inside, squeezed among extra blankets, a tin of shortbread cookies, and a bin of holiday decorations. She hunched in, knees to chin, as Bass closed the top, leaving her in semidarkness.

She peered through the crack between the lid and seat, watching Bass spin on his heel just as the POO stomped in.

He stopped in the doorway, eyes roaming the parlor until they fell on Bass. "Where's your little friend?"

"Don't know what you mean," Bass said in a very unconvincing voice.

His gaze pinched into suspicion. "When's your birthday?"

"Um—next summer."

"Huh." The POO surveyed Bass up and down as if he could find the truth of his age in the length of him. "You're one of those Montgomerys, aren't you? My pop's a big fan of your grandaddy. Played his record every night over his evening cigar. Let's hope you carry on the line, yeah? It'd be a shame to come visit you next summer. My pop won't be happy at all."

Bass's gulp was audible even to Begonia. Her fingers curled around her knees, nails biting into her skin.

The Oddslayer huffed a laugh, walked across the room, then bent down to Bass's side. A shadow fell over the slit of Begonia's view, leaving her in complete darkness. The POO's breath snaked through the crack of the seat, his words oily.

"Tick-tock, little one. Tick-tock."

Begonia's eyes sealed shut, heart a bird in her chest. She gripped her locket tight, waiting for him to throw the lid up and lock her away until midnight.

But he did no such thing. Instead, the light returned as boots squelched from the room. A moment later, Bass flung back the seat.

"He's gone!"

Bass offered an arm to Begonia, which she took and climbed out, closing the lid softly so as not to wake her grandparents. Legs weak, she sank back against the seat.

"Thanks," she said, shivering. "It felt like a coffin in there."

Bass sprang from his seat. *"That's it!"*

"What's it?"

"Begonia," he said, holding her arms in a python's grip. "What are lockets for?"

Begonia flipped through her mind's trivia stash.

Fact: Lockets became popular after priests started keeping the finger bones of supposed saints locked inside.

Fact: Lockets can be used as a good-smelling alternative to body sprays when a small square soaked in perfume is kept inside.

Fact: Instead of a loved one's picture, some choose to keep a lock of their beloved's hair inside a locket.

None of those seemed to fit what Bass was looking for.

"I don't know," Begonia said, flustered. "Wearing?"

"Keeping things inside. Just like a coffin." Bass gestured to the window seat.

Begonia tried to follow, but the clues were fireflies zooming around her head. "So, what? Like a picture?"

Bass shook his head, his whole body vibrating with excitement. "If the ghost's body is in the grave, then what could possibly be left that could go in the locket? *What is she taking from the residents?*"

A light flickered before Begonia's eyes. She caught it.

"Her soul."

"And *that's* what's inside the other locket! The one that matches yours!"

Begonia stood and began to pace. "That's what the Foxglove key must lead to. A chest or cabinet or something that holds the other locket. Edith's locket." A thought struck Begonia and she turned to Bass. "What's the difference between a soul and a ghost?"

Bass's brow creased. "I don't know. The ghost is whatever Edith is—a shadow or impression of her former self or something. The soul is something more than that, and I think she wants it back. That's why she's stealing the souls from residents. She's angry. Vengeful. Looking for her own."

Dry lips scraping against Begonia's ear. Mumbled words lost to the wind.

Begonia pushed the memory back into her collection of unanswered questions. Her hands curled into fists. She glanced up at Bass, a new fire in her eyes.

"And she'll keep hurting my grandparents until she gets it. We have to find the locket and give it to the ghost so she can rest in peace."

"When we touch it, we'll get our Oddity? Then we find the ghost and give it to her?"

"I don't know," Begonia said. "But somehow we will do all three—get our power, put the ghost to rest, and stop the auction."

Bass's expression told her he was less sure of this last fact, but he glued his lips shut. Begonia was glad of it. Another wave of exhaustion hit her and she sank back into the pillows.

She glanced out the door, gauging how long a walk it would be to David's office. Wondering if her legs could make it.

Bass seemed to understand immediately. In less than two minutes, Begonia was in one of her grandmas' spare wheelchairs, Bass at her back, zooming down the hall. They burst into David's office, scaring him half to death.

They launched into their story, David's angry frown lines drawing so high up his face they all but disappeared. His hands never stopped moving on the goggles around his face, refusing to take them off even to work on them. Begonia was beginning to think this was a new nervous tic of his.

Silence rang when they finished their tale. David's lips were tight in concentration, whirring the cogs and gears around that ridiculous contraption.

Waiting for him to speak, Begonia watched his hand twiddle, dark with grease and something green caked into the lines of his palms.

Bass couldn't wait any longer. He pointed to the goggles.

"Are those going to help you fight off the ghost, Mr. Klein?"

David stood. "Yes, something like that. Thank you for sharing this. Now follow me. I'm taking you two back to the parlor."

"What? Why?" Begonia asked, outraged. She found herself standing.

"Because I obviously can't trust you to go by yourself or stay where you're told. Grandpa Wilbur will keep a special eye on you tonight; you know he doesn't sleep well during the full moon, so it should be no problem for him to babysit."

"But—"

"No *buts*, Begonia. I told you not to pay attention to the rattlings of Babette, and by doing so, you have put yourself and young Barnabas here in danger. I'm quite disappointed."

Begonia's body was aflame. "She's just trying to help us, to help the nursing home! Unlike you, sitting up here, fooling with your gadgets, doing nothing while others get their souls sucked out."

Bass bit his lip beside her, looking anywhere but at David.

Begonia knew she'd gone too far, but she didn't care. Her pulse raged, her heart fluttered, her chest heaved. She was sick and hurting and tired and far too overwhelmed for someone not even eleven years old.

David's face reddened. "I know you are upset about the nursing home closing—"

"This has nothing to do with that!"

"It has everything to do with that!" David yelled, standing to his full height. Begonia took a step back, mouth open in shock.

"It's terrible, and I hate it as much as you, but this is reality, Begonia, and it's best you learn the lesson early that sometimes life is horribly, *horribly* unfair and there is nothing you can do no matter how much you may want to reverse it!"

David's voice broke on the last word, so loud was his tone. His hair had fallen in his eyes, which were, to Begonia's surprise, wet.

Begonia sat back in her wheelchair. She'd never seen David yell. Never witnessed him lose control.

David ran a hand down his face, scratching the stubble shading his chin. Bass was once more sliding his kazoo up and down.

"Come on," David said once he had composed himself. His gaze wouldn't meet Begonia's. "Let's get you two back to the parlor."

Begonia did not argue as David wheeled her into the parlor, Bass shuffling behind.

"And I'll be taking this," David said, slipping the Foxglove key from around Begonia's neck. "Just in case you get any ideas about sneaking off again."

With many pairs of eyes on them—a majority from Grandpa Wilbur—David left the parlor.

The absent weight of the key was an echoing wail in Begonia's chest. She tugged the pocket watch from her dress.

"On a one-to-twelve rating scale," she whispered against its face, "how likely am I to get my Oddity before my birthday?"

It is safe to assume, Dear Reader, Begonia did not get an answer.

15

Fact: Misophonia is a strong negative reaction to repetitive sounds like chewing, coughing, or breathing.

Night had fallen. Bass slept, the fire had snoozed to embers, and the grandparents' evening tea had gone cold. All the elders were asleep again. Or had died. Sometimes it was very hard to tell.

Begonia stuck a finger under Grandpa Wilbur's noses—one under each set of eyes—just to check. Breath swelled in and out. She flopped back on the couch with a dramatic sigh.

Three hours. Three hours until everything ended. She had to do something.

Begonia eased her socked feet back into her boots as quietly as she could.

"Psst!"

Her head swiveled around. Babette stood in the parlor doorway. She winked at Begonia and beckoned her on.

Begonia grinned, nudging Bass awake.

"Washappening?" he said, eyes peeling open one after the other. Begonia clamped a hand over his mouth, pointed to Babette, then put a finger to her lips in a silent *shh*.

Bass came to, fully alert. He was on his feet in no time, and the two tiptoed around the maze of sofas, wheelchairs, and in Baba Blanche's case, an aquatic tank, and made their way out the door.

"Thought we'd blow this dump," Babette whispered once they were in earshot. She turned and led them toward the stairs. "Rest our ears from the snoring and prattling."

"But what if the others wake up?" Bass asked, glancing over his shoulder.

"They won't," Babette said. She threw the children a mischievous grin. "I may have put a bit of extra chamomile in their evening tea. And if my hand slipped with a dash of cough syrup too—"

"You didn't!" Begonia whispered, half shocked, half amused.

"Their constant teeth grinding was getting out of hand! We're too old for that kind of stress! I had to get away to let my nerves relax or I was going to start predicting deaths! That's when I thought of you two poor souls, trapped away in there with all the kerfuffle."

"But what about the ghost?" Bass asked. "They can't defend themselves if she comes back."

"It's not like you could protect them. Now we all can get some peace and quiet until *David*"—here Babette said his name with a healthy dose of venom—"figures all this out."

She winced as she mounted the first stair. Begonia took her arm to help.

"So you believe us about the ghost?" Bass asked.

"Of course. I saw it with my own eyes! It whipped into the sitting room and stuck its hands into that Majorie woman's chest and put her into an oily sleep, in front of an entire room of spectators, no less. Well, not that they could see the ghost like I could, but they definitely saw Majorie's body jerking about. I tell you—I've never seen anything like it, and I've been here a quarter of a century!"

"You've seen her too, right?" Begonia asked Bass.

"For sure. And I wish I never had."

Begonia's forehead wrinkled.

They turned the corner, heading toward the residents' corridor. Begonia's room and the one David had prepared for Bass were at the end of the hall. Babette slumped at her suite, massaging her knee. "You don't mind if I stop and grab my cane, do you?"

Begonia and Bass shook their heads together.

Once inside, it became very clear Babette had spent as little time in the parlor as possible. All the lamps were on, the radio played, and a fresh cup of tea steamed beside her ginormous crystal ball.

Babette tottered in. "I've just got to remember where I left the darn thing."

Begonia sat down on the sofa and Bass on the ottoman across from her. If he kept up his nervous twiddling, his kazoo would break off the string. It was setting her teeth on edge, and that was saying something since her entire body buzzed like the inside of Grandpa Clive's turban.

"David said everyone has to stay in the common room," Bass said. "M-maybe we should go back."

Babette was doubled over, searching under her bed. "David. Bah!"

"What did he say to you?" Begonia asked her, momentarily distracted by the memory of their argument.

"*'How dare you put Barnabas and Begonia in danger! You're the adult here!'*" Babette rose, cane in hand. "But I looked him straight in the eye and said, 'Listen here, Sonnyboy. I see no problem giving those kids a bit of hope.' And if he had your best interests at heart, he'd let you be in your own bed."

She limped forward, resting her hip against her armchair, and massaged her leg. "He doesn't understand what it's like. Living with pain like that. How it's not just in your body, but exhausts the mind too. How a quiet room can be just as much therapy as a doctor."

Warmth surged in Begonia's heart. Babette caught her eye and winked.

Knowing he'd lost this fight, Bass sank low into the cushion.

"We can just head to our rooms ourselves so you can rest," Begonia offered.

"Oh, it's no trouble. Just give me a moment," Babette said, easing into her chair beside Bass. "Besides, if the ghost shows up on the way, I'd like to give her the ol' one-two with my stick!"

She brandished her cane like a sword and Begonia smiled. Even Bass's lip twitched.

I haven't forgotten about you, my Burglarizing Bookworm. Though I consider my wit quite villainously sharp, I believe sometimes it is best to let the story speak for itself. However, I would like to have a quick discussion with you about the phrase "going downhill."

You may be familiar with the term, which normally is used figuratively to mean "decrease in value, success, or overall pleasantness from what something once was." For example, Begonia had not left the manor grounds in a long time, but when she did, it was never enjoyable to go downhill, and not because the town had also gone downhill, but because the children who lived down the hill were mean, and the Never Odds reminded her of the orphanage she would live in soon that was so downhill it had probably never been uphill to begin with.

Therefore, going downhill is never a good thing, physically or metaphorically.

Unfortunately for Begonia, things were about to go downhill very quickly. The benevolent narrator that I am, I thought it was only right to warn you.

Nana Babette spoke to Bass, but Begonia missed what she said. A prickle danced on the back of her neck. The lights flickered. Static buzzed from the radio.

Then a vicious wind tore through the room.

Begonia jumped to her feet and Bass whimpered. Nana Babette frowned.

A strange sound reached Begonia's ears, like the scratching of beetle legs on wood. The sound was so small she might have missed it if not for the clawed, gray hand oozing from the wallpaper just behind Bass and Babette. Another hand broke through, a shoulder, and then at last, a head.

Edith hauled one knee out after the other, worming against some invisible force, until with a wet slither, she slid free. Her eyes rose to Begonia as if she were the only one in the room.

Begonia couldn't shout a warning to the others, so strong was her war between curiosity and fear.

Because there was something different about the ghost's face. Normally pinched with rage, Edith's expression softened and grew more peculiar the longer her gaze lingered. Her lips opened and moved against each other, but if there was sound, it was lost to the cacophony of the room.

Bass's scream pierced the air and Nana Babette turned in her chair, half-risen. The color bleached from her face, mouth hanging slack.

For a heartbeat, the four of them were stone. No one moved. No one breathed. The ghost's gaze never left Begonia's face.

Then Babette's eyes fluttered to Begonia as she uttered a single word.

"*Run.*"

Her voice broke the ghost's spell. For the first time, Edith seemed to notice there were others in the room. All her softness evaporated. Her eyes darkened, teeth sharpened, lips pulled back into a vicious wail. She glided forward, claws outstretched.

"No!" Begonia screamed.

Babette rose, shoving Bass and Begonia back. She stepped in front of them, arms wide and cane held at the ready.

Begonia grasped for her shawl, but Bass tugged her toward the hall.

"Come on, Begonia!" he yelled.

"Let—me—go!" she said, wiggling against Bass's grip.

Her head spun. Her legs shook. Her vision was the inside of a snow globe.

She swung an elbow at Bass and he dodged, wrapping his arms around her middle and hauling her back as if she were a stack of hay.

A scream of frustration tore from her lips. *"Nana!"*

Nana Babette stabbed her cane at the ghost. "Back, you devil! Back!"

Bass busted into the hall, dragging Begonia with him.

But Begonia would not leave her nana.

She writhed, kicked, raged against him. Fury seethed up her spine like snake venom, granting her strength. She dove for the doorframe, nails biting into wood, clinging to it with everything she had.

Not Nana too. Please, not Nana.

Bass's hands clawed at hers. "Come on! We have to go!"

Begonia didn't hear him. Her eyes shone, entranced by the horror in front of her.

Edith Hollowmoor stopped in front of Babette. She didn't swat away the cane at her throat, didn't even spare it a glance. Instead, she glided straight through, her edges blurring and re-forming around the wood like poison mist.

Tears burst down Begonia's cheeks. *"Nana!"*

Babette tottered back, arms flying wide. Her cane clattered against the floorboards.

And just as Bass pried Begonia's fingers loose, Edith wrapped her hands around Babette's throat.

16

Fact: Not too long ago, green clothing, wallpaper, and paints were dyed using arsenic.

Begonia fought tooth and nail against Bass as he tugged her through the hall, down a flight of stairs, and into the farthest part of the manor from Babette's room—the kitchen.

"Stop, stop, *stop*!" Begonia yelled, ripping herself free once her feet hit the tile floor. "We have to go back and help!"

Bass whirled on her, flapping his arms. Fear had turned him into a very small, bespectacled owl. "And do what exactly?"

"I don't know! You tell me! You're the one who loves dead people!"

"Yeah, the ones that *stay dead*. I don't know how to deal with an evil ghost!"

Flashes of the ghost rang through Begonia's head like a funeral bell. The claws. The teeth. The eyes.

The eyes were—well, maybe not friendly—but not evil until she noticed Bass and Nana Babette.

Nana. Her heart crunched against her ribs. She had grown used to pain, built a tolerance, but this was a different breed of hurt.

Begonia's nails dug into her fist as she forced herself to clear her head. She built a dam, stick by stick, one strong enough to hold back her grief for now.

She smoothed the hair from her damp brow and began to pace. Her words dropped slowly, deliberately. "I don't believe the ghost is evil. I don't think she was where she was supposed to be, or else she would have just floated through the wall like a normal ghost, right? I mean, it definitely looked like she was fighting *really hard* to get to us."

Bass stared and stepped away from her as if she were a rabid wolf.

"And what about how her whole body changed when she heard Nana Babette? She wasn't acting aggressively at all until she noticed her."

Bass's face was stuck in some marsh between pity and fear. "But why, Begonia? Why go for Babette and not us? And why us in the attic and at the carnivorous garden, but then not in Babette's room? That doesn't make sense!"

Begonia bit her nail, turning toward the window. The grounds stretched under fingers of fog, swirling and gray just like her thoughts. She thought of nails pried from the Weeping Tree door. Of Edith's sandpaper lips whispering lost words and soft eyes turned to flint. The answer swam up from the murk of her mind, but Begonia wanted to make sure it worked from all angles. Satisfied, she turned to Bass.

"Because she wasn't sent for us."

Bass shook his head, perplexed. Begonia resumed her pacing.

"I think someone is controlling her. Probably the same person who locked us in the Weeping Tree, who stole Edith's locket from her headstone with her soul inside. I'm sure of it."

She stopped, turned to Bass. "What if in the attic, instead of chasing us to steal our souls, Edith was actually just trying to speak to us? And in the garden too. She actually bent to whisper in my ear that time. And think about the weird way she was moving—in the attic, in the garden, and coming into Nana Babette's room. It was all slow and sticky, like she was trudging through mud. I think she's been breaking the rules to come warn us about something."

"And Mawmaw?" Bass said, glasses flashing dangerously. "I don't think she was trying to warn her of anything when she sucked out her soul!"

Begonia shook her head. "Remember the way she moved toward Mawmaw?"

"How could I forget! She glided forward, nails out—"

"Right!" Begonia said, grabbing his shoulders. "*Glided.* The same way she moved in the garden when she left us to go attack Ms. Majorie. She wasn't crawling and wiggling like she just was up there!"

Begonia whirled around, excitement fluttering under her skin.

"Whoever is controlling her forced her to attack Ms. Majorie, Mawmaw, and the others! I don't think she actually wants to hurt people—someone is making her do it!"

Bass was still frowning. "But why those specific people?"

"That's the mystery. If I'm right, the controller is the one choosing her victims, so they must have something the controller wants."

"Or know something the controller wants to stay secret?" Bass said, joining her pacing.

Begonia flashed him the ghost of a smile, happy he was now on board. "Right. So what do Dada Haneef, the Decrepit Decrescendos, Mawmaw Montgomery, Ms. Majorie, and Nana Babette have in common?"

Bass shook his head.

"I don't know either. But narrowing down the suspect list should be easy. Obviously it's someone who has something against the nursing home staying open."

"Like who?"

Begonia bit her lip, thinking. "Mrs. Pingleton? She's been sneaking around here, and on principle I never trust people with that much enthusiasm."

"No, not her," Bass said. "I just can't see it."

"The banker? Mr. Schmoob?"

"He wouldn't want the nursing home to close, though, right? Isn't David his biggest client?"

Begonia threw up her hands. "Well, then someone else! Help me think of more people. I'm not convinced it's not that shady buyer—"

"I just don't think Pingleton has it in her," Bass said, kazoo spinning.

"I don't think either of us knows what that woman is capable of, but—what?" Begonia asked as Bass's face did a somersault of emotions.

"Don't get mad, all right? But I-I think I might have thought of someone."

"Who?"

Bass shot her a sidelong look.

"*Who?*"

"David! I'm thinking David."

Begonia blinked twice. "David what?"

Bass leaned closer, dropping his voice. "David could be controlling the ghost."

Begonia huffed a laugh. "Come on, Montgomery."

"Didn't you say it was David who found you as a baby? He could have had both lockets all along and, for whatever reason, gave you one."

"That's a stretch."

"Okay, then think back to being in his office earlier."

He stared at Begonia, wide-eyed, urging her to understand. "Didn't you notice that weird green color on his hands? It's the same chartreuse color the workers painted on the halls, including the attic one, yesterday."

"So?"

"*So* someone locked us in the attic *when the paint was still wet.* And then there's how sad and distracted he's been lately—"

Begonia had heard enough. "David loves the residents! He's been doing all he could for years to keep the nursing home afloat."

Bass shrugged. "You said yourself that he was just tinkering away with his unventions while we were out doing something to save this place."

Begonia shook her head, eyes wide. "You're delusional."

"No, I'm being logical, and I'd really like it if you quit calling me names."

Begonia glared at Bass. Bass, though a foot shorter, glared back.

Finally Bass crossed his arms and gazed moodily out the window. "Fine. Believe what you want, but if the Oddject is the locket, no one would know more about it than David. I think we should take a peek around his office. He'd be in bed by now, right?"

Begonia wanted to scoff again, but something wiggled free from her memory.

A book on a desk. A hand nudging the cover away from her line of sight.

Seances and Science: Gadging Ghouls with Gadgets and Gallantry, by Flanus Thopman.

It was so unlike David not to share books with her. To keep secrets.

Or at least, it had been. Once upon a time.

Begonia suddenly felt very, very cold. David was an inventor after all, a scientist. Always pushing the limits of what Odds could do. It would just take one slip. An experiment gone wrong, some variable wrenched out of his control.

Maybe he accidentally awoke a ghost.

It would have to be something like that. A mistake. David would never attack residents on purpose and surely wouldn't want to keep Begonia from finding her Oddity.

Surely.

Begonia shook the thought from her mind.

"Fine. We'll go to David's office. And when we don't find any proof that he's the bad guy, then next time *you* can be the one to spread ointment on Grandma's bunions."

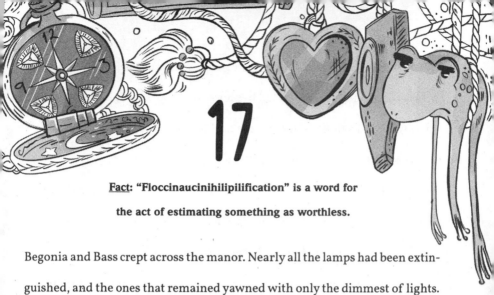

17

Fact: "Floccinaucinihilipilification" is a word for
the act of estimating something as worthless.

Begonia and Bass crept across the manor. Nearly all the lamps had been extin-

guished, and the ones that remained yawned with only the dimmest of lights.

Begonia's toes met the foyer floor and she held out a hand to stop Bass.

The entrance seemed empty apart from the grandfather clock, whose face

read one hour until midnight. She glanced side to side, making sure the coast

was clear before inching across the room.

Then three things happened very quickly. A giant crash of thunder shook

the night, lamplight flooded the room, and the manor doors swung open.

Begonia jerked to a stop and Bass shrieked, both of their heads swiveling

toward the entrance.

A group of people bustled through the threshold, drenched and sour-faced

from the storm.

The first was a tall Black woman flapping rain from her coat and water

from her shoes. Two girls followed behind her. Begonia assumed they were

her daughters.

"Bass!" the littlest yelled. Baubles clinked from her headful of pigtails as she ran toward them, cymbals crashing with every step as if a drum line hid in her ballet flats. Freckles dotted her nose, and a sucker sat in the space of a missing tooth, dyeing her lips and tongue blue.

"Look what showed up last night!"

She kicked her feet like a tap dancer, percussion pulsing up from the floor.

Bass's face morphed from fear to shock to disappointment, the last of which he quickly tried to hide. "Oh, your Oddity. Neat."

"Mm-hmm! Right in time for my eighth birthday too." She reached up and patted his shoulder consolingly. "You're next though. Don't worry."

"Wilhelmina Montgomery, what did I say about running with candy in your mouth?" the woman—one of Bass's mothers, Begonia realized—said, pushing her damp curls back into place.

The older daughter slumped in behind her in an apathetic way, as if she wished she were anywhere but here. Somewhere in the distance of her mind, Begonia recalled her name was Beatrice.

They all pointedly ignored Begonia.

"Sorry, Mom." Wilhelmina turned her big eyes back on Bass. "Mom said Mawmaw had a stroke?"

Before Bass could speak, his mother had grabbed him in a quick hug before pulling back just enough to gaze into his face. "Oh, sweetie. Where's Mawmaw? How's she doing? She's in her room, Mr. Klein said?"

Not waiting for him to answer, she took to the stairs two at a time, towing Bass along behind her. "Come on, girls."

"Wait!" Begonia yelled, running behind.

"Mom—no!" Bass wrestled free. "You can't be here. It isn't safe! There's this ghost—"

"There you are, Leona, thank God! And Barnabas too. I've been looking all over for you!"

Five necks craned to the top of the staircase as Mrs. Pingleton descended.

"Fee, I'm so glad you were here. How is she?" Mrs. Montgomery said.

Fee? Begonia's brow crinkled. She glanced at Bass for answers, but he had gone stone-still.

"Well, that *nurse*," Mrs. Pingleton said with disdain, "said it definitely was a stroke, but that it was unwise to take her to the local hospital because movement could make it worse. I've never heard such a thing, but Mr. Klein will not be swayed! And now I can't even find the silly woman! Honestly, this place has gone to the dogs."

"It wasn't a stroke!" Bass said. "There's a ghost that sucked out her soul!"

His outburst was met with silence, only broken by the pop of Beatrice's bubble gum.

Wilhelmina glanced up at her mom with a fearful expression. "Momma, is there a ghost?"

"Of course not, baby." Mrs. Montgomery's eyes flashed to her son. "Bass, this is no time for games."

"But I'm telling the truth!"

"I'll take you to her," Mrs. Pingleton said, squeezing Mrs. Montgomery's hands between her own.

Begonia's eyes narrowed on the movement.

Then her whole world tilted as shock coursed through Begonia, from the tips of her wispy hair to the scuffs on her boots.

Because the wedding ring that flashed on Mrs. Montgomery's finger had a twin on Mrs. Pingleton's.

Fact: Ants and humans are the only two types of animals that wage war on their own kind.

Begonia's body iced over in armor.

As the four women clomped up the steps, Begonia whirled on Bass. "The *buyer* is one of your moms?!"

Bass folded in on himself. "I—um—"

"You *what*? Just casually forgot to mention that to me?!"

"Well, no, it's just that you were so upset about the auction and I—"

But Begonia's mind was a tornado, speeding, churning, demolishing, ripping up every stone to reveal the ugly, wiggling truth underneath.

Bass tailing her like a flea on a possum, watching her every move. Bass casually forgetting to stand guard, letting them get locked in the attic. Bass allowing himself to get captured by nearly every plant in the carnivorous garden. Distracting her with pointless clues and accusations.

He had been stalling, sabotaging her at every turn.

The OOA had been infiltrated.

Her vision flashed red. "That's why you didn't want me to think it was Pingleton controlling the ghost! You're working with her to take down the nursing home—"

"That's not it!" Bass said.

"—and each resident gone is less work for you later!"

"Begonia—!"

"I *heard* Pingleton say this place would have her rolling in cash—and that means you too! And I'm sure the resort will be all creepy and death-themed, just like you'd like it!"

"Begonia—that's not—it got my mawmaw!" Bass yelled, arms flying wide.

"You're a liar."

"So I didn't mention that my mom wanted to buy the place! She still wouldn't hurt anyone. Plus, she doesn't even know about Oddities—she's a Never Odd! I just didn't want you to hate me. We're a team. OOA, remember?"

Begonia barked out a cold laugh. "We were never a team. You were my subordinate, and you betrayed me."

Fury flashed in Bass's eyes, something Begonia had yet to see. The next thing she knew, his chubby finger had poked into her forehead.

"*You've* been nothing but mean this whole time, but I didn't say anything because I wanted you to like me! You're the only other Oddless I know! I thought you'd get it. How everyone around you expects something of you, has powers and you don't. How alone that feels. But you're so obsessed with finding your Oddity to prove you're worth something, you don't even see everything else around you."

"That is not—I don't think—"

Bass crossed his arms. "Keep lying to yourself, then."

Begonia's fists shook at her sides. Her body ached and her stomach squirmed and her loved ones were soulless and she had an hour before she was Oddbliterated.

"We can't save anyone if we don't have the Oddject. The crystal ball said we had to find it. The prophecy, this mission, you and me—we're a waste without it."

Bass huffed in disbelief. Shaking his head, he reached up and unclasped the black cat brooch on his chest before slapping it into Begonia's hand.

"You were never a waste to me."

Bass turned and climbed the rest of the stairs, leaving Begonia alone but for the roll of thunder.

The manor was much more creepy alone. Not that Begonia would admit it, or even had space in her mind for that thought to dwell. Still, the tiny hairs on her arms stood at attention with each squeak of the floorboards, every bite of wind against the windows.

Bass didn't understand. He had a family and a house to go home to. Swamp Root Manor was all Begonia had. How dare he be so selfish as to leave her alone in this, quite literally, final hour. She straightened her shoulders. She needed to be more like Nana Babette, to channel her strength. Nana was capable of getting things done all on her own, never needing anyone.

Well, except for Begonia. She always needed her.

Tears pricked Begonia's eyes, but she swatted them away. She had a locket to find. An Oddject. And if any place had information about its whereabouts, it would be David's study.

And he had a lot of explaining to do.

Begonia turned the corner, finding the office door cracked open, light spilling out into the hall. Lightning zinged from the windows. The wall lamps flickered. Begonia's breath suddenly refused to fill her lungs.

But there was nothing to fear. She knew David. David loved her. He would never hurt her.

Begonia pushed the door. It creaked open as she stepped inside. As usual, papers and books clouded every surface, and a low fire crackled in the hearth. The smell of pipe smoke and old pages hung in the air. No bubbling witch's brew or animal heads floating in jars. Bass was ridiculous.

Begonia walked to the center of the room and slowly spun, searching for the best place to start her snooping.

She stopped, brow furrowed. David's usual evening cup of chamomile lay shattered on the floor, brown tea dripping over the side of his desk. She moved closer, careful not to step on the jagged porcelain.

Steam rose from the puddle.

It was still hot.

Spiders crawled down the nape of Begonia's neck. It was only then she noticed how quiet it was. The usual chirping, clacking, and whistling of unventions were silent as the grave.

Begonia brushed a hand over the desk, feeling where the teacup would have been only minutes before. Searching for some invisible clue. She found nothing.

She leaned into the wood, one palm resting beside the picture of her and David picnicking on their double-heart beach, frustration roiling in her gut.

Then, like a clock striking midnight, something clicked.

Her hand flew for the picture, bringing the frame so close to her nose that breath fogged the glass. Her eyes followed the familiar double curve of the beach's perimeter, lightning flashing in her fingertips.

Double-heart beach.

> *"An Oddject of power resides on this hallowed ground*
> *Where twin hearts are affixed and grief goes to drown."*

The swamp with its twin-heart beach was right on the edge of the grave-yard, and where else would grief drown but in a place where loved ones are laid to rest?

Vindication burned in her chest. She knew just where to find the Oddject.

Begonia set the frame down, spinning on her heel. She took off at a sprint toward the hall. She would drag David out of bed if she had to.

But she skidded to a halt at the door. Just before she had rounded the cor-ner, a burst of firelight caught something reflective, shining painful light into Begonia's eyes.

She peered back, squinting.

Something gold gleamed against David's armchair.

She inched closer, everything taking shape in the low firelight.

The topmost part of David's head peeked out over the back of the chair, hair catawampus around the gold band of his goggle invention. He had fallen asleep wearing them.

Begonia's shoulders relaxed. "David! I figured it out!"

She moved around the chair.

David lolled against the cushion, mouth open, arms dangling off the sides. He could have been asleep.

He could have been, if not for his eyes, which from under the green tint of the goggles dripped black, oily smoke.

18

Fact: Eosophobia is the fear of dawn.

Many people consider eosophobia to be an irrational fear, one a person could get help to overcome. But if you were expecting to meet a terrible fate come dawn, say, a trip to the gallows—or worse, the dentist—it may in fact be completely rational to fear the dawn.

For Begonia, dawn included her memory being wiped, being carted off to an orphanage, and having her home auctioned off, with family members dispersed to who knew where.

Therefore, Begonia felt very justified indeed in her eosophobia.

She trudged out on the lawn. The key she lifted from David's body now hung around her neck, and she had a shovel clenched in her hand.

Being a rather small child, she did not have much room left in her body for more sorrow. Bass had abandoned her, Nana Babette had joined the other soulless, and David—sweet, loving David—was innocent after all.

Begonia was utterly alone but for the grief she could not let herself feel. So instead, she focused on the mud under her boots and the smooth handle of the shovel in her grip.

She had a heist to complete.

She stomped ahead, glad for the shelter of the Whispering Woods as above Reba roared, weeping rain over the decaying leaves.

"Hey, Begonia," said a tree. "Did you hear the one about a weeping willow who read a *sappy* romance? He found it full of *pine*-ing."

Begonia ignored the creaking chuckles.

"Arnie, *leaf* the poor girl alone."

More groaning, woody laughs.

"Oh, do shut up," Begonia snapped.

An oak tutted. "My! Aren't we prickly this evening."

"My! Aren't you balding this evening," Begonia shot back. She was not in the mood to be trifled with.

"It's autumn!" the oak cried. "And leaf-pattern baldness is ecologically natural this time of year, I'll have you know!"

After that, no one else bothered Begonia. She passed through the towering black gates of the cemetery and down the stone path to the swamp. Bat wings tickled her stomach, growing larger and more hairy the closer she got. Now that she knew where the Oddject was, it called to her, sending a signal that beat in her chest like a second heart.

Her boots sank into damp sand. The swamp loomed like a creature before her—green, thick, and slightly smelly—only held at bay by the twin heart–shaped stretch of beach between it and the graveyard.

And in the very center, the place where the two hearts kissed, the earth was disturbed. Dark and mounded up in uneven patterns.

Begonia's heart skittered as she walked forward, floating step-by-step as if in a dream.

She stopped. Stared down. Blew out a breath deep from her belly and thumbed her locket for luck.

Once for Dada Haneef and the Decrepit Decrescendos. For Nana Babette and Mawmaw Montgomery. For David and, well, maybe not for Ms. Majorie, but definitely for the safety of the rest of Swamp Root Manor.

She plunged her shovel into the earth. Over and over, metal thwacked into sand as Reba pelted her back. Begonia did not stop. She did not wipe rain from her face.

CLUNK.

Shock waves chattered up her teeth as Begonia's shovel hit something hard. Her heart leapt into her throat. Throwing the shovel aside, she fell to her knees, sloshing the mud and stones away in handfuls. Her nails scraped against wood. Brass embellishments shone in the moonlight. She swiped the rest of the debris free until the full view of a large trunk appeared in the sand. It was old-fashioned, with a rusty keyhole on the side. A sour smell wafted up from the hole, like swamp water and rotted leaves.

Begonia didn't curl her nose. Instead she ran a hand over the muddy roots tangled in the handles.

The trunk was the most beautiful thing Begonia had ever seen.

The kind of trunk pirates hid treasures in. Treasures like a locket.

Her fingers fumbled around the handles. She grunted, she panted, she slipped in the muck a few times, but finally the trunk slid free. Begonia knelt down, chest heaving.

She looped the key off her neck. Fit it in the keyhole. Turned.

The lock clicked and dust spit as the lid cracked open.

Begonia's breath was a phantom in the air.

Gong! Gong! Gong!

Over the wind and rain and the crash of Begonia's heart, the wind carried the chime of the grandfather clock.

Midnight. Begonia's eleventh birthday.

Mouth dry, Begonia clamped her slick hands to the side of the lid, muscles coiled to push, then froze.

Needles prickled her hairline in that strange way they did when one realized they were being watched. Slowly she turned.

Lightning split the night, illuminating the figure that loomed before her.

Tall, dirty, and—strangely—blinking behind goggled lenses, the figure leaned down, electroblaster in hand.

The Oddslayer's smile was a knife. "Happy birthday, love."

19

Fact: Scopaesthesia is a phenomenon in which humans can tell when they are being stared at, as if by a sixth sense.

Begonia's tongue wore a fur coat. At least, that's what it felt like as her eyes blinked and the world spun into focus.

Stars stared down. Damp moss clogged her nose, her clothes were stiff and caked with muck, and somewhere out of sight, the sound of snoring petals tickled her ears. Somehow, she was in the carnivorous garden.

Begonia slung her woozy head forward, then nearly gasped. The POO was in front of her, working a greasy rope around her wrists. Begonia twisted, but another rope was looped around her middle, holding her tight to something cold and hard at her back.

Her heart pounded as she tried to remember what happened. She had just been digging for the Oddject when—

She spotted the trunk just beyond her ankle. Memories washed through her, colder than the downpour. The Oddslayer finding her on the beach. Kidnapping her at electroblaster point. Their wet march past the garden gates, where she bit him, trying to flee. The stinging zap of electricity, and finally, darkness.

She winced, still imagining the current in her bones.

The POO double-checked his knots, then stomped to a suitcase under a nearby tree. He rummaged around its contents with many clangs and dings as a cudgel, manacles, thumbscrews, and something that looked like the clawed teeth of a bear trap were tossed about.

Begonia went rigid. From the weapons, yes, but also from the view of the clearing taking shape around her. How familiar it was. How she had been at this very spot only yesterday, fitting her locket into the headstone now holding her captive.

Her pulse sped.

She had to get to the Oddject before it was too late.

Joints creaked as Begonia's leg stretched forward, straining for the trunk's edge. Her foot fell, finding only air. Slick with sweat, she tried again, moving as quietly behind the POO as she could. Her muscles strained, her cheeks ballooned, her face reddened, but still her boot tip only skimmed the leather, nudging it farther away.

Frustration boiled under Begonia's skin. She wanted to beat her fists, claw the dirt, scream and scream until there was nothing left inside.

She had survived four ghost attacks in two days, surfed a casket cascade, bested an insulted Foxglove, and stolen toenails from under Ms. Majorie's nose. To be bested at last by none other than a POO was nearly too much to bear.

At the moment, his backside was on full display as he bent, wrestling the clasp on his bulging suitcase around the tip of the electroblaster.

David's electroblaster. With David's goggles strapped around his head.

Steam whistled from Begonia's ears. No one stole from David but *her.*

"Those—aren't—yours!" Begonia said, fighting her bindings.

The POO turned and laughed, spittle flying from his lips. "Your friend won't be needing them now. And these"—he tapped the side of the lens—"well. Didn't know until I got them on, did I?"

Begonia had no idea what he was talking about. She still glared.

The Oddslayer finally snapped the suitcase shut and stood, pulling something from his pocket. With a *snick*, he flicked back the lid as if it were a simple cigar lighter. But it was much, much worse.

The Oddbliterator.

Begonia pressed into the gravestone, feet digging in the mud.

The Oddslayer stepped in front of her and bent down until Begonia could count every freckle on his nose. Could smell his rotten teeth behind chapped lips.

"All I have to do is push this little button," he taunted.

Begonia's teeth chattered. Her palms sweated. Her throat bobbed like a boat in a storm. But she was still the granddaughter of Nana Babette, Mawmaw Montgomery, and fifty-six other brave, stubborn, and rather cankerous elders. She carried gumption in her bones.

Begonia took a deep breath, squared her shoulders, and forced herself to meet the POO's gaze.

If he was going to use that thing on her, then he would have to look her in the eyes and feel every bit of her scorn until the last of her memories faded away.

The Oddslayer's sneer lost its bite. Perhaps he had hoped she would whine and plead, no doubt like other Oddless had in the past before their memories were stolen. She would not grant him that.

He growled and straightened, snapping the cap back on the Oddbliterator.

To Begonia's bewilderment, he walked back to the tree, picked up his suitcase, shoved the Oddbliterator inside, and snapped it shut.

Begonia's heart raced, confused. Surely the POO was playing some mean trick. Surely he wasn't picking up his suitcase. Surely he wasn't walking out of the clearing.

But he was.

Just before stepping through the vines, he turned, pulled up the goggles, and stared at her with his naked eye.

"'Mazing," he said, huffing in apparent disbelief.

Then he turned and lifted the curtain of green.

"Wait!" Begonia said. "You're—you're just leaving?"

"Don't worry. Your friend's coming soon. Paid me a pretty penny to collect you too." The Oddslayer tapped the corner of the goggles and rattled his suitcase, no doubt filled with more of David's prized unventions.

Begonia was slack-jawed. "But I'm eleven now! I'm still Oddless!"

The Oddslayer turned, about to throw some rude retort, no doubt, when something caught his attention behind her. He grinned, gold teeth flashing in the moonlight.

"There you go," he said. "Delivered her like you asked. Safe and—well— maybe not sound, but—"

"Thank you, POO," a voice said. "Your services have been most helpful."

Iced beetles crawled over Begonia's skin.

No. It couldn't be.

The Oddslayer smoothed his dingy shirt collar and sniffed. "I still prefer to be addressed as Pursuant of Oddless—"

"Leave the electroblaster."

He looked longingly at the barrel of the blaster, lip pooched. "I thought this was part of the spoils."

The POO must have received a subduing look because he suddenly hiked up his breeches and cleared his throat. "Very well, very well. Keep your wig on."

He propped the blaster against a tree and ducked out of the clearing, lost to the vines and fog.

The world went quiet. The rain dulled to a drizzle, and not even the daffo- dils seemed to be snoring anymore. No sound but the roar of Begonia's heart.

For, Dear Reader, she knew the owner of that voice, and if you are as good an investigator as you are a grave robber, I would say by this point, you may have guessed who it belonged to as well.

Clump-slop. Clump-slop. Clump-slop.

Footsteps squelched in the mud, punctuated by the unmistakable thud of wood sinking into damp earth.

Begonia looked up to meet the figure before her, the blood fleeing from her veins like cockroaches before a torchlight.

Nana Babette smiled down.

20

Fact: You are just as likely to die from a trolley accident as at the hands of a colony of ants, but more likely to die from a coconut falling on your head than both combined.

"My dear, dear pet. What a mess you've gotten yourself into."

Begonia's mouth opened and closed several times before she got control of it.

"But you—the ghost! We saw it get you!"

Nana Babette smiled, the wrinkles around her eyes spreading like spiderwebs.

She bent to untie Begonia, who flinched away as if burned. Her grandmother tutted at her behavior as the ropes fell to her sides, but Begonia might as well have been a gravestone herself, frozen as stone.

"Oh, my sweet girl," Babette said, wiping her hands clean on the handkerchief she pulled from her pocket. "You saw the ghost come toward me, but the ghost would never harm me, pet. I control her, after all. My dear grandmother Edith, who I believe you've already had the pleasure of meeting?"

"Your—you?" Begonia shook her head, trying to knock the fuzz from her brain. *"Who even are you?"*

"Your nana, of course, dear. That will never change. We share a name, in fact, you and I. Hollowmoor, after my ancestors who built this manor."

She gestured to the ground before them, simpering at the shock on her granddaughter's face.

"*Why?*" Begonia said. "Why—to all of it?"

Babette's grin sharpened. "Because the townspeople didn't like us, those mushroom-brained Never Odds. Thought we were too odd. Witches, they called us. This was of course before Odds hid themselves away. Before the world began to reject the idea of the unexplainable and *science* took over."

Babette spat the word as if it were covered in pustules, no doubt thinking of David and his tinkering. As she circled the grave, Begonia got the impression her nana had sealed away these memories tighter than any potion bottle cork.

But now the spell was broken, the glass shattered, and the story flooded out like a dark elixir.

"My family's Oddities have always brushed the line between this world and the afterlife. My mother could slip through the realm of the dead. My great-aunt was rumored to be Death *herself*. And I—" Nana Babette lifted her face to the moon, reaching up as if to brush the clouds. "I see the secrets that hang in the air like cobwebs. The wishes thrown down wells to rot. And the ghosts that speckle the world like dandelion weeds."

She turned to Begonia, gaze wistful. "When my grandmother died, our family was in danger of losing the manor to those terrible Never Odds in the village. I knew I had to do something to keep it, and luckily for me, my aunt had taught me a spell to conjure the imprint of a departed loved one."

"Edith," Begonia whispered.

Babette nodded. "She wasn't the same as she had been in life, more of a puppet in a lot of ways, but I could control and use her to haunt the grounds and scare prospective buyers away."

Begonia's stomach soured. She too would have done anything to save the manor.

Or, at least, she'd thought she would.

"So I did the spell, but I was just a child and didn't realize that those with Oddities could take my home too. A man by the name of Yu bought the manor and turned it into a nursing home for Odd elders, while my family was evicted—cast out on the street like a sunken holiday gourd. There was nothing I could do but leave my grandmother's soul in limbo until I could return to control her once more.

"Time passed. I grew into an adult—penniless, forced to live among the Never Odds, surviving by telling fortunes in back alleys and shady taverns for those that thought my talents seemed almost like *real magic*. But I knew if I was to get my home back, I needed money. Lots and lots of money. That's where all seven of my beloved husbands—with their poorly timed deaths, of course—came in."

Nana Babette giggled to herself, sounding much younger than she was. She waved a hand.

"Life insurance, wills, inheritance—the paperwork was all so tedious. But it granted me all I needed. Well, all I thought I needed."

Babette's revelation tickled something free from Begonia's mind. "... *Of course I'm still keeping my part of the deal ... five resident attacks ...*"

Schmoob's mysterious nighttime meeting—it had been with Babette all along.

Begonia's neck flashed with heat. "Mr. Schmoob has been in on this since the beginning, hasn't he? Is he—I don't know—a cousin or something?"

"A cousin?" Babette's laugh was as dry as loose stones. "Heavens to Betsy, no! He's a nasty Never Odd like the rest of them. But they do have their uses. He's been helping cover up my money trail for years. Not to mention steadily increasing David's expenses."

A flood of images raced past Begonia's eyes. David, flour on his nose, kneading bake-off dough to help pay for medicine when money ran low. David, fingers blistered and red, knitting fifty-eight pairs of thick wool socks when there were no funds to fix the radiator. David, who was willing to sell off his pocket watch—his most cherished possession—for just one more month of mortgage.

David, lying soulless.

"You've been playing him all along!" Begonia said. "You and Mr. Schmoob!"

"Yes, yes," Babette said, casting out the words as if they were of no importance to her. "Like I said, he's been quite useful."

Begonia's fists shook at her sides. "Why on earth would Schmoob risk everything to help you? He could lose his job—go to jail!"

"You forget I see the unseen, pet. I saw all his crooked dealings and fudged numbers when I did his reading years ago on the streets. Would have been a terrible thing if someone told the authorities of a banker with heavy pockets."

Begonia thunked back against the tombstone as she shook her head, eyes roaming the skies for wherever her good opinion of adults fled to. "Of course. You're blackmailing him."

For the first time, Nana Babette's face soured. "Well, I was until he let that nurse overhear our meeting the day before last. She was about to run and tattle it all to David. Nasty woman. Since then, I've felt his usefulness has nearly run out."

Begonia closed her eyes. Of course—that's why Ms. Majorie was attacked. She had eyes and ears everywhere.

A strange thickness sat on Begonia's tongue, a feeling she couldn't quite swallow. She wouldn't name it, and it most *definitely* wasn't respect, but she couldn't deny no matter how awful Ms. Majorie was, she always put the nursing home first. In that, at least, they were aligned.

Begonia peeled her eyes open. Her head might permanently be stuck shaking in disbelief the rest of her life. "You're a crook."

Nana Babette's brow quirked behind her glasses. "You would know all about that, wouldn't you?"

Something twitched in Begonia. Babette's smile grew roots.

"Yes, I see all your secret thieving. The little trinkets you surround yourself with to feel more important. I guess you inherited a little of your—let's say—*opportunistic tendencies* from me."

Begonia tried to get to her feet, but her knees wobbled. She settled for a half crouch, clutching the headstone for support and leveling Babette with the very glare she'd taught her.

"*You're* not my grandmother. Not anymore."

"Actually, I'm more your grandmother than you know."

Nana Babette reached into the collar of her robe and pulled out a silver chain.

A silver chain holding a locket.

Begonia's heart skidded to a halt.

The Oddject.

"This," Babette said, holding the necklace up in the moonlight, "is a piece of Swamp Root history. It's tradition for every Hollowmoor daughter to get a locket at birth, then have it placed in their gravestone at death. This one was my grandmother's. And that one"—she pointed a crooked finger at Begonia's neck—"was my daughter's."

Begonia clutched the pendant under her smock. "It's—it's not true!"

But even as she said it, the words felt wrong on her tongue. Something deep inside her had known since Babette showed up in the clearing. Maybe even before.

But the Oddject. It was right *there*. She only needed her legs to work well enough for her to grab it. She tried once more to stand, but she was as weak as a faun.

Babette sighed theatrically, as if she couldn't wait to share a piece of bad news. "I'm afraid it is true. You see, sacrifices had to be made. I couldn't spare any money for a daughter if I was to buy Swamp Root Manor back. So I renounced her, refused to give her any inheritance, including the traditional Swamp Root locket. In the end, she was too poor to raise you herself and left you under that horrid begonia bush."

Begonia swallowed once. Twice. There appeared to be a very large, very hairy ball of yarn in her throat that refused to go down.

In a small voice, she asked, "What happened to her?"

"She died. Her and her husband. Trolley accident years ago."

Begonia licked her lips and nodded, waiting for the hammer of emotions to fall. But they didn't come.

Perhaps she had always known her parents were dead, perhaps she was just as cold and uncaring as Nana Babette, or perhaps—and here, her thoughts turned to David and her grandparents inside—she wasn't as fussed because she had never found herself wanting for another family at all.

And with that, Begonia's hand drifted from her locket to the pocket watch.

More questions than answers fought for space in her skull. "Then why give me the locket?"

Babette shifted her slippered feet, glancing widely at the garden as if, for the first time this evening, she couldn't meet Begonia's eye.

"It was perhaps a moment of weakness when I saw you there, under that bush. I would have known who you were even without the note my daughter left—your wispy hair, your angry little fists, that unfortunate Hollowmoor chin."

She laughed, and it sounded so much like the Nana Begonia had grown up with, it sent splinters through her heart.

"I'd grown sentimental in my older years, I suppose, but a piece of me loved you. So I burned the note my daughter left, slipped the locket around your neck, then told David some story about there being an injured cat loose in the garden, knowing he would find you."

Nana Babette finally turned to her granddaughter, eyes misty, face lined with the years of laughs and kisses and bedtime stories.

Begonia looked away. She didn't want to see the love there. Whatever kind of love it was. Her heart was breaking.

Babette walked forward, tone gentle. "As you grew, I realized how much alike we are. Both alone in the world, both in love with the manor, both ill in our own ways no one else could understand."

She gestured from her cane to Begonia's temple, then brushed damp hair from her granddaughter's face with warm, dry hands. It was only a heartbeat before her grandmother's eyes slipped from her face and swam back to the manor.

"But my first and truest love will always be Swamp Root." Nana turned and walked back to the electroblaster, heaved it up on her shoulder, but not before tossing a trite smile at Begonia. "No offense, dear. You are a lovely girl."

Despite her quivering, Begonia's voice came surprisingly steady. "You've won. David's gone, the nursing home is being auctioned off, and you have all the money to buy it back. Why not let me find my Oddity in peace?"

This time, Babette's face showed genuine sadness. "I'm afraid I haven't won, pet. Did you know David has willed you part of the nursing home grounds? It's all here, in this document from Mr. Schmoob."

She tugged an official-looking paper from the inside of her robe, adjusted her glasses, and read,

"*I, David M. Klein, being of sound body and mind and of my own free will, leave the estate and grounds of Swamp Root Manor to my charge, Begonia Hollowmoor, except in the unlikely event that her death and departure transpire prior to mine.*"

Begonia's head, already spinning, folded inside and out like old origami. Her nostrils flared.

"So take my soul like you did David's and Mawmaw's and all the others! Or kill me like all your husbands!"

Babette gave her a sad smile. "I'm afraid it's not the death part of the clause that concerns me, pet. On the contrary—well—why don't you see for yourself?"

Nana Babette gestured to the trunk.

Begonia blinked. In all the excitement, she had completely forgotten about the chest. She eyed its moldy wooden frame warily. If it wasn't Edith's locket inside, she had no idea what else the prophecy could have meant.

A chill swept over her, much deeper than anything caused by the wind or the rain or even Edith Hollowmoor's ghost. This was a bone-deep cold, and she realized with absolute certainty, she did not want to know what was inside.

"Go on," Babette said, not pointing the electroblaster at her exactly, but hoisting it higher in a way that reminded Begonia she was the one in charge.

Still too shaken to stand, Begonia slid in the grass until her knees thumped into the chest. She glanced up once more at Nana Babette, who nodded with an unreadable expression.

Begonia took a trembling breath. With numb fingers, she fumbled past the key still in the open lock, grasped the lid, and threw it open.

She stared into its depths.

21

<u>Fact</u>: In some countries, masters in martial arts must register their fists as deadly weapons.

If you have ever been on either a twisty roller coaster or in the back seat of a getaway car, then you probably know what it feels like to experience a jarring reversal. How the sudden change in direction can make your stomach drop, your head spin, or your balance feel completely off. It's an overall disorienting experience, and I do not recommend it.

Reversal can also have a secondary, metaphoric meaning. One where some kind of twist is revealed near the end of the tale, forcing the reader, character, or both to look back over the entire story through a new lens. Old things take on new meanings, new things take on old meanings, and strategically placed bread crumbs you may have missed come back to—forgive the pun—haunt you.

Therefore, if you are not strapped to a runaway railroad car or using the faucet to rinse a very large spoon, you may find objects in reverse to be a rather exhilarating experience. Even if it does cause your stomach to drop, head to spin, and balance to flounder.

Begonia stared into the depths of the trunk. Perhaps if her stomach hadn't dropped, her head weren't spinning, and her balance weren't floundering, she might have noticed the velvet purple blanket lining the wood or the plush lace pillow resting at one end.

But she hadn't noticed. She was incapable of peeling her eyes away from the face of a sleeping child within. One with a pale white face, wispy white hair, and a dingy white smock. A tarnished silver locket rested perfectly centered over her chest.

Only she wasn't sleeping.

She was dead.

Begonia's world bent. Cracked. Shattered.

Memories bled through the fissures like shards of glass.

Pain that shot across her skull like lightning. Biting, blinding, world-shattering agony. The wood floor rising to break her fall. The hammock of David's arms just before her head hit the ground. His face swimming, mouth calling for help. His voice shouting her name. Then wailing it.

The peaceful feeling of drifting.

The peaceful feeling of waking up in her bed like any other day.

It couldn't be. It *couldn't*.

Begonia's teeth chattered. Her hands—she didn't know what to do with her hands. She peeled them from the trunk and wrapped them around herself.

"H-how long?"

Babette inched forward, adjusting the electroblaster so she could rest a hand on Begonia's shoulder. Begonia did not have the strength to shove it off. In fact, she could barely feel it.

"Just over a month, pet."

A month. She had been in *there* for a month.

Begonia brought her hands up to her face, wiggled her fingers. They seemed so solid before, but now she caught a slight wisp as if smoke danced off her skin. Something she never knew to look for, and maybe the knowing made all the difference.

"How?" Begonia asked.

"Like I said, Hollowmoor women always have Oddities that toe the line between this world and the next. Yours fit right in."

Begonia shook her head. "It can't be. I'm just—"

Just plain old Begonia. Nothing special. Nothing Odd.

She didn't even have a tingle in her fingers the way she did on the cliff.

She peered up at Nana Babette. "Then what is it?"

Her grandmother's smile almost appeared genuine. "Isn't it obvious, pet? You're a ghost."

The sky, the garden, the body in front of her turned a fuzzy white. She combed over the past month of her life, needle ready to poke holes in Babette's theory, and listed every fact she thought she knew about ghosts.

Fact: Ghosts in lore are tied to a place or object.

Goose bumps trickled down her back. She couldn't remember the last time she left Swamp Root grounds.

Fact: Ghosts don't eat or drink.

Her disdain for stewed pea soup. For the crackers from Bass that rolled her stomach. It wasn't as if Begonia purposely didn't want to snack, it just never crossed her mind—and then it never crossed her mind that it didn't cross her mind.

Piece by piece, more truths wrote themselves across Begonia's heart. Her grandparents, Mr. Schmoob, and Bass's entire family ignored her, or at the very least never spoke directly to her. David's new unexplained sadness that Begonia thought had been related to their debt. The way the pocket watch never worked when she asked when she would get her Oddity.

Babette prattled on. "I suppose it's because you died before any other Oddity had time to arrive. Oddities are fickle that way. Would you still have come back as a ghost if you lived to be an old lady, never knowing your full potential until that happy day? Or did your untimely death trigger this ghost gift? We may never know."

Begonia felt her breath hitch, scared at any moment she might drift away. She touched her hands, her chest, her cheeks just to make sure she still could.

"There, there, pet. The denial is quite common, I hear. Both before and after you learn the truth. The mind does whatever it needs to in order to protect itself."

Her clawed fingers scraped Begonia's skin as she patted her back. Begonia flinched, rubbing the spot between her shoulder blades.

"B-but how can you touch me?"

Nana Babette laughed. "Never-Odd rubbish. Of course I can touch you. Ghosts aren't how they portray them in their campfire stories."

A strange emotion took root in Begonia's ribs. She should have felt special. She should have felt different. She should have had a power strong enough to save her family.

Tears filled her eyes. "Why didn't you just tell me?"

"My dear, would you have believed me?"

Begonia didn't speak. She didn't need to. They both knew the answer.

The underbrush rattled. Begonia's and Nana Babette's heads sprang up. Twigs snapped and mud splashed as two figures emerged from the vines.

Mr. Schmoob, top hat awry and muttonchops quivering with exertion, wrestled a squirming Bass into the clearing.

"Found this one trying to sneak into the garden, ma'am. He had this."

Metal clunked as Mr. Schmoob threw Begonia's shovel to the ground.

"Begonia!" Bass yelled, kicking wildly. "Code red, code red! Undertaker! Undertaker!"

Begonia's heart swelled. "Bass! What are you doing here?"

Bass struggled to get another word out as Schmoob's meaty fists circled his airway like he was trying to control a deranged chicken.

"Saw—POO—from—window!"

He might have been steadily turning purple, but Begonia had never been more happy to see his face.

Mr. Schmoob cursed, losing his grip, as Bass's incisors found his arm. Bass gulped in a lungful of air before rounding on the banker and executing a series of rather elaborate martial arts moves.

It is impossible to describe what happened next, mainly because no one understood—least of all Bass—but after much twirling, spinning, and hair pulling, Schmoob was on the ground, gasping for air.

Begonia whooped. Just the sight of Bass—his round cheeks, his crooked glasses, his ridiculous orange kazoo—blew the dust from her brain. She held out a hand for him, and Bass ran toward her, his smile mirroring hers.

"Will you get control of him?!" Babette barked.

Slightly green, Mr. Schmoob lurched forward, hog-tackling Bass just before he made it to safety. Even with his apparent secret jiujitsu skills, Bass was no match for Schmoob's girth.

Schmoob grabbed the ropes at Begonia's feet and began to wrap him up like a mummy.

"Bass!" Begonia said, lurching forward.

Babette pointed the electroblaster at her. "Back!"

Begonia froze, eyes flying between the blaster and Bass. Bass caught her gaze and, with a near imperceptible move of his head, shook it once.

Begonia's heart stuttered. Helpless, she sank back to the ground as Schmoob coiled the rest of the twine around Bass and brought him before Babette.

Her grandmother stalked forward, finger waggling. "Barnabas Montgomery. Nosiness must be catching in your family."

Bass glared at her with shiny, dark eyes, chewing on the rope in his mouth.

"That grandma of yours—always listening in doorways and peeping through blinds. She somehow found out about my family connection to Swamp Root and couldn't wait to run and sing it to David. Another little job for the ghost."

Begonia's head whirled to Nana Babette. "Is that why you attacked them all? Because they learned about your dirty deeds?"

"Alma, yes, and Haneef too. He knew my plan as soon as I did with that nasty secret-hearing Oddity of his. The a capella group, on the other hand, was just for a spot of fun. You know how I *despise* show tunes."

"And David?" Begonia asked, anger once more seething up her neck. "What did he do besides be the best thing that's ever happened to this place?"

"The best thing, bah! David wanted to keep the truth of your *condition* from you. He wanted to lie to you forever. He guessed after you told him the prophecy that it might lead you to your body and didn't want you to find it. It was *David* who locked you in the attic, not knowing Edith was in there with you, of course. *I* wanted you to discover the truth so you could move on and leave me to my manor."

Move on.

Begonia didn't have the space to process what that meant.

"You hag!" Bass yelled, his mouth free of the rope. Mr. Schmoob yanked him back with a *"shh!"*

Babette's eyes narrowed. Mr. Schmoob's eyes kept flicking in Begonia's direction, never quite falling directly on her. With a chill like a dousing of water, Begonia realized he couldn't see her. Maybe he couldn't hear her either.

"Pity you don't have your family's Oddity," Nana Babette said. "It's quite powerful, you know. But I suppose there's always a dud in every generation."

"I am not a dud!"

The words tore from Bass's throat, so loud and powerful they rattled around Begonia's chest like a deep drum of thunder.

Babette raised an eyebrow, taken aback. "Then what are you?"

Bass's eyes, his face, his very essence radiated like the coming dawn. He leveled Babette with a glare even she would be proud of.

"I am a mortician."

Begonia's heart might have burst with pride.

Babette laughed. "The black sheep is what you are. Least loved, least Odd. Worthless."

"Don't listen to her, Bass!" Begonia yelled. "You're worth every bit as much as the rest of them! More, even."

Bass's shock turned soft. With growing horror, Begonia saw his eyes go misty behind the orbs of his glasses. She was suddenly very involved with a loose string on her sleeve.

"Don't cry all over me, Montgomery. I've got enough going on at the moment," Begonia said, but there was a smile behind her words.

He hiccupped a laugh, then his gaze dipped down to the ground. It froze on the open chest.

"Um, Begonia?" he asked.

"Yeah?"

"What am I looking at?"

"Um, me. Long story. Will explain later."

Bass's voice quivered. "Okay."

Begonia turned to Babette, needing to ask the question eating at the back of her mind. She pointed to Mr. Schmoob, his gaze still roaming the headstone behind her. He jumped as an owl hooted in the distance.

"Why can some people see me and others can't? You, David, Bass . . ."

Nana Babette smiled and patted the electroblaster, quite at ease. "Those goggles David's been toying with? They're some sort of ghost unvention that allows him to see and hear you. As for Bass and me, we can because of our Oddities."

"I don't have an Oddity, as you keep pointing out!" Bass said. Mr. Schmoob hushed him again.

"Of course you do, you cabbageheaded child! How do you think you can see Begonia with a naked eye when others can't?"

Bass's brow crinkled. "I don't—"

"*You can see ghosts.* That's your Oddity. That weird obsession of yours with death must have overwritten your family gift. It's rare, but it happens sometimes."

"No—I—that's not true!"

"Think of what you are seeing now, child!" Babette pointed to the body in the trunk and then to Begonia. "What other logical explanation can you give?"

A book cover swam behind Begonia's closed eyelids. *Seances and Science: Gadging Ghouls with Gadgets and Gallantry,* by Flanus Thopman. That ghost book in David's office. Not a book he had used to awaken Edith Hollowmoor, but one he used to construct the apparatus that allowed him to see her.

Come to think of it, she couldn't remember the last time she had spoken to him without goggles.

No wonder the POO stole them when he was tasked with finding her for Babette.

"Then why did the prophecy tell us to hunt for an Oddject if we're already Odd?" Bass asked.

Lightning glinted in Babette's glasses. "Don't you see? *There never was an Oddject.* I made it up. I needed Begonia to follow clues to this trunk so she could find her own body."

"But *why*?" Begonia asked.

"Because of David's will!" Nana Babette rattled the paper in the air. "Death *and* departing! Such a silly little embellishment of words that should have meant nothing. But you surprised us all and came back as a ghost. Dead, but not departed! While you haunt these halls, the manor will never be mine. And you couldn't move on, not until you learned the truth of your death for yourself."

Babette stroked the silver locket at her throat, expression wistful. "And once you are gone, my dear grandmother can be reunited with her soul and depart as well."

Begonia's breath hitched. Bass was right. Oddject or not, Edith's soul was still in that locket.

Her fists balled as she turned her full fury on her grandmother. "I will *never* leave. This is my home. And I will never stop haunting you until you wake up all the souls you stole!"

"Then I will never stop until I find a way to banish you regardless! I assure you it can be done."

Begonia glared at her. Babette's chest heaved. Bass tried to hop forward and tumbled to the ground.

"I'll never let you get away with this!" Bass said, rolling very nonthreateningly in the mud.

Babette's expression cracked into something with teeth. Feral and full of rabies. "I see we must deal with Mr. Montgomery first."

22

Fact: Because of the complexities of medieval armor, it could take a knight up to twenty minutes to dress for a single fight.

Begonia's blood—*did she still have blood?*—iced over at Babette's words.

"What do you mean?"

Babette gestured lazily around the clearing. "We can't have little Barnabas spilling all Nana Babette's secrets, now, can we? Not when I'm so close to reaching my goal."

Her grandmother set the blaster against the tree, pulled the locket from her neck, closed her eyes, and with her thumb, rubbed the pendant.

"No!" Begonia yelled.

An unnatural wind howled through the clearing. Bats skittered from the trees, frost spiderwebbed down vines, and the stars blinked out one by one.

Begonia's pulse raged in her ears. She climbed to her feet, leaning heavily on the gravestone. Babette hid the locket behind her back with a smirk.

Edith's ghost materialized. Her gray shoulders were as tense as the trees around her, as tight as the strings of a twisted marionette. Completely under Babette's will.

Mr. Schmoob's head whipped back and forth, eyes wide with terror. Though he could not see, he definitely sensed something was wrong, and with a very loud, very undignified squeal, he tore off through the clearing, fleeing the garden.

Babette paid him no mind. She growled, "Get the child," and at once, Edith glided forward.

Bass yelped. He rolled onto his front, flopping like a catfish as he tried to wiggle away.

"No!" Begonia screamed. She lurched forward, knees trembling like beetle wings.

"Yes!" Babette said, and slammed her cane to the ground. Wisps of bright green shot out from where wood met earth, clanking around Begonia's ankles like phantom chains. She tried to lift her foot, but it was like wading through a stew of maple syrup and tar. She wobbled back against Edith's tombstone.

Bass had somehow gotten to his feet, ropes still around his legs and face slick with sweat. He jumped like he was in the world's most high-stakes sack race, one arm wide for balance and the other holding his glasses to his face. Glancing back at the ghost on his tail, he stumbled over a branch and fell.

Begonia had to *do* something.

Words called to her from across an ocean. A vague memory of David and his less-than-helpful encouragement.

"I learned some truly valuable life lessons while I waited for my Oddity to show."

"Being resourceful is an important skill, with or without powers."

Begonia's spine snapped to attention. She scanned the clearing, analyzing every angle with a scientific eye. Like an inventor. Like David.

She saw Bass squirming on his back, saw the ghost towering over him, saw Babette's cackling, the blaster propped up against the tree beside her—

Begonia didn't think, she just dove. As if it were a second nature, her legs disappeared and reformed around Babette's magic chains, cutting through like a knife to butter, a hand to a cobweb, a bat's wing to a midnight fog. Her feet half glided, half pounded against the soil, flickering between a solid boot and white mist. She moved faster than she ever had in her life.

Begonia latched a fist around the blaster as Babette turned.

"Hey, now!"

But Begonia had already rolled to safety. She thunked against the tree completely solid, all ghostly powers evaporated.

Remembering how David had taught her, she flipped the lid, turned the nozzle, pressed the button, slid the lever, pinched the coil, and tickled the trigger. The gun purred to life, a blue current racing up and down its side.

"Begonia!" Bass screeched. Edith bent over the top of him, a hand stretched for his ribs, to the heart pounding inside.

"Sorry, Edith," Begonia said. Closing one eye, Begonia took aim and fired at the ghost.

The bolt flashed out, striking Edith in the center of her back.

White-blue light ricocheted around the ghost like lightning in a jar. The trio watched the display, eyes wide, blue light reflecting on each of their faces.

All at once, the volts died, Edith's body swallowing them whole. Edith didn't seem to notice any of it, so tight were her master's strings. Her wiggling fingers sank closer to Bass.

Babette laughed. "Did you really think—"

Begonia fired the gun a second time. The shot beamed toward Babette's chest. The smile slid from her grandmother's lips, and she screamed in outrage.

In half a blink, Edith had flown in front of Babette, arms splayed, absorbing the shock.

Just as Begonia hoped she would.

Babette's leer returned. "You forget she is under my control, pet. I can use her as a shield all day if I need to."

But the ghost was away from Bass, which was all Begonia could do at the moment, giving him time to untie himself, and her more time to think.

Babette sighed, propping herself casually against the tree and crossing her ankles.

"So what's the plan, Begonia? Are we going to spend the rest of our days sending the ghost gliding back and forth across the clearing?"

Begonia ignored her as Bass finally ripped the last of the ropes from his ankles.

"Go get help!" she said.

Babette clucked her tongue. "Oh, how I would love to play one last game with you, Buggy, but time is of the essence."

She slammed her cane into the ground once more, and green lights shot to Bass. His scream died as he froze in the glow, his body levitating off the ground.

Then, like a giant fish hook, Babette began to reel him in. Back toward Edith.

Begonia's heart stuttered. Her vision narrowed. Her mind slowed. All she knew was the cool metal of the blaster between her hands.

And as she always did in times such as these, Begonia whirled through the deck of trivia cards in her mind.

Fact: A platypus's bill is covered in nearly forty thousand electricity sensors.

Fact: Pure silver is the strongest metal for conducting electricity.

Fact: David's electroblaster can issue fifty thousand volts of electricity.

No, no, no. None of them were facts she could use.

And still Bass floated closer. Closer.

Her panic boiled hot, weight shifted side to side, breath coming too fast.

"Come on, *think*!" Begonia whispered.

Then Nana Babette spoke, voice sweet as butterscotch and gooey as oatmeal cookies. "Don't you want to move on, pet? Rest in a place where there is no pain? Where you can have endless peace? You can be a normal child. You can run, jump, and play whenever you like. Have an afterlife that matters."

A life that matters.

Memory whirled past Begonia's eyes, a kaleidoscope of grief. Mawmaw's smoky eyes. Edith's screech. Envelopes stamped OVERDUE. The leering faces of village children. The bottom of her puke basin.

All moments that made up Begonia's history. A history where she was taught to hate herself for what she couldn't do before she learned to love herself for what she could.

But there were so, so many more *could*s.

Flour on her cheeks as she baked naan with Dada Haneef. Tears of laughter in her eyes as she butchered another piano lesson but put a goofy smile on Mawmaw's lips. Trivia nights with David, hot cocoa on their shirts and lazy grins on their faces.

And if she had to admit it—OOA missions with Bass, even with him displaying that ugly brooch on his chest like it was the queen's jewelry.

As if jolted there by electricity, a final fact sparked and melded to the others.

Fact: On average, each year 55,700 people are grievously injured by jewelry.

Begonia set her jaw. "I *have* a life that matters. Right now. Even if it's different from others'."

Babette's grandmotherly expression cracked, shattered into something with teeth. She threw back her head and cackled.

Begonia's vision took on a dreamlike quality, white and soft. Bass moved in slow motion, drawn to the ghost like metal to a magnet. Babette laughed wildly, chin thrown back, hands flung wide, cane in one, silver locket in the other—

Dangling just outside the protection of the ghost.

Begonia took aim and pulled the trigger. The bolt sang through the air. It shot right under the outstretched arm of Edith and buried itself deep in the locket in Babette's hand.

The clearing flashed blue. Babette screamed as her entire body went rigid. Her eyes rolled. Her muscles spasmed. Her hair strained with static.

The hollow dimmed as the light faded. Babette collapsed to the ground, locket flying. Bass followed behind, falling to the earth with a thump and a loud "*oof!*" as the spell on him broke.

Begonia traced the locket's arc across the sky. She backpedaled, reached out a hand, and grinned as its weight sank into her palm.

Babette weakly pushed herself up on her elbows. Her face was caked in mud. Grimacing, she addressed the ghost. "Get . . . the boy."

Edith, once frozen, now sprang to life, darting for Bass.

Begonia launched herself forward, once more feeling that strange ghostly pull. She was wind. She was air. She was everything and she was nothing.

But mostly she was fury.

Bass wiggled back into the tombstone, but there was nowhere to go. Edith had him pinned. She raised her hand, fingers outstretched, a breath from his chest.

Begonia slipped between them. Distantly, she felt Bass shiver, but her eyes were only for Edith.

Edith stopped, head tilted. She considered the locket as if trying to sense the soul inside.

Begonia's breath was a caged thing in her ribs. She didn't dare break the spell.

And then, between one heartbeat and the next, Edith's gaze softened. With a bow like a conductor after an encore, she stepped back and lowered her head. Almost like a Foxglove.

At once Begonia understood. She slipped the chain around the ghost's neck, the silver pendant falling just over the place where Edith's heart would have been.

Edith's fingers snaked up to the locket, pressing it close as she inhaled.

The breath left her body and she changed. Her skin lost its gray hue and the holes in her dress knitted together. Her teeth squared, her hair glossed, and what were once chipped claws shrank to rounded, gleaming fingernails.

Edith opened her eyes. They were kind, a gray silver like the ringlets on her temple that crinkled at the edges. They found Begonia and some kind of coil loosened in Begonia's spine.

Her great-great-grandmother smiled in a shy, melancholy way. She bent forward and kissed Begonia's forehead. Her lips weren't cold as Begonia would have guessed, but dry and soft. Just like a grandmother's ought to be.

"No!" Babette's mouth was open in horror. Her fingers clawed in the mud as she tried to pull herself to her feet. All three heads shot in her direction.

A storm cloud moved back into Edith's face. Before Begonia could breathe, Edith was in front of Babette, glaring down at her granddaughter flailing in the mud.

"No!" Babette screamed, worming back, hands shielding her face.

With a snarl, Edith grabbed Babette by her robe's collar. One moment they were there, rising up from the ground, feet dangling in the air, and in the next, a burst of light, then nothing. All that was left of the two was the echo of Nana Babette's scream. It lingered in the air like humidity, like smog, imprinting itself on the inside of Begonia's skull. Begonia knew she would carry that sound with her for the rest of her days.

Something warm moved at Begonia's side, and then Bass's hand was around hers. He squeezed once. She squeezed back.

One by one, birds began to sing. Fingers of sunlight wiggled on the horizon, heating Begonia's toes and shooing away the night's fog. A far-off deep creaking sound signaled the Whispering Woods had awoken, the first pun already floating across the morning dew.

Bass nudged Begonia. "You okay?"

Her body and mind were still numb. "I—I don't know. You?"

"I think so."

For a moment, the two of them stood there, just breathing, watching the drowsy daffodils yawn and stretch their petals.

Begonia glanced down where her hand met Bass's. It was slightly transparent, not how her feet had been when she had, for lack of a better word—ghostafied—but less solid than before. She closed her eyes as a tear snaked down her cheek, but there was a smile inside her too.

She was Odd. And in truth, it didn't matter to her at all.

She had released Edith and stopped Babette just like she would have if she were a Never Odd. Strangely, the feeling warmed her insides, a purring cat on her chest. She wasn't worthless and didn't need an Oddity to prove it.

Branches snapped and feet pounded. Begonia's head jerked up as Mr. Schmoob tore into the clearing. He looked once over his shoulder, then sped past them without so much as a blink in their direction.

Bass's voice was half-confused, half-laughing. "I thought he would be in the village by now."

"Me too," said Begonia. "What—?"

The ground shook as out of the mist charged a gaggle of grandparents. They were armed to the teeth with cross-stitching needles, kitchen utensils, and in the case of Grandpapa Sir Walter Philips, a giant broadsword that was so heavy that both Grandpa Forty-Eight and Grandpa Forty-Nine—or perhaps it was Grandpa Forty-Nine and Grandpa Forty-Eight—rolled on either side, helping him bear the weight.

Mixed in the mob, to Begonia's shock, was Swamp Root Manor's entire pack of elusive dust bunnies. Most of her grandparents ignored them in their fury, or at least tried not to be trampled by their many legs, stingers, and tentacles. The more bold rode astride them, like Grandma Peterson, perched between one's wings, and Mimi Carol, whose motorized scooter bounced behind as if it were a carriage pulled by the strangest collection of horses the world had ever seen.

I am sorry to tell you I will not be sharing the description of said creatures with you, my Nosy Reader; I have already established dust bunnies prefer their secrecy. But as you have already created an image for Ms. Majorie in your mind's eye, these beasts shouldn't be difficult for you.

Grandpapa Sir Walter Philips, iron knees freshly oiled, clanked to a stop before them. "Grand morning! Where goes the treacherous villain?"

Begonia and Bass both pointed right.

"To battle!" Grandpapa said, heaving his sword into the air before losing balance under its weight and falling backward into a shrub. Grandpas Forty-Eight and Forty-Nine heaved him out of the groaning bush before the trio was off again, sword in tow.

Bass and Begonia shared a shocked look before taking off after them with a giggle.

In no time at all, they skidded to a halt at the front of the gaggle.

Mr. Schmoob and Mr. Schmoob's muttonchops were locked in a corner, both quivering and quite sweaty. Grandpa Bonic's rats circled his feet, snapping at his ankles until the banker looked like he was playing a vicious game of hopscotch.

The elders gritted their teeth, both natural and garden grown. The dust bunnies' eyestalks swayed menacingly. Mr. Schmoob grabbed a stick and swung it wildly.

"Back, you freaks! Back, all of you!"

But the elders only raised their spatulas higher and stalked closer.

Grand Da O'Flannery whispered at Bass, "Close yer eyes, wee one."

Before Begonia could react, the banker's scream caused her head to snap up, and she was met with one of the strangest sights she had ever seen— and for growing up in a sentient nursing home for magical elders, that's saying a lot.

Mr. Schmoob dangled by his ankle like a very hairy piñata, held aloft by an enraged Foxglove. Growling and tentacles writhing, it swung the squealing banker over the horde. As most of the elders were already carrying some form of stick-shaped weapon, I need not explain what happened next. But don't worry—both Mr. Schmoob and his muttonchops made a full recovery after a well-deserved trip to the barber and extensive psychotherapy.

"How did they know?" Begonia asked sometime later as the children made their way back up to the manor.

"I told them!" Bass said. "When I saw the POO kidnapping you from Mawmaw's window, I ran downstairs and woke Sir Philips for help. He said the moment his hips were greased he would rouse the infantry. I ran ahead of him and grabbed the shovel, but Schmoob found me first."

Begonia's heart throbbed. It must have taken Bass so much courage to do what he did, especially after how she had treated him.

"Here," she said, stopping at the base of the stairs. Begonia took the cat brooch from her pocket and pinned it back in place over Bass's heart.

Bass ran his thumb over it, voice soft. "You kept it."

"Of course I did. And mine's still on, see?" She pointed down so Bass could see.

After a moment, he smiled and extended a hand. "OOA?"

Begonia grinned and slipped her fingers in his. "OOA."

At the same time, they met each other's excited expressions.

"Begonia!"

"Do you think—?"

"Now that the ghost is gone—?"

Begonia put her hand back in his and squeezed. "Let's go see if our grandparents are awake."

23

Fact: In antiquity, it was common for an auctioneer to drive a spear into the ground to start and stop bidding during an auction instead of today's use of a much more benign—albeit boring—gavel.

The front lawn was filled with very shiny, very unfamiliar automobiles and their coffee-sipping drivers leaning against their hoods amidst yawns and puffs of their cigarettes.

As soon as they caught her eye, Begonia's spit lodged in her throat like an acorn. She couldn't be too late. She couldn't have gone through everything only to have the manor auctioned off.

Before she could worry about it further, Bass pulled her up the stairs and onto the porch. The manor swung open its front doors for them, revealing the chaos inside.

The foyer was a hubbub of harassed-looking workers and fancy-looking buyers in expensive-looking suits.

At the foot of the stairs, a well-manicured hand grabbed Bass's shoulder. Begonia couldn't blame him for screaming. They had been through a lot.

"Goodness, it's just me, Barnabas! You okay?" Mrs. Pingleton said, hair freshly floofed and in her most vibrant pink power suit yet.

She plowed on before Bass could answer. "Good, good. Oh, I'm just so nervous for the auction! I've been waiting for your mom to come down, but you know how squirmy Wilhelmina is about getting her hair done. Might take all morning!"

She gave a nervous peal of laughter that didn't reach her eyes. She hadn't acknowledged Begonia at all, but now that Begonia knew why she was being ignored, it didn't seem to bother her as much. In fact, since it was Mrs. Pingleton, it didn't bother her at all.

"I wonder where Mr. Schmoob is. I was hoping to get everything squared away as quickly as possible." Her neck craned around the banister.

Bass glanced at Begonia from the corner of his eye. "He's a bit—ah—detangled right now."

Mrs. Pingleton patted Bass's arm with a simperingly sweet smile. "You mean detained, dear."

"Uh, yes. That too."

Begonia bit her lip to keep from laughing as Mrs. Pingleton clomped off into the Odditorium, tottering slightly in her bedazzled heels. Begonia and Bass ran to catch up.

The Odditorium was spit-shined—every cobweb removed and every dust mite expelled. Folding chairs had been unfolded, rugs had been unrolled, and an auctioneer's podium stood atop a platform like a towering guillotine. To Begonia's right, a table groaned under the weight of refreshments and bidding paddles.

The auctioneer—a large man with a large scowl and even larger mustache—paced at the front. He kept twirling his whiskers around the edge of a pencil and checking his reflection in the window.

Some of Begonia's early-rising grandparents were present as well, all doing their best Never-Odd impressions. Grandma Minnie sat sourly in the corner, her bulk taking up two chairs. Begonia wasn't sure if her glower was because it was auction day or because of the very tall, very pink wig smashed on her head that David had given her a week before to conceal her horns.

Begonia's eyes roamed the rest of the Never Odds in the crowd, all schmoozing and hors d'oeuvring with their diamond-clad fingers draped around bidding paddles.

"Bass!"

Begonia turned to see Bass's little sister, Wilhelmina, running toward them. One side of her hair poofed up in a cloud while the other was knotted into a twisty braid. She skidded to a halt, hair beads flying, looking Bass up and down with her eyebrow raised.

"Ooh, Mom's gonna kill you. How come you're so dirty?"

"Shut up, Mina. Have you seen Mawmaw?"

"*Wilhelmina.*"

Bass's mom—Mrs. Montgomery—appeared, a brush in one hand and a bottle of hair oil in the other. She did that quiet, eyes-cut, teeth-bared whisper thing adults do when they don't want other adults to know their children are misbehaving.

Bass's older sister followed behind, nose stuck in a fashion catalog.

"Uh-oh," Wilhelmina said, slowly backing away.

"There you are, Leona! We simply must get a good seat!" Mrs. Pingleton said. She grabbed her wife's arm and led her away before she had the chance to do more than throw a scolding look at Wilhelmina over her shoulder.

Begonia appraised Bass's moms, astonished she hadn't seen it before. It was so clear how they were two halves of the same whole, polished and posh and sharp, but where Mrs. Montgomery was sleek steel, Mrs. Pingleton was a glittering rhinestone.

Without raising her head, Beatrice followed her mothers, snatching Wilhelmina by the collar of her dress and tugging her forward amidst many cries of "*Hey!*" and "*I'm telling!*"

Begonia turned to Bass. "We need to find—"

"Attention, attention! Everyone take your seats," the mustached auctioneer said, addressing the crowd in a rather curt voice. His grouchy expression was quite the contrast to his jaunty bow tie with hula-hooping penguins. "We simply must begin, even if the proprietor isn't here yet."

He walked to the podium and Begonia's stomach flopped. Plummeted. Disintegrated.

"No!" she shouted. But, of course, no one heard her but Bass.

"I'm afraid that won't be happening," came a soft voice from the doorway.

A swell of music trumpeted from the walls, the sounds of a horned infantry riding into battle.

Begonia twisted around.

Mawmaw Montgomery, Dada Haneef, the Decrepit Decrescendos, and Ms. Majorie stood at the threshold, teeth gritted, fists clenched, war stamped on their faces.

They parted, and as a figure emerged into the morning light, dawn broke across Begonia's heart.

David was lanky, stooped, and pale as ever, but behind his goggled eyes there was no smoke. No oil. Only a fierce determination Begonia had not seen in a long time.

"The auction is off," he said.

Through the crowd, his eyes met Begonia's, and in that single second, they held an entire conversation. His gaze spoke of relief she was safe, of pride in her for being so brave.

But mostly it spoke an apology.

"Mawmaw!" Bass said, launching himself down the aisle. An extra note, light and sweet, arced from the walls the moment she folded him into her arms.

"Excuse me—what is the meaning of this?" Mrs. Pingleton asked.

"Why are you so late?" an auction worker asked.

"Mom, what are you doing out of bed?" Mrs. Montgomery asked.

"How did that nurse get her mustache so curly?" the auctioneer asked.

But David only had eyes for Begonia. "I'm sorry, Bug. I should have told you sooner." He pulled his hands out of his pants pockets and addressed the room.

"Everyone. I'm sorry to say I've been dishonest with you all. But before I explain, there is something you need to see to understand."

He gestured to Ms. Majorie, who had a large wooden crate at her feet. She flung off the lid.

Begonia gasped. Inside were piles and piles of—

"Goggles? Ew," Mrs. Pingleton said, peering into the trunk with a wrinkled nose.

"Please take a pair, pass them around," David said. "I'll explain in a minute."

Ms. Majorie trudged row to row, thrusting goggles into hands and chests, and, in the case of the dissenting Mrs. Pingleton, snapping them directly on her head.

"But these clash terribly with my culottes. These cost eighty-seven dollars, you know!"

"Shh, honey, just put them on," Mrs. Montgomery said, adjusting the strap on her own pair.

Wilhelmina snapped hers over her eyes as well as Beatrice's.

Begonia suddenly felt nervous, like Grandpa Clive had released his hive of bees loose in her stomach. After being invisible so long, she didn't think she knew how to be seen.

Her stomach gave another squirm, but no one was looking at her. They all gazed expectantly at David.

His voice carried across the Odditorium. "It will come as no shock to most of you that times have been hard for Swamp Root Manor. Knowing this, I wanted to do anything in my power to keep the nursing home from closing and displacing our residents, many of whom I have come to consider family.

"I spent many nights researching by candlelight, searching for any loophole, any miracle that might save us. The answer, unfortunately, came to me on the wings of a tragedy."

David's eyes flicked to Begonia's before he continued.

"I found that the only way to stop the bank from auctioning off the manor was to split the property, keeping part in my name and granting part to another."

The crowd gasped. Mrs. Pingleton's jaw dropped.

"You see, under decree number forty-seven, section F, class nine, the law clearly states that—"

Let me spare you, Dear Reader, from all the boring law jargon. I assure you, you're missing nothing. Just know that David spouted a list of very technical, fancy-schmancy-sounding words that no one other than him—and maybe

Mrs. Montgomery, as she was a lawyer—understood anyway, but nonetheless proved his claim to be true.

"So you see," David concluded, half an hour later, to those in his audience who had not fallen asleep, "the auction legally cannot go on."

Begonia didn't understand any of it, but she knew David, knew his tics and tells, and in this he was confident. Her breath ballooned too big for her chest.

There was quiet for a moment, pierced only by an elder's echoing snore. Slowly, drowsy members of the crowd blinked back to life, wiping drool from their chins.

The disgruntled auctioneer, who had been one of the few who remained awake, charged forward. "Then this has all been for nothing! Is my line of profession a joke to you, Mr. Klein?"

"I have only the highest respect for you and your profession, Mr.—er—Auctioneer. I did plan on coming forward with my findings sooner but have been ill, you see."

"I'll take a look at that," Mrs. Montgomery said, all business now. David handed her the document and her eyes whizzed down the page.

"It looks legitimate to me," Bass's mom said after a time, glancing up at the auctioneer, who huffed in anger. "He's right. This auction cannot go on."

"In fact, from hearing what Alma and Ms. Majorie have told me, the bank actually owes *us* money," David said. "Not the other way around."

"But who," Mrs. Pingleton snapped, startling awake the rest of the guests, "owns the other half of the grounds?"

David gestured to Begonia with a small, gentle smile. "Ladies, gentlemen, and other friends—allow me to present to you the Ghost of Swamp Root Manor."

The crowd parted around Begonia like a raging sea before a lighthouse. Gasps rang out from the crowd.

"Where did she come from? She wasn't standing there before!"

"I didn't see her either!"

"A ghost! That's highly unsanitary!"

"Still the wrong word, Frank!"

"Ew," Mrs. Pingleton said, backing away in disgust. "It's just a moldy little girl."

"Yes, no mustache at all," said the auctioneer.

"Begonia!" Mawmaw Montgomery said.

She rushed forward and fell to her knees as her arms curled around Begonia. Other shouts of delight and surprise followed, and soon Dada Haneef, all three members of the Decrepit Decrescendos, Grand Da O'Flannery, Grandpa Emery (who had chosen an anteater nose today), and her fifty other grandparents with their arms, lips, and tentacles were on her in the warmest hug she had ever had.

Begonia's heart might have burst.

"But how, David?" Mamaw Myrtle asked, fingers wrapped in their dust touch–proof gloves and pinching Begonia's cheeks.

"Begonia has received her Oddity," he said with pride. "She's a ghost."

"She got—she got to come back?" Dada Haneef asked, touching Begonia's shoulders, her hair, her chin as if he couldn't believe his eyes.

"She never left," David said. "You just couldn't see her. Which is why I've been working day and night to perfect these phantomoculars." He glanced down at Begonia, his next words just for her. "So all your grandparents could see you again."

Begonia's heart swelled; her eyes filled.

Grandma Minnie bulldozed her way in front of the others and lifted Begonia into a bone-crushing hug. Grandpa Bonic's rats danced around their heels, occasionally leaping up to nibble at her bootstraps.

When Begonia was finally placed back down, David moved forward and the crowd parted around him. He knelt before Begonia, taking one of her hands in his.

"I am so, so sorry. I should have told you. You deserved to know. I can't imagine the pain you must have gone through this last month not knowing why no one would speak to you."

"I thought it was because I wasn't Odd," Begonia said. "Nana Babette told me everyone knew I was going to be Oddbliterated, so they were slowly distancing themselves to make it easier."

Tears were in David's eyes. He squeezed her hand, unable to speak.

Begonia went on. "It was all her—the ghost attacks, the mortgage being raised. She knew you put half the land in my name."

"I know, Bug. She told me as much when she and the ghost appeared in my office."

"More ghosts?!" someone asked from the back of the room.

Gasps rippled through the Never-Odd bidders. A few ripped off their goggles and ran from the room. From the front of the house, automobile engines roared to life, tires squealed, and gravel rained against the side of the building as they raced away.

"Oooh, I hope they don't come back with pitchforks," Grandad Merl said, peering nervously out the window. "I just buffed my mushrooms."

"It's the torches I hate," Grandpappy Burl said. He shivered, sending a cold blast of snow whizzing over the floor.

"Seriously, David," Mawmaw Montgomery asked, hand on hip, "what about the Most Important Odd Secrecy Law? The Extraordinarily Bad Infractions Committee will be on all of us."

The remaining Never Odds glanced at one another, confused and a little scared.

David stood, addressing his residents. "I think it's time, don't you? If we aren't the change, if it isn't now, then when?"

There was a beat of silence. Begonia held her breath.

Then, with a reverberating *"yahoo!"* Grandpa Clive ripped the turban from his head and launched it skyward. His bees arced across the room, humming sweetly, forming hearts and smiley faces in the air.

A tremendous cheer rang up from the Swamp Root residents and staff. Grandpa Bonic flung open his trench coat, rats skittering in every direction; plump portobellas erupted on Grandad Merl's arms; and Grandma Minnie's face reddened in concentration just before her wig exploded into smithereens, horns growing twice as large in its place.

Bass threw back his head and laughed. Begonia joined him. The feeling in her chest must have been what it was like for the first finger of moss to find Swamp Root walls. Safety. Stability. A good place to grow roots and settle.

A scream rent the air. The celebrations died. Begonia whirled.

The remaining Never Odds huddled together in the center of the room, eyes round, mouths trembling.

But one woman fought against the crowd. She pushed against the barrier of bodies, struggling to reach something just outside the line of protection.

Begonia craned her neck.

On the floor, crawling steadily away from his mother, was a Never-Odd toddler. He rose to his feet, very pink cheeked and drooly. He tottered foot to foot, eyes wide as buttons, gazing around the room of new and wonderful peculiarities before setting his sights on Nini Zehra.

As always, Nini Zehra was oblivious to the kerfuffle, gently smiling away under a beam of light from the window.

The boy made a beeline to her, cooing and slobbering and stomping his shiny white boots.

At the sound, Nini Zehra turned. She looked side to side for the cause of the noise before her eyes sank to the boy on the floor. He blabbered up at her, hands grasping at the air above his head.

A smile bloomed on Nini Zehra's lips as she bent before him. The toddler's mother cried out, but an older Never Odd held her in place, her lined eyes full of wonder.

Mouth an open ring, the boy cooed at the dandelion fluffs swaying from her scalp, always blowing as if caught in a gentle breeze. Nini Zehra dipped her head and the boy ran his fingers over the silky stalks, completely enraptured.

Straightening, Nini Zehra then plucked a stem from her head, holding it out for the boy. He wrapped his tiny hand around it, brought it to his mouth, and blew.

The puffs glided skyward. He laughed, clapping his hands, making a game out of scooping them from the air. Nini Zehra joined him, the two dancing in a swirl of dandelion snow and sunshine.

Begonia's heart throbbed. She felt like she was standing on the edge of something new and warm and right.

The Never Odds relaxed; a few of them even smiled. The boy's mother disentangled herself from the older woman, but her fearful urgency was gone. She looked to Nini Zehra and, almost shyly, gestured at the flurry around them. "They are beautiful."

Nini Zehra took the woman's arms and squeezed.

It was difficult to say who made the first move, Odd or Never Odd, but suddenly the two sides were so thickly mixed among each other it was hard to move through the crowd.

The Decrepit Decrescendos sang show tunes to an onlooking crowd snapping their fingers—or pincers—to the beat, Grandpappy Burl chilled warming cocktail glasses to applause, children swung from Grandma Minnie's horns like a jungle gym, and in the corner, the auctioneer hastily jotted down facial hair styling tips from Ms. Majorie.

And Begonia was covered in hugs. Coated in kisses. Smothered and seen and loved.

Sometime later, when the now canceled auction was in danger of becoming a full-on party, Dada Haneef approached Begonia pushing a walking stroller with—of all things—Nana Babette's ridiculously large crystal ball resting on the seat. He rolled it in front of her.

"What's this?" Begonia said.

"Many of Babette's treacheries whispered in my ear the night I was attacked. They have all quieted since. All but this one." Dada Haneef gestured down to the crystal. "I believe you might find what's inside rather helpful."

"Inside?" Begonia said.

She hunched over the crystal, rolling it this way and that, until on the bottom, she found the slightest indent. One would not have even noticed it if they weren't looking for it. If they didn't have a thief's eye.

The imprint of a heart.

She looked up at Dada Haneef—nodding—and David, who had not left her side, brow quizzical the way it always was when he had a tricky device to solve.

Begonia pulled her locket from her neck, placed it over the indent, and pushed.

The top of the ball cracked open. An invisible door.

Begonia peered inside, the winter pit of her chest filling with springtime flowers. She glanced up at David.

"I think our fortune is about to change."

24

Fact: Etterath is the melancholy emptiness one feels after a long, difficult process is finally complete.

Through the flap of the tent, rain drizzled down from Reba, coating everything in glittering diamonds—the grass, the automobiles, the manor shingles. Well, until the manor shook off the droplets like a wet dog, drenching the visitors below.

The perfect kind of day for a bake-off, in Begonia's opinion.

Sure, the nursing home now had enough funds to pay off what was due on the manor—thanks to the wads of cash Babette had hidden inside her crystal ball—but there were mouths to feed. Begonia had suggested a community bake-off to raise money, and David had loved the idea.

Which is why, a week after all the rather unseemly events concluded, Begonia found herself seated behind a booth, in a very large, slightly smelly tent that stretched over the manor's front lawn, passing out raffle tickets. Never Odds from the village ambled around in their raincoats and rubber boots, tasting free samples and dropping off some of their own. A redheaded girl around Begonia's age had donated prizewinning macarons that everyone said were delicious. Even though Begonia couldn't taste them herself, she thought she sensed a hint of sugar on her tongue when she zoomed by, mouth open.

Swamp Root workers and residents flitted around the tent, tending to customer desires or complaining loudly about the weather, many times doing both at the same time. All were recognizable by the green-orbed phantom-oculars strapped around their skulls.

"Thank you for your donation," Bass said beside her, ripping a red voucher off a massive wheel of tickets and handing it to the man next in line. "The raffle begins at four o'clock. Enjoy your visit!"

"Bass, look what Mom got me."

Cymbals crashed from her heels as Wilhelmina sauntered up, dangling a cake pop in his face. Begonia didn't miss how she positioned Bass between the two of them, no doubt to use her brother as a human shield if Begonia suddenly decided to possess her or something. She had a pair of phantom-oculars on—Bass's whole family did—but Wilhelmina averted her eyes from Begonia.

Bass groaned. "How much longer until my lunch break?"

Begonia checked David's pocket watch, which, yes, she had returned, and he had then lent back to her only for today so she and Bass could take breaks from the ticket booth. This was after a firm talking-to and making her return everything she had stolen with an apology to the original owners.

"Another twenty-seven minutes."

"I'm wasting away to nothing!"

"As your ghost friend—no, you aren't."

"Mmm," Wilhelmina said, dramatically munching the cake pop. Her eyes rolled back in her head.

Bass sucked his teeth. "Get out of here before I tell you how many dead people I see in this tent."

The cake pop fell to the ground as Wilhelmina's mouth opened in terror. She trampled off through the crowd, cymbals crashing all the while.

Bass wore a satisfied look as he leaned back on his heels, hands behind his head. "Sisters."

Then the chair leg slammed back to the ground as he pushed up, an idea crossing his face.

"Hey, now that you're, you know, wearing a 'pine overcoat' and all—"

Begonia choked. "Excuse me, what?"

"—you don't think you could learn the whole soul-sucking-freezing thing, do you? Just for a few hours, then—"

"*Bass!*" Begonia said, swatting his arm with a laugh.

"Oof! Okay, okay! Kidding."

They shared a smile.

"You really have to go back home?" Begonia asked.

"Yeah, but I'll be back for winter break. Your grandpa Bonic said he'd freeze the next dead rat he finds so I can practice my autopsy skills. Although we can't tell Mawmaw. Or my moms." Bass looked around furtively. "Let's just keep this between you and me, okay?"

Begonia tried very hard to keep a disgusted expression off her face. "Trust me—I'm not explaining that to anyone."

Bass was ridiculously happy to have a dead friend. And if she was being honest, she was happy to be his dead friend. Even if she had to spend her existence making up for how she'd treated him.

David appeared from the crowd, hunched, cloaked in brown, and slightly damp. His hands toyed with the buttons on his jacket the way they always did when he was busy or nervous.

The new secretary he had hired, Mr. Cattlewool, followed him around, rattling off what Begonia was sure was a list of boring tasks that had to do with running a nursing home.

David nodded, no doubt half listening the best he could over his smiles and handshakes to the bake-off guests.

"And lastly, sir," Mr. Cattlewool said, "we have finally located the dirty man with the foul temper you sent out a search team for. Mr. Poo, I believe you called him?"

Begonia's ears perked. Bass went still, as well as a passing group of grandparents, no doubt listening hard. Gran-Gran Violet even whipped out an ear trumpet.

"He's being held hostage by the trees of Whispering Woods. For his safe return, I am to notify you that they demand a ransom of four thousand eight hundred and twenty-three pine cones of only"—here he stopped to clear his throat—"the highest *qualitree*."

The entire group of eavesdroppers groaned.

David pondered for a moment before brushing off the thought. "Eh, well. He'll be there tomorrow. We'll deal with it then."

Mr. Cattlewool made a note on his clipboard, then the two of them were off once more.

"Uh-oh," Bass said, sinking down in his seat.

Begonia looked up. Mawmaw Montgomery marched for them to the beat of a war drum, mouth set in a reproachful line. She was followed by a very smug Wilhelmina.

"Barnabas Lee Isaac Montgomery the Third! What is this I hear about you bullying your sister?"

"Mom, what happened?"

Bass's moms appeared, steel and diamond, but literally so in the case of Mrs. Pingleton, who it appeared had glued rhinestones to the rims of her phantomoculars. Beatrice tailed them, snapping her ever-present piece of bubble gum.

The entire party wore their ghost goggles but didn't spare Begonia a second glance. Undead or not, she was no match for juicy drama.

"Momma, Bass is being a meanie-head!" Wilhelmina said in a ridiculously high-pitched voice. Even with all the morality work Begonia had been doing the past week, she was instantly reminded why she hated children.

Mrs. Montgomery pinched the bridge of her nose and closed her eyes. "We are about to leave for vacation, Mina. I need you all to figure out a way to behave and get along, just for seven days, okay?"

Wilhelmina crossed her arms, lip pooched as she stared at the ground. Bass shot her a *ha-ha* face.

Mawmaw's pinched-eyed glare could have melted iron. "I'm going to go find the refreshment booth, and when I come back, you both will be acting right. Begonia—keep them in line."

Begonia gave her a hardy salute before Mawmaw walked off, Beatrice at her side.

Ever chipper, Mrs. Pingleton put a hand on Bass's shoulder and squealed, practically oozing confetti and rainbows and all those other heinous things.

"I can't *wait* to go on our little trip together! Did you know, Begonia, that Bass has offered to visit local properties for sale with me that boast of haunt- ings? Isn't that exciting?! We only want the real deal, of course."

Mrs. Pingleton pinched Bass's cheek and he playfully batted her off, grin- ning in a shy but self-satisfied way.

"The point of the trip is to have a relaxing family *vacation*," Mrs. Montgomery chided, rolling her eyes. She then glanced at Begonia. "Remind me where the bathroom is?"

"To the left of the foyer."

"Thank you, sweetie. Come on, Mina." Wilhelmina stuck her tongue out at Bass before disappearing behind her mother. Mrs. Montgomery shot a warning glance at her wife, then ducked out of the tent. "Vacation, Felicity. Not a work trip."

"Of course." Mrs. Pingleton smiled innocently until Mrs. Montgomery was halfway across the lawn.

She had taken to the knowledge of Oddities quite well once she understood Mrs. Montgomery had kept it a secret to protect them. Apparently, all along Mrs. Pingleton just thought Wilhelmina liked noise.

Once her wife was out of sight, Mrs. Pingleton lowered one thick lash in a dramatic wink. "Oh, we will have so much fun!" She squeezed Bass's shoulders once more, then was off, fluttering table to table like a bedazzled butterfly.

Blushing, Bass caught Begonia's eye. "Momma P. was super cool about the ghost-Oddity thing. I mean, that was probably just because she's excited I'll help her with her bed-and-breakfast, but still! And Mawmaw and Mom didn't seem to care either. They just wanted me to be happy."

Begonia gave him a playful elbow. "I told you! It was all just self-floccinaucinihilipilification."

He grinned.

Another family arrived, and Bass busied himself with administrational duties. They weren't wearing the phantomoculars, and Begonia was quite fine being ignored.

Rain tapped a lazy rhythm on the tent roof, and Begonia's eyes roamed the bake-off, the perfect recipe of Odd and Never Odd. They really weren't as bad as Nana Babette made them out to be.

Nana.

A chasm had opened in her chest, rife with so many emotions—most of which Begonia didn't know what to do with. It was times like this, when she was alone with her thoughts, that the hole inside rumbled, cracking just a bit bigger, just a bit deeper. Her hand, as always, found the locket at her neck.

The urge to be by herself soon became overwhelming, and Begonia worked the new muscles she had been stretching the past week. Invisibility, speed— she had even begun to practice moving through walls, which was a lot harder than the storybooks had led her to believe.

A burst of cold inched over her skin. For a moment, the molecules that made up who she was glimmered as they broke apart, a swirling constellation, before she was swallowed up by nothingness.

She basked in the newfound power of it all. The peace it brought her.

Before Bass could notice, she slipped off her seat and out of the tent.

The carnivorous garden was quiet other than the patter of rain and the grumblings of weeds, flattened after the Foxglove was coaxed into releasing Mr. Schmoob and he was dragged off by the constable.

Begonia smiled to herself, pulling back the vines to a familiar clearing. Inside, she shook off the cold, body tingling as it reformulated around her. She had no one to hide from here.

Her great-great-grandmother's grave stood in the middle of the hollow, freshly scrubbed and free of moss. Begonia walked to it and knelt, running a finger along the grooves of the stone heart.

Whatever halls Edith Hollowmoor now roamed were surely peaceful.

Beside it, a second gravestone slumbered.

IN MEMORY OF BABETTE HOLLOWMOOR

FRIEND. GRANDMOTHER. PROBABLE MURDERER.

RIP

Begonia slid her locket back and forth on its chain. For a while she just breathed from her belly, letting the sounds of rain and smell of earth wash her clean.

When she was steady in her soul, she opened her eyes, glancing at the newest addition in this makeshift graveyard. Headstone number three.

HERE LIES BEGONIA HOLLOWMOOR

GRANDDAUGHTER OF MANY

SAVIOR OF SWAMP ROOT MANOR

AWAKE IN PEACE

It still didn't seem real sometimes, being both in the ground and not. Mourned and not. Dead and not. Even seeing—or really, not seeing—herself becoming transparent in the mirror didn't seem real, almost like she was watching someone else's story in a village play.

Footsteps sloshed in the mud behind, coming to a stop at her side.

"Thought I might find you here," he said.

Begonia continued toying with her locket, listening to a lone bird calling on the wind.

"I just finished handing out the rest of the phantomoculars. Gran-Gran Violet needed hearing trumpet modifications, and half the residents needed bifocal adjustments, so . . ."

David rambled on. He was the type of man that if he had something hard to say, he would speak of absolutely everything else until he worked up the courage to get it out. Always tinkering around, even with words.

It was quiet for a time, then David's warm hand found Begonia's back.

"You're allowed to have complicated emotions about family, Bug. It's okay to feel whatever you're feeling about her."

Begonia wiped her cheek clean. She didn't quite know how to respond, but she leaned into his touch. He seemed to understand, rubbing soothing circles between her shoulder blades.

"I brought these," David said after a time, revealing three purple begonias from behind his back. "Fresh from your bush."

Begonia plucked two from his hand, breathing in their fresh petals. The scent of spring showers and old lady perfume. Two of Begonia's favorite smells. She smiled.

Bending down, she placed one on Edith's grave, and the other on Nana Babette's.

"And this one's for you." David handed her the last flower.

She took the begonia and bent to put it beneath her headstone, when David touched her arm. She stopped, looking up.

"No, no. For *you*. Not some rock in the ground."

Gently, David slipped the flower from her hand and tucked it behind her ear. "Perfect."

Begonia's eyes were heavy with unshed tears. She brushed the flower, heart full.

David worried his hands, then forced himself to meet her gaze. "Bug, I know it wasn't right. Not telling you. I just—I can't—I *wasn't* ready to let you go."

His voice broke on the last word. Begonia took his hand in hers.

"I know."

They studied each other. Just like Nana Babette's crater, there was one in her chest for David too. Small, much less deep, but aching nonetheless. It pulsed as she watched him, filled with both love and betrayal and understanding and sadness.

She would give him the chance to make it right. If she had learned any-thing, it was that families were like gardens, and though there were thorns between them, there were roses too. The evergreen kind.

David cleared his throat and took on a false, cheery tone. "So, Your Royal Scariness."

Begonia sob-laughed and gave him a playful nudge.

"Do you think you'll—I mean, when will you—ah—"

"Move on?" she asked.

"Yes. Move on." He blew out a deep breath. "It's a big decision, but I want you to know that your grandparents and I one hundred percent support whatever you choose."

It's not like she hadn't thought about it, or dreamed about it, really. A grand adventure into the Beyond, surely filled with a tremendous amount of new trivia to acquire. She could meet her parents. Her parents' parents' parents. Never have to endure another ounce of pain again.

Rest in peace.

Grass swayed in the wind around her grandmothers' plaques. In the sky, a second bird joined the first. And then another. Soon an entire flock sang together in the tree above them.

David's face turned sunward to watch, and the chasm in Begonia's chest knitted the smallest bit along its frayed edge.

She nudged David and he glanced down. "Why on earth would I leave my family after just winning them back?"

David's answer was a sunlight smile.

They walked over the sodden grounds back toward the bake-off tent, not talking but content in each other's company.

A thought struck Begonia.

"David?"

"Yes?"

"Does Ms. Majorie *have* to have the phantomoculars?"

"Yes, Begonia. She does."

"Come *on*. She already has two hundred and seventy–degree vision!"

David ruffled her hair, an exasperated tug on his lips.

A twitch of pain behind her eye. A hook of nausea around her navel. Begonia winced, then quickly tried to cover it up. But David had seen.

"Migraine?" he asked, brow lowered in concern.

Begonia nodded.

Dead or not, the migraines hadn't left her and probably never would. An Echo, David had called it. A memory of pain from her former life imprinted on her new one.

David knelt before her, not caring that his trousers got caked in mud. He took both of her hands in his and gave her a knowing smile.

"List three facts."

And in her head, Begonia listed the following:

1. Apple seeds contain cyanide.

2. Octopuses have three hearts.

3. Begonia Hollowmoor is more than just her pain.

She had a life to—well, not live, exactly, but—*experience.* The pain and happiness and sadness and anger and glee. She had her home, her family, her friends, and the knowledge that she was Odd enough.

That she was strong enough.

That she *was* enough just the way she was to deserve a long and happy existence.

And that, Dear Reader, made it all worth it.

A FINAL NOTE

If you have found this book, then you are probably just like him. Talented and kind. Bespectacled and way too talkative. A lover of the dark and twisty. You did pull this book from my cold, dead corpse, so either you really are just like him, or are perhaps rather queasy.

Either way, you've followed the clues your grandaddy Bass left for you about this book and our journey together so many years ago.

Now, I hope you aren't spending too much time wondering about my story beyond this one. I'm sorry to disappoint if you expected some sweeping adventure, but truly it was nothing out of the Oddinary, which was exactly as I preferred it. I enjoyed my role as Swamp Root's resident ghost and took my responsibilities rather seriously. They included protecting the residents, pruning the Foxglove—as no living soul would go near it—and perhaps the most crucial task of all: haunting Ms. Majorie, as at one hundred and fifty-eight years old and still refusing to retire, she continues to haunt me.

Dutifully, I watched over Swamp Root Manor for generations. Watched new residents come and go, mourned their loss, celebrated new arrivals.

259

Watched your grandaddy grow up, become the finest mortician ever known, and have a slew of annoying children of his own. I loved each of them.

I watched him become a resident himself, wrinkled and bald as an old plum, but never losing that toothy smile or that silly old cat brooch he wore on his chest every day. He was as Odd and annoying and wonderful as the day I met him. Right until the very end.

Now, now—I did not share all of this for you to feel bad for me. In fact, I have experienced more love and life than most, especially for one so dead.

You are probably wondering why Grandaddy Bass and I devised a plan to send you on the same wild goose chase my nana Babette sent us on all those years ago.

The answer, Dear Reader, is that sometimes you have to go on a journey to *go on a journey*.

You have to travel through terrifying attics; battle your ghosts; brave the wild; dig yourself out of metaphorical—and sometimes physical—graves.

You have to be daring and witty, pure of heart and mind, and a little obsessed with the morbid to make it in this world.

You may be well or not well. Liked or not liked. Odd or Never Odd or just really, *really* super odd, but the point is you are here and worthy of space and time and effort and love.

When I gave that fact in the beginning of this story that the true gift of adventure is not the friends we make along the way, but the lies we uncover about our enemies, I want you to understand that sometimes we are our own enemy, sealing our own coffins with our own hammer and nails.

Your grandaddy and I left you this story as a proverbial crowbar, if you will. I shall close out this tale with a happy goodbye, both in the ending of this story and a new chapter in mine. At long last I feel ready for that final great adventure. And don't worry—I'll be sure to tell your grandaddy you said hello.

So I leave you with one last piece of parting trivia, in the hopes you will go forth and live your wild, or not so wild, adventure:

You are Odd enough.

And—never, *never* forget, Dear Reader—that is a fact.

The End

ACKNOWLEDGMENTS

There are many facts in this book, but the truest fact for me is that I couldn't have done this alone.

To Brian—I can't wait to grow old with you, wreak havoc in our nursing home, and then do it all over again once we are ghosts. There isn't another person I would want to be odd with for all eternity.

To Dad and Mom—I hope you behave better in your nursing homes than your parents did. But then again, I might not have this book without their ornery antics. Love you both.

To Samantha Fabien and Tiffany Colón—Thank you for having enough faith in me to let me cut loose and write something so absolutely zany and silly and 100 percent ME. You are the reason *The Odds* is an actual thing!

To Jessica Froberg—I wrote every punch line with you in mind, knowing you would just *get it*. Thank you for all the late-night critiques, your encouragement, and your friendship.

A special thank-you to Aunt Judy and Uncle Mif for all the love, enthusiasm, and pulled pork; to Abby who's always down for bookshopping and pho when I need a break; to my Authortube Ladies—Kevin, Laura, Lainey, and

Liselle—for their support and laughs; to Vanessa Morales and Sephanie Yang for their amazing design of this book; and to the entire team at Scholastic for their dedication to get my stories into the hands of the children who need them.

And, of course, to Mamaw. A piece of you makes it into every book I write, and somehow that makes you feel a little less far away. Miss you always.

ABOUT THE AUTHOR

Lindsay Puckett lives in a tiny apartment in Ohio where there are too many books, just the right amount of pet hair, and never enough houseplants. Or peanut butter. She has a bachelor's in psychology and enjoys creating videos for her YouTube channel, where she shares her publication journey and helps other writers along their own.

Don't miss Lindsay's first novel, *The Glass Witch*!

Chloe and Cracker

Kelly McKain

Stripes

THIS DIARY BELONGS TO

Chloe

Dear Riders,

A warm welcome to Sunnyside Stables!

Sunnyside is our home and for the next week it will be yours too! We're a big family—my husband Johnny and I have two children, Millie and James, plus two dogs ... and all the ponies, of course!

We have friendly yard staff and a very talented instructor, Sally, to help you get the most out of your week. If you have any worries or questions about anything at all, just ask. We're here to help, and we want your vacation to be as enjoyable as possible—so don't be shy!

As you know, you will have a pony to look after as your own for the week. Your pony can't wait to meet you and start having fun! During your stay, you'll be caring for your pony, improving your riding, enjoying long country hacks, learning new skills, and making friends.

And this week's special activity is a challenging treasure hunt. Just imagine you and your pony cantering across the countryside together, solving clues! Add swimming, games, movies, barbecues, and a gymkhana and you're in for a fun-filled vacation to remember!

This special Pony Camp Diary is for you to fill with all your vacation memories. We hope you'll write all about your adventures here at Sunnyside Stables—because we know you're going to have lots!

Wishing you a wonderful time with us!

JOdy xx

Monday morning
At Pony Camp!

Jody, the lady who runs Sunnyside Stables, gave me this cool diary when I arrived just now. Her letter at the front says it's to write down all the adventures I have this week. It's fantastic here—there are two outdoor manèges, and lots of cute ponies, and dogs everywhere, and even a swimming pool! I'm hoping to have lots of adventures—especially jumping ones!

I really wanted to come on this week because when Mom rang up and spoke to Jody, she said they're holding a special jumping competition on the last day. In our lessons, we're going to work on building up to an eight-jump course, and it's even going to include some cross-country fences for fun—I can't wait!

I love jumping but I've only done a couple of smaller courses at clear round events at my local riding school. I'm really hoping to improve while I'm here—and I'm desperate to go clear in Friday's competition.

The reasons I want a clear round so much are:

a. because I've never had one before so it will be a big challenge for me and
b. to make Dad proud of me.

Although Dad knows how much I love ponies (I'm always talking about getting my own one day!), he's never actually seen me ride. He's always working, even at weekends. But he said he'll really, really try to come with Mom to pick me up on Friday, then he'll be able to see me in the jumping competition and I can amaze him with my clear round (fingers crossed!). I really hope he keeps his word and doesn't get stuck at work as usual.

As soon as I got here, I kept asking Jody what we'll be doing every day because I was really excited. She smiled and said Sally, the instructor, will explain that when everyone arrives, but I really, really wanted to know straightaway so she gave me a copy of the timetable to stick into my diary. She has warned me that it will change, though, because we have special activities on some days. Like, it says in her letter we're going on a treasure hunt this week—that sounds really fun!

Sunnyside Stables

Here's the timetable for the week:

Pony Camp Timetable

8am: Wake up, get dressed, have breakfast

8.45am: Help on the yard, bring in the ponies from field, muck out stables, do feeds, etc.

9.30am: Prepare ponies for morning lessons (quick groom, tack up, etc.)

10am: Morning riding lesson

11am: Morning break: drink and cookies

11.20am: Pony Care lecture

12.30pm: Lunch and free time

2pm: Afternoon riding lesson

3pm: Break: drink and cookies

3.20pm: Pony Care lecture

4.30pm: Jobs around the yard (i.e. cleaning tack, sweeping up, mixing evening feeds, turning out ponies)

5.30pm: Free time before dinner

6pm: Dinner (and clearing up!)

7pm: Evening activity

8.30pm: Showers and hot chocolate

9.30pm: Lights out and NO TALKING!

Wow! There's so much to do here! I just can't wait to find out which pony I'm getting— having my own pony to look after for a whole week will be fab!

This morning we're having an assessment lesson where we all ride in together, and then Sally will decide who goes in which group. So the timetable's different already because there's no lecture this morning. It's now 10.35a.m. and not everyone is here yet, including the girls who are sharing my room—but, oh, now I can hear talking and clomping on the stairs. Maybe it's them!

Two minutes later

It *was* them!

The two girls I'm sharing with have gone downstairs to help on the yard—we are all still waiting for a couple of others to arrive, but the adults keep telling each other that there's a hold-up on the freeway so we're running a bit later than planned.

I'm going down in a minute, but first I just wanted to do a quick profile of my roommates for my diary.

Name: Isabella

Age: 12

Lives: Buckinghamshire, which is sort of near to London, but still in the countryside.

Description: Quite tall for 12,

goes to a school for girls only, has amazing green eyes and long wavy brown hair, and plays the cello, and has packed three different swimsuits because she couldn't decide which to bring (I've only *got* one!). She says her friends call her Bella, and we can too (how cool!).

Name: Georgia

Age: 12

Lives: Georgia comes all the way from Devon, which I suppose isn't actually far from here, but it's a long way from where I live (i.e. London).

Description: Short blondish hair. She seems very sensible and mature for 12, but she's also really friendly so that's OK. She has two younger brothers and one younger sister, and says she has to help her mom and dad look after them quite a lot.

The best thing is that Isabella and Georgia are both really into jumping too, and they also chose this week specially to come to Sunnyside, so they could spend lots of time focusing on it. Also, they're both really nice and are not leaving me out just because I'm a weeny bit younger than them, which older girls can sometimes do.

Oh, I have to go—Bella's calling me down to the yard. Maybe it's time to find out which ponies we're getting. I'm so excited just thinking about it! Fingers crossed mine's a good jumper!

Still Monday morning,
in our break

I am quickly writing this because I've got something exciting to put down that can't wait till later. The girls who were delayed are here now and we're just about to have our assessment lesson. But even though we haven't been given our ponies yet I have already met the perfect one for me.

What happened was, when I got outside, Jody explained that while we were waiting for the last two girls to arrive, we could get on with some yard work. She gave me mucking-out duty with this really nice stable girl called Lydia. That's when I met Charm, who is an amazingly beautiful gray Connemara.

I fell in love with him straightaway, and Lydia
said I could lead him out and tie him up in the
yard while we did his stable. I gave him a big
stroke and pat on the way, and he whinnied
and nuzzled into my T-shirt.

While we were working I asked Lydia about
him, and she told me what a great
jumper he is. That just made me
want him to be my pony even
more!

Lydia

When Lydia and I had put the
new straw down on top of the
clean bits of bedding and spread it
all out, I got to lead Charm back in,
and I whispered to him that I really
hoped he'd be my pony for the
week. After a while, the other girls
arrived and Jody called us all back into the main
yard, and introduced us to each other and the
Sunnyside Stables team.

As well as me and Bella and Georgia there is Millie, Jody's daughter, who I read about in the welcome letter. The girls sharing her room are called Suki and Mai, and they go to an international school in London. They are both eight and three-quarters and are actually from Japan.

Suki   Mai

Then there are the little ones, Olivia, Asha, and Joelle (who is only just seven and the youngest of all), and they're in a room together.

Asha

Joelle

Olivia

Me, Bella, and Georgia are all really excited about the jumping, and we're crossing our fingers that we get put in the group to do it. Bella and Georgia have jumped a bit but neither of them have done a competition yet, so I've probably got the most experience, even though it's not much.

I really, really hope I've got Charm. I've worked out I've got a 33.3333333333% chance of getting him—he's a bit big for the younger girls and Millie has her own pony, of course, and so I reckon it will be between me, Georgia and Bella.

Still Monday,
after the ponies were given out

Well, it didn't exactly go as I'd hoped, but I'm trying not to be too disappointed. We were all waiting in the yard with our hats and crops and everything, and Sally was reading from a list while Lydia brought the ponies out, one by one. They were already tacked up, because some of the girls had been helping do that while I was mucking out.

I was really excited, and as Lydia led Charm out I had all my fingers crossed for luck, but then Sally said, "Isabella, you're on Charm. I hope you two will hit it off. Charm's a superb jumper, and he has good manners." Well, my heart sank and I had to blink fast to stop tears coming into my eyes. Bella looked so excited, and I forced myself to smile at her.

Bella thanked Sally and stroked Charm's nose before leading him over to the mounting block. As he nudged her shoulder happily, I couldn't help thinking that he should have been nudging *my* shoulder instead.

Then Sally said, "Chloe, you've got Cracker. He's a really spirited, cheeky little thing so you'll need all your experience!" She didn't mention his great jumping or good manners, but he is quite sweet, I suppose—a gray Welsh Section B, with big eyes and a cute pink bit on his nose. Lydia says he's 12.2hh and I feel a bit big for him—my heels are almost off his sides. Charm's over a hand higher. I just wish ... but there's no point in wishing. I haven't got Charm so I'll just have to try and make the best of it. I don't want to waste my vacation moping!

I'll write about the assessment lesson in a minute, but first here's my drawing of who got which pony:

Sunnyside Stables

Bella: Charm, my fave!

Georgia: Prince, a really sweet cobby piebald

Mai: Star

Olivia: Ebony

Me: Cracker!

Joelle: Monsoon

Asha: Sugar

Millie is riding her pony, Tally, of course.

Suki: Twinkle

We had the assessment lesson and it went
OK. Millie didn't ride with us—Jody said she had
to get on with her vacation homework instead.
Poor thing!

At first we just had to walk and trot, and
think about our position and making good
transitions. Then we did some turns and circles
and changes of rein, and at the end we all had a
canter to the back of the ride, except Joelle 'cos
she hasn't done much riding, and she only
knows walk and trot at the moment. Instead,
she turned Monsoon into the middle and Sally
held onto her while we cantered on one rein
and then the other.

Sally was right about Cracker, he is quite
cheeky. I really had to keep my inside leg on all
the way around or he'd fall in off the track, and
when I just gently used my crop to get him
listening (he wasn't going into trot for anyone!)
he did a couple of little bucks. I didn't really

mind, but I tried not to look at Bella trotting around perfectly on Charm, or at their effortless transitions, which didn't involve any kicking or flailing arms like mine did.

Afterward we put our ponies back in the stables (or in pens in the big barn for the ones who live out) and untacked. I gave Cracker a brush down, and made sure he had enough water. Then we came back into the yard and gathered around Sally to hear the news.

Here are the groups we're in:

Group A: Suki, Mai, Olivia, Joelle, Asha.

Group B: Me, Bella, Georgia, Millie.

Our group will be doing the jumping and entering the clear round comp at the end of the week! Group A is the less experienced group, and on Friday they're going to do gymkhana games instead of jumping the course. Sally told them they'll still get to have a go at jumping in their lessons so they won't be missing out.

When we heard that we were doing the jumping comp, Bella grabbed me and Georgia, and we all leaped up and down in a huggy group.

I was excited of course, but not as much as I pretended to be. I mean, I know it's not Bella's fault she got given Charm and I didn't, but I really, *really* wish I had him.

I thought I would've forgotten about Charm by now—but I just can't seem to. I'll have to make sure I hide how I feel. I don't want to fall out with my new friends when I've only just met them! Maybe things will be better after the first jumping lesson, when we've made a start and I'm on my way to getting that clear round. Now I've got a handle on Cracker's bad habits I'll be a whole lot stricter!

Monday 6.32p.m.
In our room

We're going swimming tonight for our evening activity, but Jody says we have to let our supper go down for half an hour first. We're all squashed onto the top bunk, which is Georgia's (Bella is below and I am in the single bed by the window), writing in our diaries. We were up here talking before, but Bella kept going on and on about how amazing Charm is, and it was really getting on my nerves, so I suggested we did some writing instead.

Pony Camp DIARY

NAME

This afternoon it was really scorching hot so Sally said we'd have our Pony Care lecture first, and then have our riding lesson afterward when it was cooler. She showed us how to tie the

ponies up correctly, and where all the
equipment goes so we don't leave anything
lying about that could be a danger, and what to
wear and everything.

Then after the break we had our first
jumping lesson. I was so excited! We had a
warm-up for about twenty minutes, working in
all the paces on each rein. When we stopped
to put our stirrups up a couple of holes,
Georgia got worried that Sally was going to
start setting up the course right away. But Sally
explained that we'll be starting with trotting
poles and singles and then building up gradually,
so Georgia felt OK after that.

We did some basic pole work, then we
practiced trotting on and going into the jumping
position down the long side, which was pretty
tricky. Cracker enjoyed it because I didn't
exactly have all my powers of steering in that
position, and so he got to cut the corner off

and wander across the manège!

Then Sally set up a simple cross pole. First we approached in trot (except Millie, because Tally just charged at it in canter!). After a couple of goes we came up in trot and then cantered away, and we had to keep the canter till we reached the back of the ride. Cracker cut the corner off the first time, but after that I got my inside leg on straight after the jump so he had to behave. There's so much to think about with him on just one jump, I have no idea how I'm going to get around a whole course!

Then we cantered the whole thing, and he cut the corner off again before I even had time to think. I got a bit annoyed with him and felt like giving up. It must have showed because Sally called out, "He's perfectly capable, Chloe, he's just seeing what he can get away with. Circle him around and go again." Then when I went over the next time, she shouted "Leg, leg,

leg!" as soon as I hit the ground, and at least I kept him on the track down the short side, although I bet I looked totally clumsy and unseated.

I've just moved over a bit to make sure Bella can't see what I'm writing. I feel really bad even putting this down, but I have to because it's what happened. We finished off the lesson by working over a double, and Sally made the second pole into an upright. Cracker did OK, but he only just cleared it, whereas Charm sailed miles over and I felt completely jealous again. I bet Bella will go clear in the comp without even trying, and she's probably not even that bothered whether she does or not! I bet her dad makes a big fuss of her whatever she does. It just doesn't seem fair that I need

Not fair!

Charm and she's got him.

Oh, I feel awful and I wish I hadn't put that now. It's not Bella's fault she got Charm. I hate feeling this way—it's just not like me at all. Right, I'm going to climb down from here right this second and hide this diary somewhere in my stuff.

And then I'm going to try my hardest to forget all about Charm.

Tuesday lunchtime

We've just had lunch and I'm sitting outside on the benches in the sun.

I was going to write in here when we went to bed last night (I've got a cool little flashlight on my key ring) but after two lots of riding, then swimming as well, I'd run out of energy. Still, even though we were all tired, we kept bursting into giggles after lights out because Bella was whispering this story to us about a boy down her road who keeps asking her out. Georgia and Bella are great fun—I'm so glad I'm sharing a room with them!

This morning we had our Pony Care lecture on tack and tacking up. I knew some of it already, but it was really good to learn about all the different bits. Also, Lydia was doing the lecture and she demonstrated tacking up on

Suki's cute yellow dun Twinkle, and then she
undid it all and told us to bring Charm and
Sugar out too. So we practiced tacking up on
them in threes, which was cool 'cos I got to
spend time hanging around with Charm and
making a fuss of him without it seeming strange.

In our lesson this morning we did flat work,
and Sally explained that it will help us with our
jumping. Apparently the three important things
you need to jump well are balance, impulsion
and rhythm. I wanted to call out, "And you
need a good pony who listens to you and picks
his feet up!" But I didn't dare say that because
Sally is quite strict most of the time, and I
thought she might get annoyed.

So we did all these turns and circles, and
some riding straight down the center and three-
quarter lines, and we worked on making lots of
transitions, which Sally says is good for
impulsion. Then we started practicing figures of

eight, dropping into trot and changing our
canter lead in the middle—we'll need to do
that twice when we jump the course. At first
Cracker just wanted to carry on up the track,
and not come through the middle at all. Then
when I finally got him to trot through the
diagonal he refused to go back into canter, so in
frustration I tapped him with my crop.

"Get your leg on first, Chloe!" Sally called
out. "You can't just sit there and
then blame Cracker when he
doesn't canter!"

me v. flustered !))

I felt really red and flustered
when she said that—I wasn't just
sitting there—to me it felt like I was kicking
away like crazy! Bella always got her canter back
as soon as she asked—and on the right leg too.
Oh, it's just so annoying! Sally probably thinks
I'm completely rubbish—if I was on Charm
she'd see that I really *can* ride, and that I *do* put

my outside leg back and everything—it's not my
fault that Cracker doesn't listen to me!

I was so frustrated I made things a bit
awkward in the yard after the lesson, although I
didn't mean to. Bella and I had tied up our
ponies next to each other to untack and give
them a brush down. The ponies have their own
grooming kits and each bit of the kit has the
pony's name on. Well, somehow
Charm's body brush had
gone missing and she asked
me if she could borrow
Cracker's. I was about to say
yes, but somehow a big "No!" came
out of my mouth.

"But you're not even using it," said Georgia,
looking confused.

I felt myself going all red and flushed again,
like I did when Sally kept correcting me in the
lesson. "But I'm just about to," I mumbled.

I wished I hadn't said no, but I didn't know how to get out of it, so I picked up the brush, planning to use it quickly then give it straight to Bella. But by that time Georgia had stepped in and lent hers, and it looked like I'd started using mine just to be awkward. Urgh!

Luckily they forgot about it over lunch and everything was fine by the time we got our fruit and yoghurt, but I can't let Bella find out how I feel about Charm—I'll have to try even harder to get over my jealousy.

Tuesday, in my room after a nice supper of baked potatoes with tuna and sweetcorn—yum!

Tonight we're having a table tennis tournament in the games room, and we've only got twenty mins before it starts so I'm going to have to write really fast! I'm alone up here 'cos Bella and Georgia are on washing-up duty.

Before we got our ponies out to mount up for our jumping lesson, Sally called us into the manège. The course had been set up! There were four fences completely up and four trotting poles to mark where the other ones would be. We all walked around the route, and Sally explained the best approach to take for each jump and where the tricky bits might be. This is what the whole course is going to look like:

The JUMPING Course

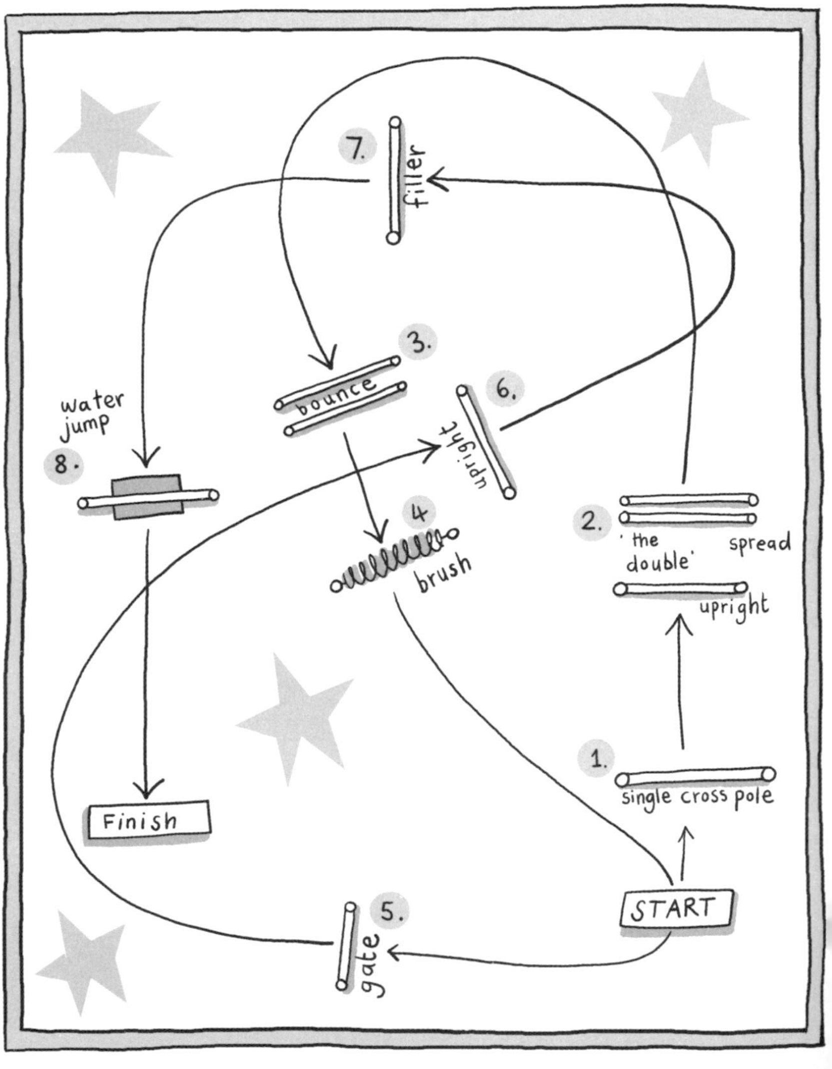

7.
filler
3.
bounce
6.
upright
water jump
8.
4
brush
2.
'the double'
spread
upright
1.
single cross pole
Finish
START
5.
gate

This afternoon the only fences up were the single and spread at the start, and then the bounce and brush in the middle. We had to practice going around the trotting pole (which was marking where the filler will be) to get a good approach to the bounce. I can see now why Sally was being so strict about me not letting Cracker cut the corner off in the flat work. It's a tricky turn and I'll need every inch I can get to line him up properly over these middle jumps. The thing is, you really have to hit the bounce properly because if you're too long you'll end up knocking the second bit of the fence down.

Sally said me and Millie were both still cutting the corner, and she put a block there for us to go around. Tally got the message quickly, but Cracker went inside it twice, and Sally made me keep doing it till I got it right. By then I had so much inside leg on I thought my calf might explode!

After ages of trying, me and Cracker finally got over the brush and back to trot in time to change canter lead (onto the correct leg at last!). We made it around the corner and over the center of the trotting pole that marked where the gate would be.

"Honestly, Cracker," I said, as we all walked around on a long rein to let our ponies cool down, "why couldn't you just get it right in the first place? We've got so much to do before the comp—and I've had to spend an hour teaching you not to cut a corner. You're such a pest!"

"Oh, Chloe, he's not," I heard someone say. I looked up and was really embarrassed to find that Sally had heard me telling Cracker off. I went red and tried to explain. "It's just, my dad's coming on Friday and I've promised him I'll get a clear round, but Cracker won't listen to me around the corners, and I'm sure he's going to knock the gate, and I don't know how I'll get him

back into trot in time after the brush to change
canter lead, and…"

I trailed off. Sally looked
annoyed. "Chloe, honestly!" she
cried. "Poor Cracker's doing his
best! You need to work on
the communication
between you, and to be
firmer when you ask for
something. If you looked up and ahead
more around the tight corner he'd understand
what you wanted better. It's true he's not a very
experienced jumper, but he tries hard and he's
getting there."

Sally CROSS!

"I know, but it doesn't seem fair that I have to
work so hard when some of the other ponies
just get it right first time and…" I began, but
Sally cut me off.

We both knew who I meant by *some of the
other ponies.*

"But you're not on the other ponies," she said firmly. "I gave Cracker to you because I thought you could bring out the best in him. I still think you can, Chloe, but you need to work together as a team and build up a partnership, like Bella has with Charm."

That really stung me.

"Just be careful that you're not so desperate to achieve a clear round in the competition that you actually stop yourself from doing it," Sally said then.

As she gave Cracker a pat and walked off, I stared after her. Even thinking about it now, I still don't understand what she meant. How can I stop myself from getting something by really wanting it? That doesn't make sense.

 Oh, Millie's just come up to say the table tennis tournament's about to start. I'd better go!

Tuesday night

When we got into our beds, Bella was going on and on about how great Charm is so I pretended to fall asleep, and after a while she and Georgia fell asleep too, so now I can write in here by the light of my key ring flashlight.

While Bella and Georgia were playing against each other in the table tennis tournament I slipped off to the yard to visit Charm. I spent ages leaning over his stable door, stroking him and telling him how much I wish he was my pony.

I felt a bit bad then, because Cracker hadn't been turned out yet, and I could see him in the barn, munching hay. I'm sure he saw me too—but I didn't go over and fuss him. I would have, if I'd had more time. Maybe. But I didn't really feel like it.

The table tennis was fun—Millie's older brother James organized it, with her dad. Millie actually won, but she said the second-place person should get the prize, 'cos she's here all the time and she plays a lot. So Mai won the *Spirit* DVD—when she gets back to school she's going to ask her house mistress to put it on for all the girls. She and Suki board at their school because their parents are in Japan. They must be used to not seeing their moms and dads much because they don't seem to miss them at all.

I'm not used to it though, and after I got knocked out of the table tennis tournament I was suddenly desperate to speak to Mom, so

Jody let me call. Dad answered, as he'd just got in the door from work. The good news is that he's almost definitely coming to the gymkhana on Friday. The bad news is that he said, "So, still reckon you're on for that clear round you promised me?"

I said, "Definitely!" but my stomach was churning. Then Mom came on the telephone and I told her all the good bits of what we'd been doing this week, and none of the awkward things like how jealous I feel about Bella getting Charm. I don't want her to worry that I'm not settling in here.

Anyhow, I have to think positively about that clear round. There are still three days to sort out my jumping before the comp—I'll make more effort with Cracker tomorrow and  hopefully everything will go well!

Wednesday, after supper

I haven't had time to write in here all day, but loads of things have happened. Our flat work lesson this morning went fine, and the Pony Care lectures on feeding and points of the horse and everything were good fun. But this afternoon's jumping lesson was a disaster.

Everything has gone wrong. I mean, *horribly* wrong. I've fallen out with Bella and Georgia. And the worst thing of all is that it's my own stupid fault.

This afternoon when we rode into the manège all eight jumps were in place, and my stomach flipped with excitement. Before starting at the beginning, though, we did some work on the last jump, which is the water tray.

Sally explained that although it's only a single it's the most challenging fence, because ponies can find the water a bit spooky. She said we'd just walk our ponies through the water first, without the pole, so they could get used to it.

Well, Charm didn't mind at all, and Tally splashed straight through it. Even Prince was fine once he'd had a good look.

But not Cracker.

He walked through it on the second try, and for a moment I thought we'd be OK. But when Sally put the pole up, even at a much lower height than it will be on Friday, he just absolutely refused to go over, even in trot. He had this way of seeming like he was going over, then scampering sideways at the last minute, and it caught me out every time. After a few tries, I felt like I was holding everyone up, and I had to do the fast-blinking thing to keep myself from crying. Sally came over and explained that Cracker was finding it easier to run out because the fence is narrower. She said, "You just have to ride forward positively and look ahead to the finish. You're looking down at the water, and that's going to make him think it's scarier than it is."

I wanted to say that I was doing my best, but I didn't dare. I tried looking ahead and riding Cracker forward like Sally said, but it still didn't work. Then I got annoyed and rode him at it quite fast, and this time when he lurched to the left I came flying off onto the woodchips.

Everyone laughed. I realize now they only meant it in a friendly way, but I didn't see it like that at the time. As I got up and dusted myself down I didn't look anyone in the eye. I got on again and trotted to the back of the ride, but what I really wanted to do was run indoors, get in bed and have a good cry with my head under the covers. I'd thought we'd only have to worry about the gate when it came to getting a clear round, but then I realized we had to deal with the water jump as well and the whole thing just seemed hopeless. It didn't help that Charm was flying over everything without even trying, and Sally kept saying, "Well ridden, Bella!"

Then things got even worse. When we tried the last couple of jumps together, I still couldn't get over the water tray. Bella offered to give me a lead so Cracker could follow Charm over, which made me feel absolutely stupid, like she was just showing off and trying to make me look silly. "No thanks, I'm fine," I mumbled, without looking at her. I know now that she wasn't being mean at all, but it's too late to take back what happened.

Anyhow, Sally said it was nearly time to finish
and let us all have a pop over a single, to end on
a positive note. I didn't feel positive though, and as
we walked our ponies around on a long rein to
cool them off, I was simmering with fury at Bella.

As I dismounted on the yard, I found her right
behind me and when I saw her happy, smiling
face I just snapped. "You were only offering me

a lead to make me look
hopeless!" I hissed. "You
think you're such a
good rider, but it's only
'cos Charm's so good
that he makes you look
good too. It's not fair that
you get the easy-peasy

pony while I'm stuck with Cracker!"

And then I marched Cracker straight through
to the barn and untacked on my own, not even
waiting to hear if Bella said anything back.

I got on with brushing him down, but my heart was pounding and I felt terrible—how could I have said something so mean? Everything had gone wrong and I wanted to ring Mom and get her to drive down here and take me home.

That was when Olivia and Asha came up, looking nervous. "Bella's crying," Asha announced.

I felt like running away, but I made myself follow them back to the main yard. When I got over to Charm's stable, Georgia had her arm around Bella, and Suki, Mai and Joelle were hovering beside them, looking worried.

But before I could say anything Georgia looked up and gave me a glare so cold it made me shiver. "How could you be so mean to Bella when she was only offering you a lead to help you?" she hissed.

The younger girls all stared at me and I felt completely awful, like I wanted the ground to open up and swallow me. I realized that there was only one way to explain how I'd acted—I had to tell the truth. I took a deep breath. "Bella, I'm sorry," I began. Georgia snorted but I clenched my fists and carried on.

"The thing is, I wanted Charm," I admitted. "I've been trying not to let it show, but when I was struggling so much on Cracker, I couldn't help thinking, if I only had Charm… I didn't want to feel jealous and I tried my best to hide it—"

But Georgia interrupted me. "It's even worse that you've pretended to be her friend all this time!" she said icily.

"But I *am* her friend!" I cried. I tried to get Bella to look at me, but I only caught a glimpse of her red, tear-stained face before she buried it in Georgia's fleece again.

"It's OK, Bella, you've got real friends, forget about her," said Georgia. "Come on, you'll be OK with all of us." And with that she led Bella off toward the farmhouse. The others followed, giving me very cross looks. I started crying then and hurried back into the house. I tried to creep through the kitchen to get upstairs, but Jody was at the sink, testing Millie on her times tables. As soon as she saw my face she made me sit down and tell her what had happened. While I was explaining it all, and trying to stop crying, I realized that I've been so focused on Charm I haven't even given Cracker a chance. I felt like I'd been mean to *him*, as well as Bella, and that made me cry even more.

I don't blame Georgia for being so angry either. She must think I'm such a horrible person after today. "I said sorry," I sniffled, "but

I don't think Bella will want to be friends with me anymore."

Millie got me some cookies even though it was nearly time for supper, and Jody gave me a hug, saying, "I'm sure deep down Bella knows you didn't mean it. You can always try apologizing again later. Just give her time to calm down and it'll blow over, you'll see. Now how about helping me get the supper ready?"

So I did, and then I set the table.

I dreaded having to face the girls at supper, but Millie sat next to me and no one said anything nasty. I tried to smile at Bella a couple of times but she still wouldn't look at me. I didn't dare smile at Georgia in case she did her icy glare and it made me start crying again.

It's so lucky my washing-up duty tonight was with Millie. After we'd cleared up, she had to carry on with her math practice, so when I'd put everything away I just sat down next to her and

got my Pony Camp Diary out, and I've been
writing in here ever since. I should have gone to
the games room for the movie, but I sort of
haven't quite made it yet. There's someone else
I need to say sorry to (as well as Bella), and it
can't wait till tomorrow, or even one more
minute.

I just went to ask Jody and she says I can go
up to the field because Lydia's there, but I have
to come back when she does. And Jody's given
me a carrot from the fridge.

Got to go now!

Wednesday, after lights out

I'm in bed, writing by the light of my key ring flashlight again. I tried to hang around in Millie's room for as long as possible after lights out, hiding under the covers at the bottom of her bed, but when Jody came up to check on us all she made me come back in here. Luckily Bella and Georgia were asleep, so I didn't have to face them.

At least me and Cracker are friends now. Luckily he came when I called him over. I leaned over the fence, gave him a big pat and said sorry for being so mean, and especially for spending time with Charm when I could have been with him. I ruffled his mane and whispered, "Cracker, I'm so sorry for blaming you for our bad jumping when I should have been thinking of us as a team, and riding you better and more positively."

Cracker looked at me with his big black eyes, and I'm sure he understood. I added, "I've brought you a carrot to say sorry." When I held it out he munched it right up, so I know it's all OK between us now.

I wish I could just give Bella a carrot and then she'd like me again. I've just thought, maybe I should be calling her Isabella now because she is only Bella to her friends, and maybe I'm not her friend anymore. Urgh! I hope Jody's right and that things *will* blow over tomorrow.

Goodnight!

Thursday 11.12a.m., before the treasure hunt

We're just having some drinks and cookies before we go out on the treasure hunt. My timetable from Jody has changed again today because we had our lecture first instead of the lesson. Sally said we'd need the skills for going on the treasure hunt.

I thought that meant the lecture would be on solving clues, but actually it was about road safety and first aid, and how to put boots and bandages on your pony, and what to do if you get lost in the countryside. I've bandaged Cracker's legs because Sally said we might be going through the woods, and we have to be as prepared as possible. We also put our ponies' bridles on over their head collars, and each clipped a lead rope onto our D-rings so that we could dismount and have a picnic without the ponies galloping off. When I'd finished all the preparation, I made a big fuss of Cracker and told him how smart he looked.

I have sort of smiled at Isabella a couple of times, and Georgia hasn't made a horrible face at me or anything, so that's a bit better at least. The other girls seem to have forgotten about our falling-out because when I helped Asha to do Sugar's bandages and Olivia to put on Ebony's boots they were both chattering away to me as if nothing had happened.

Oh, hang on a sec...

Jody just called us all over to her and announced that we're being split into three teams for the treasure hunt. I'm in her team with Isabella and Joelle. When she read out the teams, she gave me a secret wink, so I know she fixed it like that on purpose so that me and Isabella will have a chance to make up. I hope we do!

Thursday 8.41p.m., waiting for my turn in the shower

I have volunteered to go last so I can write in here.

Guess what? Me and Bella have made up! And guess what else? Our team won the treasure hunt! Well, one special pony in particular won it, but I'll tell you about that in a minute.

Before we left the yard on the treasure hunt, Sally gave each team a map and their first clue. She explained that there would be three different sets of clues, and three separate routes to follow, but that we would all meet up at the same final place to search for the treasure. Our team leaders had a cool saddle-bag each, packed with our sandwiches and water

and the cell phone and first-aid kit. Then Lydia
handed out fluorescent bibs to wear over our
riding clothes so we could easily be seen by any
passing cars.

Sally said the only rule was that we had to
stop for a half-hour lunch break so the ponies
could have a rest. Our team went into the
kitchen with Jody and worked out where the
first clue was telling us to go, and then we got
our ponies out and headed off.

Johnny's team had gone already,
but Sally's was still in the yard.
We'd worked out that we
needed to head for the church
in the hamlet marked on the map.
We walked along the road for a little
while and then turned up a track. It was good
because we all talked together, and even
though Bella didn't say anything exactly *to* me
she wasn't ignoring me either, and after a while

I didn't feel so nervous around her. We trotted on, and when we hit a nice wide uphill bit next to some fields we persuaded Jody to let us have a canter, to help us get ahead of the other teams. "OK, then," she said, smiling. "Millie and her dad will be dragging their team across the countryside at high speed, so we might as well try to compete!"

Cantering up the hill was fantastic, and I could tell that Cracker really loved being out of the manège!

It took about half an hour to get to the church, and we found our next clue pinned to the noticeboard in the little stone porch. I dismounted and held Joelle's pony while she jumped down and ran to get it. It said:

> Follow the green arrows.
> Stick to the path.
> Be good.
> Or you'll end up like Little Red Riding Hood.

"Whoever wrote this isn't very good at poems!" I said, giggling. It was nice that Bella giggled at that too.

"Oh, thanks very much!" harrumphed Jody, but she was laughing.

"*You* wrote it!" I cried. "So you must know the answer!"

She nodded, but of course she wouldn't tell us where to go next or help us with the clue at all.

So we all dismounted and huddled around the map. After a while, Bella cried, "Aha! I've got it! Little Red Riding Hood was told to stick to the path through the woods in the fairy story, wasn't she?" She pointed at the woods marked on the map. "If we ride to the edge I bet we'll find that they've put some arrows up, maybe pinned to trees. Then we'll just have to follow them through the woods. As long as we stick to the path as the rhyme says we'll find our next clue."

"Well done, Bella, that's great," I said.

"Thanks," she said, smiling, but she still didn't look exactly *at* me.

Jody said, "If that's what you girls think, then let's get going!"

"But are we right?" Bella asked. Jody just made a zipping her lips sign. She wasn't giving anything away!

"What do *you* think, Cracker?" I asked, and he actually whinnied right at that moment, making everyone laugh. "Cracker thinks you're right too," I told Bella. This time when she smiled, her eyes met mine and I started to think that things might turn out OK between us.

So we set off for the woods and sure
 enough there was a green arrow on a post where the path entered them. We had to duck a bit under the trees at times, and I was glad I'd put the bandages on Cracker, as there was

a lot of bramble around. After a few more green arrows, we came out the other side onto a nice grassy bit by a field, where we found a piece of paper pinned to a tree. Our next clue!

Jody said we should have our lunch first before working it out, and even though we were keen to keep going, we were all pretty hungry too. We dismounted, took off the ponies' bridles, and clipped our lead ropes to their head collars—then the ponies could have lunch too! Joelle needed the bathroom, and Jody took her back into the wood to go in private while Bella and I held Bonny and Monsoon for them. I knew it was my chance to talk to Bella—and I took it.

It was really awkward at first and I didn't know how to begin, but then suddenly I found myself blurting it out. "I really *am* sorry I was mean to you," I gabbled. "I did want Charm, but now I'm so glad I got Cracker and I'm just very,

very, *very* sorry and…" I trailed off then, not knowing what else to say. There was a horrible moment when I thought she was going to tell me to get lost and never speak to me again, but luckily she didn't. Instead she said, "That's OK, Chloe, I forgive you. And, well, you know *why* you got Cracker and not Charm, don't you?"

I shrugged. "Just the way things turned out, I suppose," I said.

"Chloe!" she cried. "Don't be dense! It's because Sally thinks you're a good rider. That's why she gave you a pony who needs more guidance."

I couldn't help but feel pleased. "Thanks," I said, "but maybe Sally thought I was a better rider than I am. I still can't get Cracker over that water jump. I'm going to have to wear a swimsuit in the comp tomorrow, because something tells me I'm going to get wet!"

Bella laughed at that and everything was OK between us again, but we still shook hands to make it official. By the time Jody got back with Joelle, we were chatting away and she gave me a secret wink and looked really pleased.

We all sat down together and had our lunch, which was egg mayonnaise or ham rolls, and bananas for afterward—of course, Cracker managed to pinch half of mine! While we were eating we worked out what the next clue meant and where we should go. The piece of paper said:

> If you take the correct path,
> The next clue you will find.
> But don't go the wrong way,
> Or you'll get left behind!

Sunnyside Stables

"That's not very helpful!" said Bella at first, glancing up the bridleway ahead of us, which forked into two paths. "It doesn't tell us *which* is the correct path. It's impossible!"

But I just grinned. I do crosswords with Mom all the time, and they quite often say "correct" to mean "right", as in left and right. "It means take the right path, not the left," I explained. "'Correct' means 'right', and 'you'll get left behind' means if you take the left path you won't reach the treasure first. I'm pretty sure that's it."

"Chloe, you're a genius," said Bella, and I blushed with pride.

So we got back on our ponies and rode through the fields in walk, chatting. After ages of not finding the next clue, we got a bit worried we were falling behind the other teams, so we trotted on.

Luckily we soon found it, tacked to a fence post along the path. It said:

up and down
And up again.
Not where fish fly,
But where birds swim.

Joelle got the giggles about that. "That's silly, birds don't swim!" she said.

"Ducks do," said Bella, smiling and pointing at the map.

There was a village with a duck pond marked on it about a mile away, and no sooner had she pointed it out than we were off. The path took us up a hill, then down a valley and up another hill, just as the clue said. We trotted as much as we could, and had another canter when we came to a nice wide bit of path. Jody even let

Bella and I jump a couple of low scrubby bushes, and it was so cool just doing it for fun and not worrying about knocked poles or clear rounds or anything.

We got to the village quite quickly and saw Johnny's team so we knew the treasure was nearby. On a post by the duck pond was our team's final clue. It said:

> Look for a red box,
> But don't rush
> Or you'll miss what's missing
> (In the . . . . . .)

We didn't know what the end bit meant, but we looked on the map and there was a red phone booth marked in the center of the village. Bella and I started heading for it

straightaway, but Jody called us back and made
us calm down and get in a line with us girls in
front of her. She said that there would be a few
cars in the village and we had to be sensible. So
we were careful, even though we could see
Johnny's team trotting on toward the phone
booth, and all I wanted to do was to break into
a canter and get there first. Then we saw Sally's
team come around the corner and trot toward
the church, so we knew they were on their
second to last clue, and would find the final one
at the church somewhere.

When we got to the phone
booth, Mai was holding
Twinkle for Suki. I felt
disappointed that we'd lost, but
then Suki came out empty
handed! "There's nothing in
there," she said. "Sally's
team must have got here first."

But we told her that we'd seen them by the church, so they weren't even on this clue yet, and we were all really puzzled. Jody and Johnny just looked at each other, grinning. I knew by now they weren't going to give anything away even if we begged and pleaded. We all looked at the clue again. "It's warning us not to rush, but we all rushed to the phone booth," said Mai. "Maybe we need to think again."

"How can you miss what's missing?" Bella wondered aloud.

I was confused for a moment too, but then I got it. "We mustn't miss that there's a word missing," I said. "It must be the end of the last line, because it doesn't make sense as it is. What rhymes with 'rush'?"

"Mush? Gush? Nothing!" cried Bella, getting frustrated.

I was busy trying to think of more things that rhymed with "rush", but Cracker had other ideas. He started wandering over to the hedge, and I gathered up my reins and tried to steer him back to the group. "No, Cracker!" I told him. "Stop ignoring me! We're supposed to be a team, remember?"

But he just stuck his head in the hedge, and when I finally managed to pull him up, he was chomping on a carrot! Well, it only took me about five seconds to realize that carrots don't grow on hedges, and I laughed out loud. "Over here!" I called out. "Cracker's found the treasure!" I leaped down and pulled a red box out of the bush, as everyone trotted up to see. There was a carrot or apple for every pony in a tray on top of the box and I had to quickly hand it up to Jody to stop Cracker from scoffing the lot!

"The missing word was 'bush!'" I told them.

"The phone booth was a *red* herring, get it?" said Johnny.

"We would have got it sooner if the rhymes were better!" Mai replied, and we all giggled.

"Stop knocking the rhymes, they took me ages!" cried Jody, but she was laughing too.

"Well done, Cracker!" I said, giving him a big pat and a stroke. "You found the treasure. Clever boy!" He nuzzled my arm, so I knew he was happy too!

Sally's group caught up with us then, and she asked who found the treasure. "Chloe did," said Bella, with a  smile. I glanced nervously at Georgia, but she smiled at me too. She was obviously happy to forget about the falling out if Bella was—what a relief!

"Actually, Cracker found it," I said.

"It sounds like a case of excellent teamwork to me," said Sally, and I just couldn't stop grinning.

Inside the red box were three cool pony notelet and envelope sets for the winning team. We let Joelle have first choice because she's the youngest, then I picked the one with the bay Welsh Section B on, because he looked a bit like Cracker—well, not the color but the same cheeky eyes. There were mini chocolate bars in there too, one for everyone. We all got off to stretch our legs and ate them while feeding our ponies their prizes (except Cracker, of course, who'd already scoffed his. I made a big fuss of him though, in case he felt left out). Jody put our writing sets in her saddle-bag until we got back to the yard. Then off we went, one long string of happy riders and ponies with no disagreements.

Sunnyside Stables

When we got back and untacked, I had to give Cracker's carrotty bit a good scrub under the faucet. But instead of thinking *urgh what a horrible job* it felt like one of my happiest moments ever—it was so fantastic just being on the yard in the sunshine with my friends, caring for my fab pony. I wish I could stay here forever and never go home!

Oh, the shower's free. Bye for now!

Very early on Friday morning!

I was going to write more last night but I fell asleep. I worked out that altogether we did two hours and twenty minutes of riding on the treasure hunt—no wonder I was tired out!

I woke up early, thinking about the jumping comp. Then I crept around getting dressed, but it still wasn't time to get up so I've got back into bed in my clothes!

Me and Bella shared out our notelets between the three of us so we all have the same, because we didn't want Georgia to feel left out. Then we had a fab idea—we're going to write thank yous to the Sunnyside staff for our fabulous week at Pony Camp. I can hardly bear to think that it's our last day, it's all just gone so fast! It's the jumping comp today—I can't believe it's come so quickly. Luckily we've got another lesson to work on it this morning. I just hope there's still time to turn things around with Cracker before the comp this afternoon. Dad's expecting to see me get a clear round, and it will be awful if I get dumped in the water tray instead!

But whatever happens, I'm really looking forward to having a good time with my friends and my fab pony. I can't wait to fetch Cracker in from the field and get going.

Oh, cool, the alarm's just gone off. I know—I'll lie down and pretend to have just woken up, then Bella and Georgia will be amazed to see me in my clothes—ha ha!

Morning break on Friday

Hurrah! We finally made it over the water jump! My beautiful Cracker is such a star!

After we'd warmed up, we went over all eight jumps at a lowish height, to get into the swing of things. Georgia got muddled up, and she and Prince went the wrong way at first, and we all had poles down—so at least I didn't feel like the only one getting in a mess.

At first Cracker wouldn't go over the water jump, but I didn't get annoyed, because I could see everyone was having their own problems. And I knew he was trying—it wasn't his fault he didn't like the look of it.

After a few goes, with him running out every time, I was getting a bit downhearted. That's when Bella offered me a lead. Of course this time I said yes please! I followed a few paces behind Charm as we went around the corner and toward the water jump. Charm popped it easily, and Cracker just followed him over, almost before he realized what he was doing! I gave him a big pat and thanked Bella loads. Sally told me to take him straight over again on my own, and sure enough he jumped like a dream! I still had the gate down though, so no clear round yet. We'll just have to try extra hard this afternoon, and hope for the best.

Oh, gotta go, we're all going to tie our ponies up in the yard and make them look extra smart for the comp!

Just to quickly say...

...how beautiful Cracker is looking! I've done some cute little mane plaits, all I've got to do now is wind them up into neat knots. I've given his coat a really good brush, and even put some bright blue ribbons in his tail. Now I've just got to get into my jodhs and sort my hair out, and we're ready.

Oh, I've just looked out of the bedroom window and our car has pulled up. Mom and Dad are both getting out!

Friday night, snuggled up in my own bed!

Well, even though I'm not at Sunnyside Stables anymore (boo!), I wanted to finish off my Pony Camp Diary by writing about what happened in the jumping comp.

It was so exciting riding into Group A's manège, which was set up as a practice area with just one jump in. We warmed up and had a couple of turns over the upright, then Sally explained that in the comp we would have two turns each, and as they wouldn't be timing us the aim was to get a clear round. We all wished each other luck, and then one by one we were called into the arena, where we had to bow to the judges (who were Lydia and Johnny).

Cracker and I started off OK. We were very close on the gate, but I couldn't look back to

see whether it was down. I needed all my focus
to get the turn right. We came through the
middle of the arena and over the upright
without a hitch, and I changed my canter lead.
We approached the water jump straight and in a
nice rhythm, but Cracker still ran out!

I was really disappointed because I thought
we'd got that sorted out this morning, but I
tried to keep calm and turned him around.
We'd only had one refusal. We still had another
chance. I was a bit nervous though, and Cracker
picked up on it, because he rushed at the jump,
then swerved out again at the last minute. I
managed to stay on, but I felt my heart sink—
we hadn't gone clear. We weren't alone
though—no one had managed a clear round
except for Georgia.

After I dismounted I stood fiddling with
Cracker's girth for no reason, to avoid having to
go over to my parents. When I saw Dad coming

toward me, I was going to pretend I had something urgent to do in the tack room. But in the end I stayed put because I didn't want to miss any of my time with Cracker.

As Dad reached us, I stiffened and Cracker gave me an inquisitive look and nuzzled my arm. He could tell something was wrong. I looked up at Dad and decided to get the first word in. "OK, so I didn't get a clear round, but so what? It's really hard, you know," I mumbled.

But instead of being cross, Dad just held his hands in the air. "Chloe, calm down!" he cried. "I think you're doing really well and so does Mom."

"But I promised I'd get a clear round, that's why you came..." I began.

"It's you who kept talking about getting a clear round," said Dad, "not me. Honestly, I just want you to enjoy yourself. We all think you're doing amazingly."

"Really?" I mumbled.

Dad put his arm around my shoulder. "Maybe I don't say it often enough, but I'm so proud of you, Chloe," he said. I looked up at him, and his eyes were twinkling. I could tell he really was.

Sally called over to us that it was time to begin round two, and I got Dad to hold my other stirrup while I remounted.

"Good luck, we'll be rooting for you," he said, with a big smile on his face.

I looked over at Mom, who waved and gave me a thumbs up.

Georgia went first this time, and she had that horrid spread down, but at least she'd gone clear in the first round, so she didn't mind too much.

Bella got a clear and I expected a little bit of my old jealousy to come back, but none did. I just felt really happy for her and Charm. Millie looked very determined in this round, and we were all cheering for her, but Tally picked up too much speed on the first corner, did a handbrake turn to the bounce, and ended up jumping quite long and knocking the second pole. We all gave them a big clap, though, for a good try. Millie didn't look remotely bothered about not going clear. But she's lucky, she'll probably get another chance next week!

Then it was my turn.

Everyone was cheering and clapping as I rode by, but when I got into the arena I didn't hear a thing. All there was in the world were me and Cracker and the jumps. I remembered to look up and ahead, and concentrate on where we were going this time, and I just let Cracker get on with jumping.

We started off a bit messy over the cross pole and spread, but everything stayed up (phew!) and we got into a good rhythm around the nice wide arc at the top of the arena, which set us up much better for the bounce and brush. We got over the middle jump without a hitch, but I only let myself be pleased for a split second, then refocused and

asked Cracker to trot to change our canter lead.
Then we were off around the tight bend and
over the dreaded gate. This time Cracker
seemed to know it was a danger zone and did a
huge leap over, more than clearing it. He started
getting really excited after that, but I kept him
nice and steady around the bend and over the
upright. Then we were setting ourselves up for
the water jump. I consciously breathed out and
sank into the saddle. I had to let Cracker know I
was relaxed, and then he would be too. I looked
up and ahead at the finish, as if the jump wasn't
even there, and before I knew it we were over!

We'd done it—a clear
round!

Mom and Dad
were cheering like
crazy, and I rode out of
the arena grinning
from ear to ear.

In the practice area I leaped off and made a huge fuss of Cracker—what a total star pony! And what a fab team we'd made!

All us Group B girls said a big well done to each other, and as I was walking Cracker back into the yard, my parents came up to meet me. Mom gave me a hug and Dad said, "Well done, Chloe, that was excellent."

When we'd put our ponies back in their stables for a rest, us Group B girls got our drinks and cookies from the kitchen, then we all sat at the edge of the other manège together to watch the younger girls play some gymkhana games. It was great fun, and we cheered wildly for all of them.

Then later there was a prize-giving, and we brought our ponies out again and collected our

 rosettes. I felt so proud of the clear round. And I felt even prouder that me and Cracker did it as a team—together.

I tied the rosette onto his bridle, and Dad took some pictures of our group and our ponies all together, and then we asked Lydia to take one of my whole family with Cracker in the middle. Cracker nuzzled Mom's arm, and she looked a bit nervous in case he nibbled her sleeve!

When it was all over, I led Cracker to the barn. I gave him a carrot I'd scrounged from Jody, and spent ages fussing and stroking him while I brushed him down.

I felt upset about leaving him, but I'm planning to go back next year—I'm already trying to persuade Mom to book it! It was really sad saying goodbye to Bella and Georgia. Dad took loads of photos of us three though, and I'm going to send some to them tomorrow, with my first letter.

We've all promised to write to each other using the pony paper and envelopes!

Just as we were heading to the car with all our bags we remembered the thank-you letters we'd written, which were in my bag. I heaped all my stuff onto Dad and ran back over to the yard. Sally was there in the office so I gave her the letters.

As she opened hers, her face lit up. "Oh thanks so much, Chloe, that's very kind of you!" she said. "Thank the other girls for me, won't you?"

I nodded and made for the door. "Chloe," she said then, and I whirled around in the doorway. "You've totally turned it around this week," she told me. "I'm so proud of you, well done."

I couldn't help beaming. "Thanks, but it was all down to Cracker!" I said, and I skipped out and across the yard.

I really learned a lot at Pony Camp, and not

just about jumping! I've made some wonderful new friends, met some fab ponies, and found out what a true partnership is—all thanks to Cracker!

Hey, I've just realized that Sally was right—when she warned me not to be so desperate to achieve my goals that it actually stopped me succeeding I didn't understand what she meant. But I do now. As soon as I started to relax and work as a team with Cracker, we did so much better—and I had a lot more fun, too! How funny that nearly all week I thought I had to teach *him*, but actually he's taught *me* loads!

Now, I wonder which pony I'll get next year?!

To George, with love—thanks for all those
trips to Redwings Horse Sanctuary!

With special thanks to our cover stars,
Chelsea and Dusty, pony guru Janet Rising,
star instructor Jody Maile, and all
at Ealing Riding School.

www.kellymckain.co.uk

STRIPES PUBLISHING
An imprint of Magi Publications
1 The Coda Center, 189 Munster Road, London SW6 6AW

A paperback original
First published in Great Britain in 2007
This edition published 2011

Text copyright © Kelly McKain, 2007
Illustrations copyright © Mandy Stanley, 2007
Cover photograph copyright © Zoe Cannon, 2007

ISBN: 978-1-84715-218-3

The right of Kelly McKain and Mandy Stanley to be identified as the author
and illustrator of this work respectively has been asserted by them in
accordance with the Copyright, Designs and Patents Act, 1988.

Printed and bound in China

STP/1800/0009/0911

2 4 6 8 10 9 7 5 3 1